Greeley's Spyce

ALIYAH BURKE

Greeley's Spyce

Aliyah Burke

Greeley's Spyce

Editor and Formatter: Savannah Frierson

Cover Artist: MMJ Designs

ISBN: 978-0-557-01286-2

To my readers, who never gave up on me. Ms. Savannah, you know what you did; thanks for being such a great friend. To my husband who's been nothing but supportive of me following my dreams. And last but definitely not least, to the brave men and women who protect their country at the sacrifice of being away from their loved ones and risking their lives for those they may never meet.

Acknowledgments

Allow me to give credit where it's due. Any mistakes in this are mine and not to be blamed on the ones who do this for a living.
Thank you to my cover artist, I couldn't have asked for a better one. You listened to what I said and took it to the next level. Thank you!
To my editor, for all the patience and diligence you've shown me, I thank you.

CHAPTER ONE

Hawaii

Strolling down the street and minding her own business, Koali Travis was nearly bowled over by a group of men coming out of a bar. One of them reached to steady her and her insides flipped at his simple touch. "Excuse me," she muttered as she removed his hand from her arm and walked around them.

Keeping her head down, she tried to get away, but to no avail. "Hey wait," a deep voice called to her. Closing her eyes and praying that this interaction wouldn't be trouble, she turned around.

The men approached, all of them good looking, but one stepped forward even more. He was over six feet, had flaxen-blond hair, and his eyes...dear God...they were amazing. A hauntingly pale blue. "Are you okay, ma'am?" he asked.

She knew it was the same one who had run into her. Not wanting to meet his gaze any longer, she nodded. "Fine. Thanks for asking." Turning back around Kacy walked off.

As she rounded the corner, masculine laughter followed as they teased the man who had spoken to her. "Looks like she couldn't get away from your pale ass fast enough, Ghost!"

"What the hell did you do to her, Ernst, to make her run like that?"

"Shut up, guys," the voice that had sent tremors through her commanded. Then she was too far away to hear them any longer.

Ernst "Ghost" Zimmermann couldn't get that woman out of his thoughts. Admittedly, he'd been a bit tipsy when they'd left the bar, but he hadn't meant to scare the poor woman. She'd seemed frightened out of her mind.

He liked her looks. A lot. Her hair was dark brown; she wore it straight and partially obscuring her right eye—eyes that were the color of burnished copper. Her smooth skin looked like a cup of coffee with a splash of cream in it, and he guessed she weighed about one-sixty and was around five foot nine inches.

Ernst conceded that until his teammates had begun getting married, she hadn't been the type of woman he would've given a second glance. Apparently, there was something very special about black women, for two of his teammates had married them and a third was hopelessly in love with his woman, just hadn't married her yet. And he liked each of them very much and found them very beautiful.

This one though…when he had touched her it, was like someone had turned on all the lights in his world, making him realize things were bright after all. The feeling confused him for he'd truly believed he was happy. He loved his job; being a SEAL was a lifelong dream and he lived it everyday.

He'd felt the loss when she'd removed his hand from her arm. Followed by the fact she hadn't looked him in the eyes had made him want to run after her and grab her, if only to see whether he'd imagined the spark he had felt.

He hadn't. Koali was an electrician and she definitely knew sparks. She knew voltage and wattage. What had passed between her and that stranger on the street had been a spark. A very large spark.

As she walked quickly back to her hotel, she still trembled from the brief contact. *Ernst.* "His name is Ernst," she muttered to herself, needing to feel his name on her tongue.

Entering the lobby of the hotel she smiled at the people waiting for her there. "Hey, y'all," she said with semi-forced lightheartedness. "Sorry, a couple of guys ran into me as they were leaving a bar."

"Are you okay?" the leader of the group asked.

"Fine, I'm fine. My nerves are a bit high still, but fine," Koali assured them.

"Well, let's get going to the last meeting, then, so we can still have two days to enjoy this island," the leader suggested, gesturing them all towards the conference room.

Koali had come to this conference in Hawaii with a group of electricians from Virginia. They were in the nationwide guild, and the meetings brought attendees up to date on new codes and procedures. She was one of two women in her immediate group, and many of the men had initially been pretty condescending towards them. Thankfully, they had softened over time, and now it was like going somewhere with twenty overprotective brothers.

It was ten o'clock at night when the presentation finally ended. They hadn't even stopped to break for dinner. Food had been delivered and they ate through, taking notes as the night progressed.

Stretching and groaning, Koali looked over the crowded room. The lack of women still amazed her. *I need to get out of here.* Gathering her things, she dropped off her dinner tray on a cart by the door and pushed through.

"Kacy," a voice stopped her.

Koali Cynemon Travis, more commonly referred to as Kacy, turned to find Brett Thacker walking up to her. "Hey, Brett." He was a tall, thin black man with kind eyes, and one of the few who'd been nice to her from the get-go. "What did you think?"

"I think it's a good thing we have the next two days off or I would go postal!" He sent her a conspiratorial smile. "I came to see if you wanted to take a walk around the water?"

If it had been anyone, else she would have refused. But she liked Brett, and considering her earlier incident, having a man with her might not be such a bad idea. "I'd like that. Just let me run up and drop off this stuff. Meet you back here in fifteen minutes?"

His brown eyes twinkled. "Sure thing."

Koali stepped into the elevator and grinned at him. "See you in a few." As the door closed, she shook her head. Brett was always making her smile. Opening her room door, she dropped her notebook on the dresser and quickly changed into a black V-necked shirt, a pair of khaki Capri pants, and exchanged tennis shoes for flat sandals. After applying lotion to her body, she ran a brush through her hair briefly and then slipped her key and identification into her pocket and left the room.

Brett was waiting for her as promised. He'd changed into a pair of white Bermuda shorts and a blue shirt. On his feet was a pair of flip-flops. His lips lifted, sending her a smile as she stepped off the elevator. "Are you ready?"

Tucking her hair behind one ear she answered, "Absolutely. Thanks for going along with me. I am still a bit on edge after today."

"I know how much you like your nightly walks, and I was hoping to go along the harbor and see some of the ships."

"Sounds like a plan." They fell into step beside one another and began the walk toward the where the Navy ships pulled into Pearl Harbor port.

❋ ❋ ❋

"Two ice creams, please, in cups. One chocolate and one strawberry. Sprinkles on the chocolate one. Lots of sprinkles." A voice intruded into the kiss Ernst was sharing with his date for the evening; however, the one that followed that made him pull away from the lips he was kissing as the sultry voice said, "Brett, you don't have to buy me an ice cream."

His mystery woman. Every one of his hairs stood on end as the electrical currents flowed through him. His date was trying to start the kiss again, but his pale eyes were searching the streetlight-lit area for someone else completely. "Stop it," he ordered.

He knew his date whined, but he didn't know what she said for he had found her — the woman from earlier. She stood beside the cart eating her ice cream with sprinkles. His eyes softened as they looked upon her dark beauty, only to harden moments later as the man with her leaned down and whispered something that made her laugh out loud.

Eating their ice cream, they walked off down the pier. Pulling on his date Ernst said, "Let's go." For the life of him, he couldn't remember his date's name, but he knew before the night was over, he would know his mystery woman's.

Latching onto his arm with hands topped by blood-red nails, his date followed him down the pier, chatting on about something. His spectral powder-colored eyes were glued to the firm khaki-covered ass that swayed in front of him.

When the couple stopped and leaned along the railing, he did the same a bit further down, still watching the woman out of the corner of his eye. She appeared to be on a date, a thought he didn't like at all. *When the hell did I become so possessive?* Turning his head, he watched her gesture to the ships with her spoon and speak to the man beside her.

The fifth time a smile graced her lips, he pushed away from the rail. "Excuse me for a second. I see someone I know and I want to say hi." Without looking to see if his date cared, Ernst walked off.

"Pardon me," he said when he approached, leaning on one arm next to the woman resting against the railing.

Those copper eyes turned and met his directly. She wasn't quick enough to hide her surprise at seeing him again. Something that pleased him very much.

Koali's body quivered at those two words. That sinful voice was back in her head. Turning, she found herself staring at the man who had turned her world upside down with just a touch. Blinking, she swallowed and asked as calmly as she could, "Yes?"

"I just wanted to make sure you were okay," he murmured, touching her bare arm.

Trembling again from the contact, she nodded. "I'm fine. Again, thanks for asking."

"What's he talking about?" Brett asked.

"A group of idiots ran into her outside of a bar today. I wanted to make sure she was okay," Ernst answered before she could say a word.

He called himself an idiot. "I'm fine, really. You saved me before I hit the pavement," Koali said.

Brett reached around her and offered his hand. "Thanks, man, I wouldn't want anything to happen to her. My name is Brett Thacker. I guess you know Kacy."

Ernst shook his hand. "Name's Ernst Zimmermann. And, no, I haven't had the pleasure of meeting this lovely lady." Ernst turned those unforgettable eyes back to her. Then he offered his hand.

Forcing a calm look on her face, she shook his hand and said, "Koali Travis, nice to meet you, Mr. Zimmermann."

His finger trailed along the inside of her wrist as he let go of her hand, although appearing reluctant to do so. "Where do they get Kacy from?"

"My middle name. It's Cynemon," she answered before she could stop herself.

"Like the spice?" Ernst questioned, as if he could envision her being just that.

"Yes. But spelled C-Y-N-E-M-O-N," Koali explained.

"Ernst," a whinny voice reached the group. "I don't want to share you tonight. Meet them later, we have plans." A slim redhead sidled up and latched onto him.

"We should get going as well," Koali murmured, even though she didn't want to leave his presence. "It was good seeing you again, Mr. Zimmermann."

"Nice to meet you," Brett added. "Ma'am," he said to the woman holding onto Ernst like he were a lifejacket and she were drowning.

"Have dinner with me," Ernst blurted, seeming totally oblivious to the gasping woman beside him. "Tomorrow night. I would love to talk some more."

"Okay," Koali responded, shocking herself. "How about *Jack's* at seven?"

"See you then," he said with a smile.

"Until tomorrow," she responded, then walked away with Brett, ignoring the other woman completely.

When she slid between the cool sheets in her hotel room later that night, Koali wondered what she had agreed to. It was just dinner. Wasn't it?

All the next day, Ernst had a smile on his face. His teammates just assumed it was because of the redhead he had gone out with the previous night.

"Wanna grab a bite, Ernst?" Osten, a teammate, asked his as his dark head appeared in the doorway.

That grin got wider. "Sorry, man, I have a date."

"With that redhead? You seem awfully happy about it. A hell of a lot more than last night," Osten observed.

"Nope." Blue eyes turned to his friend. "Do you remember the woman from the street yesterday?"

Osten's jaw dropped. "The black chick you ran into? Her? You're going out with *her*?"

Those eyes narrowed. "What about it?"

"Hey, I just remember her trying to get away from you. How'd you finagle a date?"

"I saw her last night and asked." Ernst shrugged and smiled, remembering how cute she looked. "After I got her name."

Osten busted out laughing. "You asked her out while you were on a date?" More laughter filled the room. "Damn, and I thought Maverick was bad."

"I am not that bad," Ernst protested.

Rolling his eyes, Osten shook his head. "If you say so. Well, have fun." Then he was gone.

"I fully intend to," Ernst said to himself as he smoothed out his crewneck shirt and slid his wallet into the pocket of his khakis. Clipping the beeper to the inside of another pocket, he walked out the door.

The teammates that were there waved and barely managed to keep their mouths shut. As the door closed behind him he heard laughter. Ernst loved his friends, but even he had to admit there were times they were pains in the ass.

Some time later, Ernst entered *Jack's*, a bar and grill he knew very well. The regulars waved and called out greetings to him as he passed.

His pale gaze ran a gamut of the room. When his eyes fell upon Kacy sitting alone at the bar absently stirring her drink while looking out over the water, Ernst felt his pulse race.

What was it about this woman? Why does she make me feel this way?

For a brief moment, he just stood there and filled his vision with her serene beauty. Suddenly, two men leaned against the counter, one on each side of her. That got a different reaction from Ernst. His eyes hardened to ice chips and he moved swiftly towards them, waving off the bartender who had made to interrupt the men bothering her.

CHAPTER TWO

Koali sat at the bar drinking a club soda with a lime twist, her stomach in knots as she waited for Ernst. She'd arrived early to try and calm her nerves.

The ocean helped. It always had. Her body tensed again, however, when two men settled beside her, one on each side of her corner seat.

"Evening, gorgeous," the larger of the two men said. "Can I buy you another drink? What did you have? Martini? Gin and tonic?"

"No, thank you," Koali said, her hand tightening around the glass.

"Well, now," the second man said, "that's not nice. Here we are trying to be nice to a sister sittin' alone."

Where was he? "I'm waiting for someone." She met the gaze of the smaller man. His face was baby smooth with skin was so dark it was almost black. "But thanks for the offer anyway."

The other, larger man tsked, bringing her attention to him. He looked Hawaiian, although she wasn't positive. "We've been watching you for about thirty minutes. Whoever you're waiting for isn't coming, so you can be our date."

"Sorry I'm late, baby," a sinful voice broke in as Ernst turned Koali around on the stool to face him. "Who are your friends?" He leaned in and kissed her briefly on the lips.

Koali was so relieved when she heard his voice, and when his hand landed on her hips, her insides melted. His kiss made her feel she'd died and gone to heaven; she had to stop herself from following his retreating lips with her own. "I don't know them."

"This is your date?" Tall Hawaiian man asked.

"Yes. I am," Ernst responded assuredly as he helped Koali off the stool before reaching around her and grabbing her drink. "Evening, gentleman."

One hand resting on the small of her back, Ernst walked them into the grill area toward an empty table. Ernst held out her chair for her and enjoyed the gentle scent that wafted from her hair and body.

"I'm sorry about that," Ernst said as he took his chair. *Not about the kiss though.*

"It wasn't your fault. Thanks for saving me," Koali spoke easily.

"I should've been here earlier to protect you." His eyes traveled over her off-the-shoulder, pale-yellow blouse. It went well with the dark-blue skirt she wore that was cut at an angle to display one shapely leg. "You look beautiful."

"You are looking pretty fly yourself." She flashed him a grin as her eyes moved over his attire.

At her grin, Ernst felt his heart skip a beat. *Did this woman have any clue how beautiful she was?* "Glad you noticed." He winked at her in the dimly lit room.

Their waiter arrived and asked, "Can I get you a drink to start?"

Ernst nodded at Koali. "Get whatever you want."

"Another club soda with lime please."

"Do you mind if I have a beer?" Ernst stared directly at Koali as he asked.

"Go ahead," she said, shaking her head.

"One beer please."

"I'll be right back," the waiter said, "do you want menus or the special?" Meeting Koali's eyes again they both said "the special" at the same time. With a chuckle, the waiter nodded and left.

"Do you prefer to go by Koali, which is a beautiful name by the way, or Kacy?" Ernst queried as their drinks were brought along with a mixed tray of appetizers.

"Here you go, Ghost," the server said as he set it down. "Meal'll be up soon."

"Thanks, Drey." Ernst took a swig of the cold beer. "Well," he prompted when they were left alone again.

Her brows furrowed as if confused, but she shook her head. "I answer to either, but most people call me Kacy."

Rolling the bottle between two fingers, he nodded. "Kacy it is, then. Tell me about you, Kacy Travis."

"Looking for anything specific, Ernst Zimmermann?" Kacy asked, sipping her drink and reaching for a piece of fried calamari.

"Who was that guy you were with last night?"

"Brett is one of the guys who came for the conference." Her eyes closed in pleasure as she ate the squid.

"Something between you?" Ernst leaned forward, resting his strong forearms on the table as his eyes bore into hers.

"Nothing other than friendship."

"Good." He took a pan-fried oyster and ate it.

"Good?" Kacy's eyebrows rose in confusion.

Ernst nodded. "Good."

They sat in silence for a while eating. Ernst watched Kacy and Kacy watched the ocean. When their food came, she turned her attention to it.

"Are you nervous?" His voice broke the silence.

"A bit," Kacy admitted.

"Hey, don't be. I'm not going to hurt you in any way." He reached for her hand, squeezed it once and released it.

All Kacy did was tremble at his touch and smile, then eat more of her seafood special.

"You should smile more often," he commented, taking another swig of beer.

Blushing, Kacy took a sip of her drink and asked, "So what do you do, Mr. Zimmermann?"

Absorbing the sight of the woman across from him he said, "I'm in the Navy."

"I see. Do you like it?"

Ernst smiled. "I thank God everyday I get to do what I do."

The noise in the bar area increased. They both looked and saw that a pool game was beginning between two guys. Over the noise Kacy said, "I'm glad to hear that."

His blond brows narrowed and he wondered, "Why?"

Setting down her fork, Kacy leaned in closer to him so she wouldn't have to yell. "You risk your life for me. If you love your job, then you do it well and that...makes me feel even more safe."

He moved closer. "For all you know, I could work in admin."

"Doesn't matter. It's all important. Although, I don't see you shuffling papers." She winked.

He was intrigued. "What do you see me doing?"

Her brown eyes grew two shades darker before she brought herself under control. "I see you—"

"Ernst!" a voice interrupted, jerking them back from each other.

Pale eyes swung to the man who had come between him and his date. Merlin. "What, Dimitri?"

Dark, golden eyes roamed over Kacy appreciatively and he whistled low. "Aren't you the chick from yesterday?"

"Dimitri." The name was growled. "What do you *want*?"

"Come help us win at pool. We're about to lose," the tanned man groaned.

Kacy watched the interaction curiously, but Ernst finally said, "I'm busy."

"They're Deltas," Dimitri threw in disgustedly.

"Looks like they need your help," Kacy observed, clearly not under-standing the dislike between them.

"It would be rude of me..." he began.

Kacy shrugged easily. "I wouldn't mind watching a game or two of pool."

An unknown emotion crossed Ernst's face. "Okay." He grinned, stood, and walked around the table to assist Kacy.

"She's a keeper. Marry her, Ernst." Dimitri said, "or better yet, I'll marry her. Name's Dimitri, beautiful, who are you?"

"Kacy."

"Back off, Dimitri," Ernst warned as they wove through the dining area back to the bar side.

Dimitri led the way to the farthest table in the back where the tension was so thick you could chew it. Ernst had his hand on Kacy's arm as they approached.

"Here's my partner," Dimitri said to their opponents as he reached for his pool cue.

Ernst briefly met the eyes of his teammates. "Guys, this is Kacy Travis. Kacy meet," he began and pointed to each one as he said their names, "Osten, Tyson, Ross, Scott, Aidrian, and Maverick."

"Ma'am," they all said, shaking her hand.

"Nice to meet you," Kacy responded with a shy smile.

The game was under way, and Kacy stood with the guys and watch-ed. *This has got to be one of the weirdest dates I have ever been on. Fun, but weird. And amazingly, I don't feel scared.*

A skinny waitress came by and Kacy noticed three of the men and Ernst didn't give her a second look. The others did, especially when she came back with the drinks.

The daisy-dukes–wearing, midriff-showing woman walked up to Ernst to hand him his drink, but he nodded towards Kacy.

"He says he wants you to hold it for him," the waitress said.

Kacy took it wordlessly and kept watching. The drink was pulled from her hand as Ernst appeared beside her. "Bored?"

Shaking her head, Kacy smiled at the man next to her. The scent of cologne mixed with his unique smell created one hell of an aphrodisiac. "No, I like watching pool. You're very good."

"You have no idea," he whispered in her ear, giving birth to a whole swarm of butterflies in her belly.

"Ernst," Dimitri said as he approached. "It's your turn. I'll stay here with Kacy and keep her safe."

Narrowing his glacial eyes, Ernst quipped, "Who's gonna protect her from you? She'd be safer with Scott, Tyson or Ross." As if it were so natural, he leaned in for the second time that night and brushed his firm lips across her soft ones. "Be right back," he murmured.

Striving to regain emotional control, Kacy asked Dimitri, "Why would I be safer with those he mentioned?"

"'Cause two are married and Ross is hopelessly in love," Dimitri said with an eye roll.

"That's wonderful. And none of the rest of y'all are married?" Kacy asked.

"Correct," Dimitri said, "Wanna get married?" He winked.

Kacy laughed; she couldn't help it. "Sorry, I don't know you well enough."

"So? Tyson married his wife and they hadn't known each other much more than twelve hours."

Her eyes grew wide. "And they're still married?"

"Disgustingly and happily so," Dimitri admitted.

"Wow. I don't think that would work for me."

"Marriage or that short of time?" Dimitri asked.

"The time."

"What are you two talking about?" Ernst queried when he returned, butting in the conversation.

"Marriage." Dimitri smirked as he walked off.

Ernst's gaze locked on hers as he stepped in close. "Out with me and talking marriage with another man?" he asked in a deceptively calm voice.

Arching a brow, she leaned in even closer, her eyes falling to his lips before returning to his eyes. "You asked me out when you were on a date."

"I don't want to marry her," he growled, reaching for her arm and pulling her closer.

"Who said I wanted to marry him?" Her fingers trailed along his exposed forearm.

"Thought you were discussing marriage." Neither of them noticed how those around them were watching avidly.

"We were." She smiled brilliantly. "He was explaining why I'd be safer with Scott, Tyson, or Ross." Kacy nodded in the direction of the table. "I believe they are waiting for you."

His eyes turned to blue fire as he looked over her body seductively. "The question is will *you* wait for me?"

Something in his tone made her feel he was talking longer than the pool game. "For the evening," was all she could allow herself to say.

"That's a start," he said with a predatory look in his eyes. "Here." Ernst handed her the beer. "Do I get a kiss for luck?"

"Do you need one?" She was no dummy; she knew he was an excellent player.

"Definitely," he answered immediately.

"Well," she purred, "I wouldn't want you to lose to a couple of Deltas." Quickly, she leaned in and kissed him. "Even if they are good looking," Kacy said as she began to move away from his lips.

His eyes flashed with what she could only describe as possession. Ernst pulled her back in and kissed her again. This kiss was different. It wasn't to save her from unwanted attention, it wasn't just because.

This kiss claimed her. His thick tongue swept into her mouth, tasting her, branding her. One hand slid around her waist as the other held the back of her head.

There were sparks flying between them as he teased her tongue. Her body trembled as did his. Never before had Ernst lost control like that. He almost lowered her to the ground right then and there. The chill of his beer against his arm as she clung to him snapped him out of the haze.

Drawing her full lower lip into his mouth he slowly ended the kiss. His teeth grazed her lip as he released it totally. "Don't go anywhere," he rasped as he picked up his pool cue and walked to the table.

Don't go anywhere? It was only by the grace of the good Lord she didn't collapse into a puddle on the floor. Without thought, Kacy took a drink of his beer and leaned back against the wall to watch the rest of the game.

"What do you do?" a voice asked her.

Kacy turned to find herself staring directly into the black eyes of the man next to her. Aidrian. "I have my own business." A big cheer went up and she looked back at the table to see Ernst and Dimitri taking money. Ernst met her gaze and raised a finger. She nodded.

The man handed her a stool. "Here, have a seat."

"Thanks." She climbed on. "So, do all of y'all work together?"

"Aye. Dinna he tell you what he did?"

She smiled over his accent. "No, just that he was in the Navy."

"Dinna you want to know more?"

Kacy grinned even as she shook her head. "Look, I'm only here because he asked me out. I didn't need to know his life story."

"I'm thinkin' he's gonna be wantin' more than one date," the large man said, breaking into a smile.

If only. "Well, people want a lot of things." Kacy shrugged it off. A relationship was not something she was after right now.

Ernst sank three balls and lifted his eyes to see Kacy talking easily with Aidrian. She wasn't even looking in his direction, just keeping her warm gaze on the handsome black man beside her.

A growl rose from deep in his chest. They made a very attractive couple and he hated it. Two seconds before he could quit the game and march over there to put his fist in the senior officer's face, she turned, meeting his gaze and smiling as she toasted him with his beer.

"Relax, man. She's been watching you. Don't worry. And you know Hondo isn't like that." A Southern voice broke in.

Ernst looked to see Ross standing beside him holding a longneck. "They look good together."

"So do the two of you," his friend assured him.

"I think I understand what you feel for Dezarae," the blond said, "I wouldn't hesitate to protect Kacy."

Ross nodded. "It's a scary feeling because you don't want to leave them in case they need you."

"She doesn't know I'm a SEAL," Ernst admitted as he lined up for his next shot.

"Why not?"

"I don't know what she does, either. But she knows I'm Navy." He sank the ball and moved to the next one.

"Worried about her reaction?" Ross questioned.

Turning his head, he met the gray eyes of his friend. "I don't know. I do know I don't want her smiling at Hondo that way. I don't want her looking at anyone but me. I don't get it. I just met her yesterday!"

"Sometimes, our hearts and souls know before our brains can catch up," Ross said.

Ernst sank the eight ball and said to the others, "I'm done playing. I'm not spending my evening with a bunch of men when that gorgeous woman is waiting for me."

The Deltas paid up what they owed and Ernst took his cut. Then, he gave his pool cue to Ross and walked over to where Kacy sat still talking to Hondo.

"Hey," Ernst said as he approached.

"Hey, yourself," Kacy replied, handing him his beer.

"Let's get outta here," he uttered, nodding to Aidrian.

Sliding off the stool, she put her hand in his outstretched one. "It was really nice talking to you, Aidrian. Goodbye."

The large black man flashed her a smile. "It was my pleasure. Good-night, Kacy. Ernst."

"Goodnight, Aidrian. Let's go, Kacy." Ernst led her away, smiling as she waved to his teammates. After a stop off to pay for dinner and drinks, he pushed open the door, walking into the night.

Placing his pale eyes on her warm beauty, he asked, "Where would you like to go?"

"How about the park that overlooks the water?" Kacy suggested.

"Okay." He took them a few steps and spied the ice cream stand. "Do you want some dessert?"

CHAPTER THREE

Back and forth.

Back and forth.

The gentle breeze that flowed over her face partially made up for the high humidity that filled the air. Kacy tipped her head back, closed her eyes, and laughed at the pure joy that filled her.

"You do realize I'm eating all of your ice cream," Ernst said as his otherworldly gaze watched the beautiful woman beside him.

Glancing at him as her body swung back and forth, she asked, "Why are you?"

"Because it's melting." He shrugged. "And mine's gone."

Slowing the swing, Kacy reached towards him and wiggled her fingers. Her face was flushed; it was obvious she loved to swing.

Taking a spoonful, he slid it between his firm lips and groaned with pleasure. "Oh, damn, this is good!"

Leaning farther on the swing, she grabbed the plastic spoon and pulled it out of his mouth. He arched a brow but handed her the cup of ice cream.

"You probably ate all the sprinkles." She sent him a playful frown. *I am having so much fun with him. It is like being carefree.*

He smiled. "I will get more if you think it needs it."

Shaking her head, she took a bite and grinned. "I love ice cream, and this…this is prefect." *Especially since your mouth was on the spoon earlier.*

Kacy felt his eyes on her and suddenly felt self-conscious. Her hair was loose, her smiles often and free. She had her skirt tucked so it wouldn't fly up when she swung on the playground equipment. Her copper eyes shone in the moonlight. She'd not felt this open in a long time.

"What do you do?" he wondered, leaning his body against the chain of the swing he occupied as he faced her.

"I run my own business back on the mainland."

"What kind of business?" He pulled her swing closer and took a spoonful of ice cream for himself.

"I'm an electrician." Her body tensed as she waited for the normal male response of disbelief. It never came.

"Awesome."

Slanting her reddish-brown gaze at him, she watched him as if uncertain he wouldn't say something else, something condescending. But all he did was point to her ice cream and open his lovely shaped mouth.

"Thank you," he mumbled after she gave him a bite.

Kacy licked the spoon clean, not seeing the flare of heat in his eyes. Resting her head on the chain she watched the lights of ships in the harbor as her bare toes dug in the sand. "What do you do for the Navy, Ernst?"

His eyes roving over her profile, he said, "I'm a SEAL."

"Well, I guess that *should* explain the dislike with you and the Deltas." She scraped the bottom of the cup getting all she could. "It fits."

We fit. Touching her arm, Ernst waited for her to look at him. "Why do you say that?" He got off the swing and beckoned her to do the same.

"You are very confident. Self assured, not in a bad way." She slid her arm through his as her feet found their reluctant way back into her sandals. "The ones you played against also seemed such a way."

Ernst took the empty ice cream container from her and carried it. He loved the way she fit against his body. It would be a lie to say he wasn't imagining what it would be like with her naked. His body throbbed painfully.

"Do you know many SEALs?" he asked as he tried to get his body to calm down.

"I must say you are my first," Kacy said, leaning her head against his shoulder while they walked.

Tossing the container into the trash receptacle they passed, he grinned. *And I will be the first SEAL you do lots of things with. I will be the only SEAL you do things with. The only man.* "Well, you know what they say about your first."

Kacy stopped and faced him. "No, what?"

Ernst looked down at the woman who stood on a hillside in the moonlight with him. Her beauty took his breath away, and he knew in that moment she was the one for him.

Maybe Ross was right, that his heart and soul knew before his brain could comprehend. Being there with her filled him with such a sense of peace, of contentment, of love. He barely knew her but knew she was his future.

"That they remain your true love." His callused hand stroked the side of her face. "Your only love."

"Is that what they say?" her doubtful tone rang.

He nodded. "Oh, yeah."

"Funny, I've never heard that before."

"Must be an old German saying."

Trouble lurked behind her eyes, "An old German saying, huh? Like 'Heil Hitler' is an old German saying? You do kind of fit the description, don't you? Blond hair, blue eyes."

"I am not a believer in that crap," he growled, pulling her in closer.

"But you *are* German, and according to you, that was an old German saying!"

Catching the twitch of her lips, Ernst realized she was teasing him. "It is a very famous old German saying. Don't you have any German in you?"

"I thought military men were supposed to be observant." She tapped him on the end of his Roman nose. "Do I look like I have German in me?"

His deep voice dropped even lower as he whispered against her lips, "Would you like some?"

Kacy closed her eyes and trembled against him. "Do you know where I can find a German who may be interested?"

"Open your eyes, *meine geliebte*. He's right in front of you." His warm breath brushed against her skin.

Heavy, it was so hard to open her eyes. Kacy found his haunting gaze fixed firmly on her. "I'm sorry," she mumbled. "I can't."

"Don't apologize. As much as I would love to make love to you right here, right now. I want to get to know you. But when you are ready…this is all the German you will ever need." He brushed his cheek against hers, allowing her to feel the stubble that was beginning to grow.

Any second now Kacy knew she was going to wake up and find he was all a dream. No man was this kind, this caring, or this understanding. "I shouldn't have teased you."

"I'm not a little boy. I can handle the word 'no.' Come on." He tugged her arm and led her down the hill towards the water. "I want to show you something."

Curious about what he was up to, she followed. He stopped and stepped down onto the silken sand and turned to help her. Holding out his arms, he waited for her to accept his touch.

Kacy easily stepped into his arms and closed her eyes as he lifted her with ease to the ground where he was. His hands lingering on her body, she was in no rush to move his touch from her skin. "Thank you," she said in a raspy voice.

"My pleasure. Let's go." Ernst laced their fingers and led her down around a corner of the beach into a small inlet. They found a rock that jetted out into the water. He walked to the end and sat down. "Sit here."

"What are we doing here?" Kacy sat beside him, totally unconcerned with the amount of leg she was showing.

"Wait," he said in a hushed voice. "Just watch the water."

Enthralled by the magical tone he had, Kacy did just that. For a few moments they sat in absolute silence, the waves lapping at the rock and shore the only noise aside from their shallow breathing.

"There!" His sharp whisper made her jump.

Following the line of his finger, Kacy saw a pod of dolphins swimming into the inlet. Four babies that frolicked in the waves. "Oh, Ernst, look at them!" Her voice was wistful.

She sensed him watching her, but she kept her attention forward. "It is a beautiful sight, all right."

Taking her eyes off the water creatures, she put them on the man next to her. "Thank you for sharing this with me."

"There is no one else I could imagine sharing it with," he admitted.

Kacy leaned into him and kissed him. Her full lips gently brushed his before her tongue slid between his lips. He tasted so good. Drawing away, she blinked as a blush ran over her body.

Ernst was motionless, dazed. It was a moment before he spoke again. "You're welcome," he rasped even as he pulled her back in close to his body.

They sat together on the rock and watched the dolphins play. One strong hand ran up and down Kacy's exposed arm with her body propped against his. Eventually, he was holding up more and more of her body. Kacy Travis had fallen asleep in his arms.

She was so comfortable. Feeling safe and content, she took a deep breath and slowly opened her copper eyes, which met the cobalt blue of a masculine shirt. She was sleeping with a man, her body resting fully against his chest.

Her head was on his shoulder and his body cocooned hers as if she belonged there. His arms were locked around her warmly and securely. Flickering around in growing panic, her eyes jerked upward as a rough baritone voice said, "Good morning, *liebling.*"

Kacy froze. The memory of last night came flooding back to her. Ernst Zimmermann, Navy SEAL, good-looking Caucasian male with whom she'd spent the night.

"I have to go," she mumbled, trying to untangle herself from his warm body as gracefully as she could.

"Are you okay?" he asked, concerned as she wobbled on her feet. Ernst stood and reached for her cautiously.

"F...fi...fine," she stuttered looking everywhere but at him. One hand nervously brushed her hair away from her face.

"Look at me," Ernst ordered, holding her chin in one hand. Those eyes of hers shone like polished copper in the early dawn.

"What?" Kacy met his gaze even as her hand touched the one he had on her chin, trying to move it away.

"Why are you so worried?" Ernst refused to release his hold, instead opting to use his free hand to capture hers.

"I just have to go." Her body told a different story.

"Are you leaving today?" His hand moved from her chin to sink into her thick hair.

"No, I...we leave tomorrow."

She saw desire flare in his eyes. "Spend the day with me," he coaxed as he kissed the inside of the wrist he held.

"I have plans," she barely managed to say as her knees trembled.

His strong body stepped closer. "Can you change them?"

"I don't know," Kacy sighed, looking into his amazing eyes.

"Have breakfast with me at least." Ernst leaned in, placed his nose behind her ear, and kissed her. "You smell so good."

Her hands played with the fabric of his shirt. "I have to shower and change."

"No, if I let you go now, you'll keep on running. Don't you want to spend time with me?" His arms encircled her body, bringing their chests closer.

"Yes," Kacy admitted to the hollow of his throat as her nostrils flared, carrying his wonderful scent to her.

"Let's go eat, or I am going to do what I've wanted to do since I first touched you." Ernst's breath teased her neck.

Swallowing hard she said, "I still have to change and shower."

"We could go swimming right here." His hands caressed over her hips.

"Not without a swimsuit," Kacy said with a laugh.

"Release your inhibitions, Kacy. We're the only ones here. It's barely after five." That thick tongue of his traced over the edge of her ear.

"Trying to get me out of my clothes?"

"Hell, yeah, as fast as I can," he said immediately before he sucked her earlobe into his mouth.

Kacy grabbed his waist to steady herself. "Sweet Jesus," she sighed as her body grew wet with desire.

"Not the name I want you calling out. Are we swimming?" He teased the lobe with his teeth.

A clenching need began to burn deep in her belly. "I thought we were having breakfast," Kacy panted as his right hand slipped under her soft shirt.

"I'm about to have mine." Ernst nipped her neck before soothing it with a stroke of his tongue. His hips bucked against her, letting her know exactly what he meant.

Koali Cynemon Travis...what the hell *are you doing with this man? You know better. You can't do this.* "No," she mumbled.

Ernst had his hands back on her hips before that one word faded from the air and he drew back to look at her. "No, what?"

"I don't know you..." Kacy looked over the water and tried to step away.

Ernst refused her unspoken request. Directing her face back towards him so her eyes were watching him he said simply, "So get to know me."

CHAPTER FOUR

Ernst had let her go from the rock after she'd given her word she wouldn't run from him, then had met him thirty minutes later for breakfast. Kacy had showered and changed into a pair of jean shorts and a dark-red halter top. On her feet were a pair of hiking boots, and she'd pulled her thick hair up in a ponytail. Turned out, it was the perfect outfit to wear on a hot-air balloon trip over an active volcano.

She talked with the guide, but eventually turned her attention away and looked at the man who had come with her. Her shimmering gaze took in Ernst's handsome form. He wore a pair of black shorts, a sleeveless light-blue shirt that exposed the raw strength in his arms, and hiking boots. A baseball cap adorned his head and sunglasses hid those beautiful eyes of his.

Taking off her sunglasses, she touched his shoulder and whispered, "Are you not having fun?"

A grin turned up one side of his mouth. "I'm fine."

She knew he was lying; there was a tenseness in his body she hadn't felt before. But the fact he didn't want to ruin her day made her smile. "Okay," Kacy said as she slid her arm around his waist and leaned against his chest. "Thanks for coming with me."

His lips brushed along her forehead. "You're welcome."

Kacy repositioned herself in front of his body so her back rested against his chest and began to talk to another woman in the basket, both of them pointing at various sights and laughing. Ernst didn't let her go until after they had landed back on the ground. Even as she was saying goodbye to the other people he held onto her.

Once they were alone and walking towards the café, she asked, "Why didn't you tell me you didn't like heights? You know, like back when I suggested we take the hot-air balloon ride?"

He gave her a tight smile. "This is your day. I am following you."

Kacy stopped and faced him. Putting her hands on either side of his waist, she looked at him. As if she could see that haunting color of his eyes through both of their reflective sunglasses, she stared at him. "Okay then, you pick. What's next on the agenda, whatever you want to do."

He let a soft finger drift down her cheek. "Do you like boats?" he asked.

"Yes." She cocked her head. "What did you have in mind?"

All she got was a flash of white teeth for an answer. He took her hand and the keys, leaned in for a kiss, and then walked down to the vehicle she had driven up here. Ernst got in on the driver's side and took them to his choice of activities.

"Can I ask you something?" Kacy wondered. "If it is too personal you don't have to answer."

Keeping his eyes on the road he said, "Go ahead."

"How do you manage being a SEAL if you don't like to fly?"

"Not everything is done with airplanes. Big planes are easier; it is more helicopters and hot-air balloons that get me," Ernst divulged. Kacy was mildly surprised and touched he told her.

"Are you going to tell me where you are taking me?" she asked as her eyes moved over his figure. *Damn, you are one good-looking man, Ernst.*

"Thank you, and no, I'm not telling." Ernst smiled as the look of shock passed over her face. "Yes, you did say that out loud. For the record, you are extremely hot yourself!"

Covering her face with her hand, she moaned, "I can't believe I said that out loud."

"Sweetheart, trust me, a man loves to hear that his woman thinks he is good looking," Ernst said as he pulled into the parking lot of a boat rental place.

His woman? Kacy bit the inside of her lip to keep her moan inside.

"Yes, *schatzi*, I said 'his woman.' As in you are my woman." He got out, walked around to her side, and opened the door for her. "Come on."

Hand in hand they walked up to the rental shack, not bothering to be embarrassed he heard her that last time.

"Can I help you two?" the man behind the counter asked.

Ernst took his wallet out and gave some money to Kacy. "You grab the ice cream while I rent the boat."

Though unsure of how that was going to work, eating ice cream in a canoe, Kacy nodded and said, "Okay." Taking the money, she walked towards the ice-cream cart.

"Don't forget my sprinkles!" Ernst shouted. She waved over her shoulder at him.

Ernst had rented them a pedal boat. So they cruised along the water slowly eating their ice cream. "Thank you for this, I have never been in a pedal boat before," Kacy said as she ate another bite of her ice cream. They moved through a shaded part of the water.

"You seem to have an affinity for the water. And this is a relaxing way to enjoy it." *Plus I get to stare at those gorgeous legs of yours.*

Ernst was glad he could spend moments like these with Kacy. He'd gotten so much ribbing from his teammates when he'd finally made it back to the house where they were staying, especially when he'd walked in wearing the same clothes he'd worn the night before.

"I must say, Ernst, that is a good look for you," Tyson had said as he shook his head.

"Shut up, man. We didn't do anything," Ernst had protested.

"And we should believe that why? When you come back wearing the same clothes you left in?" Dimitri had asked.

"We fell asleep down by the water. That's it," he'd insisted as he walked into his room.

"What's your rush?" Dimitri had yelled at his retreating back.

"I'm meeting her for breakfast," Ernst had hollered back as he made his way to the bathroom to take a quick shower.

Strolling back into the living area, Ernst had pulled up short at the sight of Scott standing there with a solemn look on his face. "Sorry, man," the top man of the Megalodon Team said. "We have to leave."

Ernst had frozen as if the whole world had been jerked out from under him. A million emotions had crossed his face before he could composed himself. "Okay, I'll be packed in a few." He'd almost missed Scott's wince, so dejected Ernst had been.

"Aww, man, I'm sorry. It was a joke. Go on have your fun," Scott had said, holding his hands up in apology.

Ernst was brought back to the present with Kacy's response. "I have always loved the water. I was born here in Hawaii, so maybe it is in my blood."

"What about your family?" Ernst asked, frowning over his empty ice-cream container and taking a spoonful of hers.

"I don't know them. I have a few friends that I consider family; otherwise, it is just me." Her voice had grown tense, probably with memories.

Well, that explains a lot of the trust issues you have, my spicy electrician. "I'm sorry to hear that." Ernst touched her arm, amazed at how rigid her body was. "What do you want to do next?" he wondered as he tried to lighten the mood.

Her voice was subdued. "Whatever."

Putting his empty container at his feet, he reached across the boat and turned her face to his. He removed her sunglasses and his so they were looking into each other's eyes. "No, not whatever. I'm sorry I brought up bad memories for you. I am here if you want to talk, but I want you to have fun today."

"I am having fun," she said as her finger dipped into the melted ice cream and smeared it down the bridge of his nose.

Blue eyes narrowed. "Are you sure you want to start this?"

Biting her lower lip, Kacy shook her head. "No. I thought about it and I don't want to."

Ernst wiped the ice cream off his face, dropped his hand in the water to clean it off, and dried it on her skimpy halter top. "Well, that's better."

Looking down at the damp spots on her top Kacy nodded. "I'll remember this."

"So will I," he said as his eyes filled with passion.

"I'm hungry, so take me to shore." She directed with a wave of her spoon.

He crossed his arms and shot her a look. "Oh, no, sweetheart, you have to work also."

Curling up her lip, she slid her glasses back on her face and sighed. "Okay. Probably just that you can't go the distance."

"Playing with fire, *schatzi*. You're playing with fire," he warned as they began to peddle back to the dock. "Just say the word and I guarantee you will find that I am more than capable of 'going the distance'."

"Men, always so touchy," she quipped, refusing to look at him.

"I'll touch you." He leaned over the side and splashed her with water.

"Ernst!" Kacy cried.

"Well, hon, you looked hot." He splashed her again.

"That's it!" She stopped peddling and leaned over, scooping up handfuls of water to toss at him. In the process, she drenched herself, but she laughed at the shock on his face. Forward motion stopped as they began to have a water fight. Moments later, they were nearly soaked to the bone.

Ernst's eyes flared as they fell on the dripping wet halter top that molded itself to her voluptuous body. Water ran down her face; the sunlight glistening off the droplets made her skin shine even more. She was beautiful.

Ernst helped Kacy out of the pedal boat and onto the dock. He brushed back the damp tendrils of hair that fell across her cheek to rest behind her ear. "Let's get some lunch." The stance of his lean body stated to those watching that she was his woman. As they walked down the streets and strolled through the park, the warm Hawaiian sun almost totally dried their clothes.

He took her to an outside café and they had a light lunch. As she sipped her iced tea, he smiled. "So, what's next for us, Ms. Travis?"

"I kind of want to take a walk." She looked around before meeting his gaze again. "I want to enjoy being outside here. I doubt I will be back for a while."

"A walk it is. In the park?"

She shrugged. "Just a walk." Kacy finished off her salad and drank the rest of her tea.

Ernst nodded and paid the bill. "Well, let's go for a walk then." They stood and he slid his arm around her side, loving the feel of her skin against his.

They walked in silence until Kacy suddenly veered to the doorway of a sidewalk shop. She grabbed his hand. "Wait a second. I want to go in here."

His eyes grew wide as he took in the total girly shop even while allowing her to pull him inside. There were about ten women in the shop and they all fell silent and looked at him. He was the only male in there.

"Oh, hell," he muttered. "I'm feeling a bit outnumbered here."

"Scared of a few women?" Kacy's voice teased.

Squaring his shoulders, he took a seat on the very pink frothy couch. "Nope. By all means, *liebling*, give me a fashion show." He waved one hand around the room even as he looked pointedly at the lingerie.

Blushing, she walked away from his piercing gaze and over to the window where she'd seen the frilly skirt. The saleswoman walked over to her. "You have a very brave man, my dear. Most husbands don't come in here at all."

"Oh," Kacy corrected her, "he's not my husband."

The woman picked up the skirt and held it out to her. "Really? From the way he watches you, I would have guessed you were married. Have you been dating long?"

"We've been a couple ever since we met," a deep masculine voice reached them. Ernst's arms slid around Kacy's waist as he kissed her neck and then he moved away.

Which was three days ago. Kacy just rolled her eyes and turned the skirt around, looking at it from all angles. "I'll take this in a," her brows scrunched, "a size two. Yes, that should work for her."

"I think this would work for you," Ernst muttered from behind her. In his hand he had a delicate piece of lace.

The saleswoman smiled and Kacy blushed from the top of her head to the soles of her feet. "Stop," she protested, pushing his hand away. "I'm getting this for a friend. She loves pink and skirts."

His breath teased her ear. "Will you wear this for me if I get it for you?"

"No, now go put it back," she admonished.

"Fine," he whined, moving off after affectionately patting her on the ass.

"He looks like a handful," the woman said as her gaze followed Ernst.

"He's something all right," Kacy admitted. Turning, she watched as he wove in and out of the silk, satin, and lace in the shop. Every now and then he would hold up an item and look at her. Kacy would merely shake her head.

"I will just box this up for you," the saleswoman said.

"Thanks," Kacy said, handing her money. Copper eyes narrowed as they focused on a skinny brunette who had sidled up to Ernst and talked animatedly to him. The woman was leaning into him, showing off her ample cleavage to the blond man.

Ernst could feel Kacy's gaze on him. The woman talking to him desperately wanted more than he was willing to give. Not wanting to risk his newfound relationship on the simpering woman in front of him, he turned his pale gaze to meet the fiery one of the woman he knew would be his wife.

He winked at her and watched her try to seem indifferent, but failing miserably. Moving away from the brunette, he strode toward Koali Cynemon Travis, and in front of everyone, pulled her into his arms and kissed her.

Sliding his tongue into her mouth, he absorbed her taste. Hands slid around to rest on the small of her back, teasing and caressing her skin.

Her body arched deeper into his as she purred into his mouth. Kacy moved her hands around his neck, drawing them even closer. His erection pressed against her belly.

Easing back so his lips rested gently upon hers, he murmured, "I don't want anyone but you, *schätzchen*."

Kacy put her eyes on his. "She's pretty cute."

"Not my kind of woman. Not enough curves, color, or spice." He winked at her again before lifting his head to glance around at their audience. "Sorry, ladies, I couldn't help myself."

They were treated to a round of laughter. The saleswoman brought Kacy's package to her along with the change. Carrying her purchase, Ernst led his woman out the door and back into the Hawaiian afternoon.

Sooner than he preferred, they were standing in front of the hotel's fountain, and Ernst held Kacy tightly in his arms. *I don't want to let her go in through those doors.* "Thank you for spending the day with me, Kacy," he whispered into her ear.

"Thank you for making it a day I will never forget." Her arms tightened around his waist as she pressed her ear to the "lub-dub" of his heart.

They'd gone horseback riding along the beach; biking along wooded trails; and wading in the creeks. Kacy had insisted on buying dinner, and they'd eaten at another nice outdoor café overlooking the water so they could enjoy the sunset.

Each of them had pictures as souvenirs. Ernst had a wallet-size one of the two of them standing together in front of a beautiful waterfall. He had his arm across her shoulders and she had her brown arms wrapped around his waist.

"I don't want to let you go, Kacy," Ernst told her.

"I have to go. My plane is leaving in a few hours and I still have to pack." Kacy made no move to leave his embrace.

"I want to see you again." Ernst moved them off to the side to give them a bit more privacy.

She smiled sadly and her body memorized his masculine scent. "You don't even know where I live."

His hands rubbed her back. "You weren't very forthcoming with personal information."

She shrugged. "I'm a private person."

I know that. Private and not very trusting. "Can I see you again?"

Kacy leaned back to meet his gaze. "Where do you live?"

He stared deeply into her eyes. "I have a small apartment in Virginia."

"Where in Virginia? It is kind of a big state."

"Near Norfolk."

Kacy closed her eyes briefly as if to control the swarming emotions he saw in them. "Do you know a little restaurant in Virginia Beach named *The Fisher King*?"

Ernst shook his head. "No, but I can find out where it is. Why?"

"Two weeks from now, I'll be outside that restaurant. If you want to see me again, be there." Her eyes opened again and he saw more of those conflicting emotions swirling in them.

"The only reason I won't be there is if we are sent away on a mission." His gaze begged for understanding.

"Sure," she said doubtfully. "I'll be there at seven. It's a casual place so jeans are fine."

"Why don't you believe that I want so much more from you than a one-night stand?" Ernst asked as one hand cupped her cheek.

"I have to go." Kacy said.

A sad smile crossed his face. Then it turned mischievous. "You do realize it is going to have to be one hell of a kiss to last me two weeks that you give me, don't you?"

"So you saying that I am going to have to do better?" Kacy arched an eyebrow.

"I'm saying kiss me so it will linger on my lips for the next two weeks." His other hand moved up to rest on her other cheek.

"I might need a few practice runs before I am ready for that final one," she teased as her arms slid up and around his neck to lace her fingers behind his head.

"Quite a few."

"Definitely," Kacy agreed. "So, I should begin." Her hands tugged his mouth down onto hers.

CHAPTER FIVE

Virginia Beach, Virginia

"That ought to do it, Mr. Stevens." Kacy slammed the rear door shut on her Volkswagen van and walked back toward the older gentleman who had paged her. "You can't have that much stuff hooked up to that one outlet. The breaker will keep tripping like it did. But normally, the breaker would be able to be reset; you had a bad one. If you need that much stuff there, get a power strip."

"Thanks so much, Kacy," the graveled tone said as the man shook her hand. "I know you have a bunch of more important things to do than save my bacon time and time again."

"Well," she said with a wink at his wife who had joined them on the step. "Keep this up and your wife may begin to get suspicious." Both of them laughed. "Oh, well, just my luck, all the good ones are taken." Her cell phone began to ring and so she said, "I have to get going. Take care y'all and I will talk to you soon." She grabbed her phone, walked to her vehicle, got in and said, "KT Electric."

A huge grin crossed her face as she recognized the voice on the other end of the line. "Hey, Ilanderae, how are you doing?" Ilanderae Nycks was one of the few people she considered a close friend.

"I just got the skirt and had to call and thank you. How do you always manage to find the cutest little things?" Her friend's rich voice was easily heard across the line.

"Little being the operative word. A frickin' size two. You are so small it makes me sick," Kacy teased. She knew Ilanderae didn't need clothes given to her since she was a fashion designer, but Kacy still loved to give her something from time to time.

"But you have all those wonderful curves. How are you doing? How was Hawaii? What'd we do? Hell, who'd we do?" Ilanderae asked.

There was one I wanted to "do." Kacy's body flushed hot at the memories of Ernst. "I had a really nice time."

"You know I am rolling my eyes here, girl. Any men? Come on dish."

"Well, I did meet this one guy…" She held the phone away from her ear at the piercing scream from Ilanderae.

"Details." The order rang loud.

"I didn't sleep with him…well I didn't have sex with him. I feel asleep in his arms."

"Still waiting for more details. We will get to your issues later."

"Okay, he is about six-two and I would say around one-ninety pounds. Blond hair, these amazingly pale blue eyes, and —"

"He's white?" She sounded shocked.

"Lightly tanned, but yes, technically, he is Caucasian." Kacy smiled over her friend's reaction.

"Well, you know I like my men dark, but hey…go with what you like. Now, tell me why didn't we sleep with this gorgeous man?" Ilanderae questioned.

"I wanted to, Landi, so much, but I couldn't," Kacy said with frustration.

"Still hearing Kirby in your head?" The tone was soft.

"Every time I close my eyes, or think that I may be moving on, I see him." Kacy pulled into her driveway and pushed the button to open her garage, parking next to her car.

"Sweetie, that man has ruined you for all men, but tell me more about this new man. Was he into you?"

"Kind of." Kacy smiled as she remembered the hour it took them to stop kissing before he was satisfied he would make it two weeks.

"What aren't you telling me?" Her friend demanded.

"We spent my last two days there together. Went for a hot-air balloon ride, horseback riding, pedal boating, biking, and just having fun. Landi, I have never had so much fun with a man before." Kacy admitted as she walked into her house, closing the garage behind her.

"Sounds to me like someone is in love," Ilanderae offered.

"I don't know what love is."

"Not every man is going to hurt you, Koali. I know what you went through, but you have to give this one a chance, especially when I hear the joy in your voice as you talk about him. It sounds like he was into you. What does he do?"

"He's Navy."

"Well, not a lot of money there. Unless he's an officer. Is he?"

Kicking off her shoes, Kacy shook her head. "I don't know. Landi, I barely know anything about him, except that when he touches me I feel complete and beautiful. His kisses leave me breathless and I want to be with him. I don't know about his family; I don't know anything. I met his teammates but only briefly."

"Love," Ilanderae said in a falsely disgusted voice.

"I am meeting him for dinner in a few nights at *The Fisher King*, if he shows up."

"He lives in Virginia?"

Kacy opened the freezer and pulled out a microwavable dinner. "He said around Norfolk. I said I would be outside the restaurant and if he wanted to see me again to be there at seven."

"You didn't give him your phone number or anything, did you?"

"You know me, Landi." Kacy shoved the dinner in the microwave and pushed the button before walking to the living room and sitting in her chair.

"Girl, if I were closer, I would kick your ass," the sigh came.

"Tell me how Milan is." Kacy hoped Ilanderae would get off the subject of her new man that she didn't really have yet.

Outside The Fisher King

Kacy leaned against the stone wall and brushed her hands over her thighs. They were having an unseasonably cool week, so she wore blue jeans, a honey-colored silk blouse, and a pair of sandals. Her hair hung past her shoulders, and as she ran a hand down the back of it she heard the voice of her dreams.

"You still look beautiful, *schätzchen*," Ernst said as his body appeared beside hers.

Turning her copper eyes to him, she drank her fill. He wore jeans that cupped him so nicely. A black tee shirt and tennis shoes completed his outfit. "You still look pretty fly."

"Hello, Kacy," he murmured as his body stepped in to get a kiss.

Kacy kissed him back with more passion than she could ever remember having for a man. While her number of lovers was limited, what this man made her feel was off the charts. "Hello, Ernst," she whispered against his lips.

"Didn't think I would be here did you?" His blue eyes moved slowly over her body as he committed her to memory.

"I had my doubts," she admitted, blushing and stepping away from him. "Ready to eat?"

"More than you could possibly know," he said in a low seductive timbre. Ernst reached for her arm and drew her back to his side. "I said I would be here unless we were deployed somewhere."

"So you did," Kacy agreed. "And here you are."

Ernst smiled, breathing an internal sigh of relief. For the past two weeks, he had panicked every time the phone rang, hoping beyond everything that his Team wouldn't be sent away on the day he was to meet Kacy. Thankfully, they hadn't been.

However, Ernst had been a nervous wreck as he'd driven to the restaurant. What if she didn't really like him and didn't show?

His heart had swelled when he'd spotted her leaning against the wall
in front of the restaurant. It had taken him a moment to regain his composure
before walking up to her. He had missed her so much.

But the fact that she hadn't thought he wanted to see her again threw
him. What did he have to do to gain her trust?

"Well, let's go eat," Ernst said, filing that away for later and holding
the door for her. They would enjoy their time tonight.

The interior of the place was beautifully lit with recessed lighting and
fancy chandeliers. As Ernst did a once over of the place it occurred to him he
was the only white person in there and the object of many curious gazes.

"Hey, Kacy!" a large black man yelled over the music that played in
the building. "I'll be with you in a moment; take your table."

"Thanks, Darnell," she responded with a wave. "This way." Kacy
took the lead.

At least she is still holding my hand. Ernst met the gazes of all who
stared at him. No one said anything mean, but he could see the suspicion in
their looks. "Come here a lot?" he asked as he stopped beside her in front of
the booth.

"All the time," Kacy said with a smile. "Inside or out?"

Ernst cocked his head and looked at her. "Inside or out what?"

"Of the booth." She pointed at the seat in front of her.

He looked and looked again. It was one booth seat and a table up
against a wall. They were going to sit side by side. "Well, I'm right-handed so
I will sit on the outside, otherwise we will hit each other." *I don't want the men
in here looking at you.*

"You remember I'm left-handed?" Kacy seemed impressed. She slid
across the leather seat and closed her eyes as his warm body settled next to
hers.

Leaning in close to her, he whispered in her ear, "I remember everything about you."

"So," a booming voice intruded. "What can I get you to drink?"

Ernst looked up to see that same large man standing in front of them.
Picking up the menu, he glanced over it and asked, "Kacy? What do you
want?"

The man she had called Darnell interrupted. "I know what she
wants. I was asking you."

Kacy shrugged and sent Darnell a look. "I want you to meet my
friend Ernst, Darnell."

"Friend?" Darnell asked, sounding like a schoolmarm instead of the
three-hundred-pound man he was. "I ain't never seen you bring a friend in
here to sit at your booth. Not a male one anyway." Those dark eyes moved
back to Ernst. "You must be something special. How about I bring you a

lemonade and if you don't like it, I will get something else for you." He was gone before Ernst could say anything one way or another.

"Where do you know Darnell from?" Ernst questioned.

"I did the electrical work here when they first opened, and have been eating here ever since." She frowned. "I'm sorry; I sort of just assumed you would like what they serve."

"Hey, I love food; as long as it's good, I'm happy," he reassured her, touched by her concern.

Kacy smiled at him. "Well, then, you will be happy. His wife is an awesome cook."

"I love how your eyes crinkle up at the corners when you smile," he blurted out. It was his turn to grin as he saw the blush move across her skin.

Soon, they were dining on hushpuppies, greens, fried Saba over rice, and frog legs. Darnell had delivered it on one large plate so they could take smaller portions and put it on their own plates.

"Oh, Lord, this is good." Ernst laid his fork down beside him and leaned back in the seat. "I'm stuffed. I think I am going to have to run an extra twenty miles to work this off."

"I knew I liked you," Darnell said. "Any man who eats like you and is so obviously fond of my Kacy is good in my book. Now, what's gonna be for dessert?" He tossed down the dessert menu. "I will be back in a bit."

"Dessert? After that amount I just ate?" Ernst turned his head to look at Kacy who was nodding.

"Have to have dessert. They would be insulted otherwise."

"Are the portions always this big?"

"Yep."

"Jesus, I think I should let the team know about this place. It is awesome." Ernst leaned in and kissed her on the cheek. "Thanks for sharing it with me."

Darnell returned. "What's for dessert?"

"I want Bananas Foster," Kacy said.

"I'll have an order of bread pudding," Ernst said. "And a coffee please."

"Be up in a few." Darnell took two steps and turned back. "Y'all make a great couple. I like him, Kacy; keep him." Then he left.

"He's a smart man," Ernst observed with a grin. "You should listen to him."

Kacy rolled her eyes but blushed. "I'll keep that in mind."

After their desserts had been delivered and it was once again just the two of them at the small corner booth, Ernst asked, "Do I get to know more about you now?"

"What were you looking for?" she hedged.

"I don't know…a phone number. An address." He put down his fork and placed his gaze on her face. "Look at me, Kacy," he pled.

Slowly, she met his gaze. "What?" Kacy questioned.

Ernst noticed the distrust that lurked in the back of her eyes. "I want to know where you live. I want to be able to call you. Hell, I want to call you my girlfriend."

Kacy swallowed. "I...I...I..."

"Kiss me, Kacy," he said.

That got her attention. Those dark brows of hers scrunched together as she asked again, "What?"

"Kiss me. Right here. Right now." *Do you trust me enough to do that in front of your friends?*

Not even looking around the room at the patrons who'd fallen silent and begun watching the couple in the corner, Kacy put down her fork. Getting up on her knees on the bench, she moved over so their mouths were millimeters away. Her copper eyes gleamed with the emotion he wanted them to have for him. Love. Desire. Trust.

She straddled one of his legs and her hands rested against the smoothness of his chin. As her head moved closer her eyes drifted closed. It seemed as if all her feelings were poured into this kiss. Her tongue ran over his lips before sliding between them and entering the warmth of his mouth.

Ernst let her have control of the kiss for about five seconds. His body was rock hard the second she'd gotten up on her knees and moved toward him. But when her tongue slipped into his mouth, he forgot himself. Easily dominating the kiss, he grabbed her around the waist and held her there while his mouth plundered hers.

Both of them were hot and horny when they broke apart. Her eyes were like liquid metal and his were burning with promise—a promise to finish what had been started.

Kacy got off his lap and silently picked up her fork to try and eat some more. Her hands were shaking so bad it was almost impossible.

"Let's go," Ernst said. "I want to have you to myself for a while." Kacy nodded, clearly not trusting her voice to speak. Ernst paid for dinner and soon they were back outside.

"You can follow me home," Kacy said in a quiet voice.

"Are you sure?" Ernst asked, not really wanting her to think on it and back out of the offer.

Kacy nodded and spun on her heel, apparently not willing to give herself an out, either.

Chapter Six

Getting out of his rusty pickup, Ernst shut the door, his attention transfixed. Though Kacy's house was a nice little rambler, it was her car that made him want a closer look.

"Come on in," Kacy called from the garage as she got out of her vehicle.

"That is a beautiful car you have there," he said running his hands over the light metallic gray car. On the gas tank cover was a small red-orange phoenix painted in intricate detail. She had a 1968 Camaro Z28.

She grinned. "I love this car."

"Makes sense." Ernst followed her inside the house, watching as she pushed the button to close the garage. "You have a really nice home."

"Well, it's not much, but it's mine," Kacy said. "Make yourself at home; I'll be right back."

Ernst looked around. Along one wall he saw a huge fish tank full of tropical fish and plants. "Jesus," he muttered as he walked closer.

"Those are my pets. I don't have time to take care of a dog or cat, and fish relax me."

"Wow. That is impressive." He looked down at the woman who appeared beside him. She'd put her hair in a ponytail. "Why did you put your hair up?" Ernst wondered as he touched a few strands that had escaped confinement.

He would've had to be blind, deaf, and dumb to miss the look of fear that crossed her face. "Hey," he said, moving his head to catch her gaze. "I was just wondering, I like it both ways." Slowly, he noticed the tension leave her body.

"I like it off my neck," she admitted. "Let me give you a tour, for what it's worth."

"It will be worth it," he assured her. "Lead on."

"Living room," she teased as her hands presented the area where they stood.

"I think I got that," he whispered in her ear as he pinched her butt.

"This is the kitchen/dining room." Kacy showed him a room that was pretty bare. The only appliance he saw was her coffee maker on a counter. Nothing was on the table except for one placemat and the salt and pepper shakers that were shaped like seahorses. "I don't cook."

"Nice to know there is something you don't do," Ernst joked.

Shaking her head, she led him back through the living room and down the hall. "Bathroom." She pointed. "Laundry room." Kacy gestured to a closed door.

Ernst stuck his head in each of them. Her bathroom was done in a dark emerald green color. The laundry room had pictures of the ocean hanging on the wall that was painted a pale blue.

"My office is in here." She opened the door and let him look inside.

A low whistle left him. The room was full of books on electricity and poetry. A large table was along one wall and it was covered in rolled up blueprints. On that same wall was a picture of a killer whale breaching in the sunset.

"Down here is my guest room," Kacy said as he pulled the door shut behind him and followed her into the next room.

It was a smaller room painted pale purple with a futon along a wall. Pictures of coastlines were all over. Dark purple pillows and blankets accented the room. A large, overstuffed chair was in the corner with a plush gray walrus sitting on it.

It was simple, yet there was a very comfortable feel to it. He liked it. "Very nice," he said as they left the room.

She pointed to the end of the hall. "My bedroom is down there."

"I don't get to see that one?" Ernst asked.

"It's not clean," she tried.

"I don't care."

She hesitated a second more. "Okay," she caved and led the way to the door, unaware of the possessive gaze that ran over her body.

She opened the door and stepped inside her room. Ernst brushed past her and gazed around the space that defined the woman of his dreams. The furniture looked like Ikea and it fit her. Simple and strong. The walls were covered in a mural of the ocean and coastline and the carpet reminded him of sand.

Her bed was a full size and he knew they would fit perfectly on it together. The bedspread was the color of the Caribbean, and on it were pillows of starfish, other ocean creatures, and shells.

"Like ocean life, don't you?" Ernst asked as he picked up a seahorse-shaped pillow from her bed.

"I do," Kacy said, blushing. The phone rang and she said, "I'll be right back." She headed up the hall.

Left alone in her room, Ernst picked up another pillow from the top of the bed. He brought it close to his nose and inhaled her scent. A sheet of paper caught his eye and he leaned down to see what it was.

A grin crossed his face as he looked at the picture of them from Hawaii. "I'm figuring you out, my *schätzchen*. You are as attracted to me as I am to you. This picture proves it. I just have to find a way to gain your trust," he whispered to the room as he put the pillow back, not wanting her to know he had seen it.

When she walked back in the room, he was looking at a pillow trying to figure out what it was. "It's a porcupine fish," Kacy said. "Pull on his tail."

Ernst did and laughed as the quills stood out straight. "That is cute." He put it back on the chair. "You have a lovely home."

"Thank you," she said.

They moved to the back porch overlooking her backyard and sipped on iced tea. Ernst snuck a look at the woman sitting next to him in a lounge. She was watching him. "So now you know where I live, Mr. Zimmermann. Is that better?"

"Don't call me that. Call me Ernst. I want your phone number as well."

"Why are you so persistent?"

Setting down his iced tea, he swung his legs over the edge of the lounge he was on and rested his arms on his thighs. Putting his eyes on her he said, "I told you in Hawaii I want more from you than a one-night stand. I will go away and never bother you again if you can honestly tell me that you don't feel anything for me."

Kacy stared at him. "I can't say that, not honestly."

"Kacy, I don't know what has happened to you in your past to make you this mistrustful. But honey, I'm not going anywhere. There is something way deeper than either one of us can comprehend going on between us. You are in my thoughts all the time — the feel of your lips on mine, how you taste, how you feel in my arms."

Ernst leaned closer and took her hand in one of his. "I want to get to know you, inside and out. Yes, I want desperately to make love to you, but I want so much more than that." His lips brushed the inside of her wrist. "I want to have a relationship with you. I want to take you to functions that the Team goes to. I want to show you off to the world as my girlfriend." *As my wife.*

"Why me?" Her eyes were direct as she asked her question.

"Why not you?" He took the glass of tea from her and pulled her toward him so they were facing each other.

"Considering the woman you were with that night you asked me out, I don't think I am exactly your type," Kacy told him.

"Until I met you I didn't know what my type was. I can't explain what it is about you, but I will try." He waited for her nod before continuing.

"That first day that I ran into you, I felt something then. I couldn't get you out of my head for the rest of the day. I hadn't wanted you to be scared of me."

His fingers moved lightly over the backs of her hands. "When I saw you with Brett, I got jealous, especially when I saw you smile when all I did was make you fearful. I wanted then to carry you off to a place where no one would bother us." Ernst got off his lounge and knelt between her legs. "There is something inside you, Kacy."

He tipped her chin to meet his gaze. "Something that for some reason you try to keep hidden. A fire that burns within you. I saw it that day we spent together in Hawaii. You have a passion for life that calls to me in a way I never knew existed. I am complete when I am with you, and I know that we don't know each other very well yet. I have told myself that as well. But like someone told me, there are times our hearts and souls know before our brains can comprehend.

"I know what true love and compatibility look like. I've seen them with the men I work with. They don't know color and they don't know society's dictates. And as sure as I am kneeling between your gorgeous legs on your porch, I know you are the other half of my soul. But I am no dummy, and I know you don't trust, so I am willing to take it slow."

Kacy was speechless. "How is that a man like you is still single?" Her eyes were soft as they looked upon his handsome features.

"Because I was waiting for you."

Sitting closer, Kacy put her lips to his and kissed him.

Ernst slid her forward so she was straddling his waist before he stood and walked into the house with her in his arms and their lips still locked together. With a groan, he stopped in the living room and sat them down on the couch.

Kacy opened her eyes and looked at him.

He could see the uncertainty floating around in her gaze. "Not tonight, no matter how much I want to. Not tonight." Ernst readjusted her so they she was lying on him on the couch.

"I haven't had many men in my life. I don't want you to be disappointed in me." Her quiet confession reached him.

Brushing a hand across the top of her head he said, "I will never be disappointed in you. Can you tell me why you are so lacking in trust?"

Her body tensed but at least she didn't pull away from him. "You know how after you hear something enough you begin to believe it? Let's just say I have been told I was worthless enough that I have begun to believe it."

Eyes turned to ice shards as he thought of someone degrading his woman. "Sweetheart, you are so much more than you allow yourself to believe. Understand that I believe in you fully."

"That is very sweet of you to say, Ernst, but you don't know me." Kacy closed her eyes as if to enjoy the feel of his arms around her.

"We are dating; I will get to know you. I want to know everything about you."

"Since when are we dating?" she asked with a smile even as tears welled in her eyes.

The softness he saw overcoming her features melted his heart even more. "Don't you remember what I told that woman in the store in Hawaii? We have been dating since we met." His fingers began to tickle her.

"Stop!" she squealed as she tried to get away.

"Admit it; we are a couple." Ernst captured her with his legs and held her there while he continued to tickle her.

Struggling to get free, the tears began to run down her face. "O...o...okay. We're a couple. Stop! Please stop!" she panted.

He lifted her and turned her so they lay chest to chest. "Now that wasn't so hard to admit was it?" Ernst arched a blond brow.

Jumping off him she said, "It doesn't count. That was admitted under duress." Then she ran out into the backyard as he bolted after her.

Ernst ran through the door and found her bent over trying to catch her breath in the far corner of the yard. "What did you put yourself into the corner for? First rule of combat: never let yourself get backed into a corner." He sauntered down the steps like the predator who knew his prey was out of options.

Kacy looked at him and begin to move sideways as he approached. His steps were sure and confident as he flowed toward her. For a second she imagined him wearing combat gear and honing in on his target, and she could understand the fear that person would experience.

As she moved a bit more, she saw a glimmer of desire flare in his eyes at the prospect of a hunt. He slightly shook his head at her and flashed a crooked half smile. "I think you are out of options, *liebling*."

While she wasn't as athletic as the man stalking her around her yard, Kacy was in decent shape. Feinting one way, she bolted off in the other direction and almost made it to the steps when she was tackled.

Ernst took the brunt of the fall and then rolled her over so he was on top. Nose to nose with her, he clucked. "What do I get for capturing you?" His hands were beneath her shoulders as his lips moved over hers.

Breathing hard for more than one reason, Kacy shook her head at him. "A glass of iced tea?"

"Well something sweet was on my mind, but I don't think tea will do it. I was thinking of some brown sugar and cinnamon." His eyes darkened as his mouth claimed hers.

Her body arched against his as wetness flooded it. *I want you so bad, Ernst. But I don't want you to tell me how horrible I am in bed.* Kacy didn't even realize her body had stiffened.

Ernst did. Drawing back from the kiss, he rolled off her and got to his feet, pulling her up after. "What wicked thought crossed your mind this time, Kacy?"

She shook her head and refused to look at him.

Gathering her to his chest, Ernst put his chin on the top of her head. "Do you not see how perfect your body fits mine? We were made for each other Kacy. Nothing that fits like this can be bad. Let go of this fear you have; we will be wonderful together. I know this for a fact."

Kacy opened her mouth to respond when the phone rang from inside. Her body slumped for a moment before she untangled herself from his embrace and walked up the steps to the porch. With one last glance at him she walked in the house and picked up her cordless phone.

She made some notes on a pad of paper as she listened to her potential client. "Sure thing. I can be there in about thirty minutes. Electricity doesn't care what time it is, sir. See you soon. Yes, sir." She clicked off the phone and stood. "Damn."

"What was that about?" Ernst asked from behind her.

Jumping, she turned. "I didn't know you were in here. I have to go." Kacy walked to her bedroom ignorant of the fact that Ernst was once again following her.

"Where are you going?" he questioned as she entered her closet and pulled out a pair of jeans and a tee shirt.

"About thirty miles from here. I don't know him. New client." Her fingers were on the buttons of her shirt as she began to undress.

Ernst continued watching her and Kacy tried to stay calm. The fact he kept his distance spoke volumes. "Let me come along," he said as gently as he could.

For a moment, Kacy worried the inside of her lower lip, unsure if she should keep undressing. When he made no further movement, she decided to proceed, especially since she did feel comfortable with him. Safe even. Shrugging out of the silk blouse, she pulled on the tee shirt and began to change pants.

"Is there a particular reason you want to come along on my call?"

"Not really, other than the fact he is a man you don't know, and it is ten-thirty at night," he growled, watching her slide on the other pair of jeans.

"Sure, but you can't get in the way." Her words were quick. He didn't miss the smile she had.

Ernst climbed in her van; and Kacy felt him watching as she clipped her cell phone on her side, got into her van, and backed out of the garage, driving off into the night.

CHAPTER SEVEN

Rubbing the back of her neck, Kacy restocked her van. It was one in the morning and she was exhausted. At least tomorrow was Sunday and she could sleep in a bit. Having Ernst with her had been a godsend. Mr. Sing had wanted more than just her expertise in electricity, making a pass at her the second she had handed him the bill.

She smiled as she remembered Ernst stepping between them and asking him to please not hit on his woman. Mr. Sing had apologized and paid her. The van ride back had been silent as she'd mentally run over what she needed to do.

So now, she wanted nothing more than to climb into bed. Of course, there was one other thing she wouldn't mind doing and his name was Ernst. Shaking her head to get her focus back, Kacy finished restocking the van and shut the door.

Going inside the house, she saw Ernst leaning against the wall leading to the kitchen. His pale eyes were on her from the moment she walked in the door. Kacy sent him a nervous smile. This man took her breath away.

"Thanks for going with me," she offered as she closed the door to the garage behind her.

"You get hit on a lot?" he asked, unfolding his body and walking towards her.

"It happens," Kacy said and shrugged that fact off. Kicking off her shoes, she put her keys by the door.

"Well, I should get going," Ernst said as he ran his hand down her face.

"Thanks for dinner," she said.

Looking into her eyes, Ernst leaned down to kiss her. The heat immediately sparked to life. As if against his will, he drew away from her tempting mouth. "Dream of me Kacy, 'cause you know I will be dreaming of you." One more fast kiss and he was gone, slipping away into the night.

Slumping against the wall, Kacy closed her eyes and relived the feel of his lips on hers. "I am one stupid broad to let that man walk out of my door." Disgusted with herself, she turned off the lights, walked down the hall to her room, and put on her sleep clothes.

A pounding on the door startled her. Her next door neighbor, Mrs. Wilder, was an elderly woman who would sometimes come over late at night when she got spooked or needed to go to the emergency room. Heading up the hall at a jog, she jerked the door open to find not her neighbor, but Ernst standing at the other side of the door. Kacy's eyes grew wide as she backed up almost to the wall of the entryway as he followed her inside. Not a word passed his mouth as he grabbed her ass and hauled her up against him. His lips ground on hers as he claimed her mind, soul, and body. She was his and she knew it.

Clambering to get closer, she wrapped her legs around his waist as his strong hands dug into the flesh of her ass. With one swift kick, he shut the door behind him and carried her down the hall to her bedroom, shouldering his way into the room.

Lips still mashed together, he laid her down on the bed and then followed, covering her softer body with his firm one. Her hands began tugging up his shirt as her skin searched for his, desperately needing to feel it upon her own.

Ernst tore his mouth off hers and stared into her eyes as he tried to regain control of his breathing. Sitting up, he whipped off his shirt. Naked desire blazed in her gaze.

"Touch me," he rasped.

Kacy sat up as well so they were knee to knee on her bed. Eyes roving over his exposed torso, she licked her lips in anticipation of touching such a work of art. Reaching for the moderately haired chest, she laid her spread hands across his pectorals. The heat of his skin burned her palms; the coarseness of his chest hair contrasted with the smoothness of the rest.

Her hands moved down over his ribs and across his six pack, then back up again and down his shoulders and arms. "You are amazing," she whispered as she continued to touch his body. "So strong." Kacy looked at how dark her skin was against his. Inhaling, she smelled the mixture of his cologne, his natural scent, and the desire that flowed in the room.

With a direction and mind of their own, her hands moved back down across his taut stomach and to his waistband. A deep, pulling need was alive inside her. She wanted this man more than she wanted her next breath.

But the disappointment. And what came after. Her body stiffened and her eyes grew wide with fear.

Ernst noticed the change in her body immediately and grabbed her hands, pulling her body into his. Wrapping his steel-bound arms around her, his willpower just about crumbed as her face burrowed into his neck. She smelled so sweet.

"I'm sorry," she mumbled against his neck.

Praying for strength, Ernst set her away from him. "Why did you stop touching me? Do you not like my body? Do I repulse you?"

"No." Immediately she reached for his arm. "I don't want to disappoint you."

Ernst tucked her hair behind her ear. "You will not disappoint me. Can I touch you now?" he asked softly.

"Yes," she said quietly.

A grin spread across his face. "I have been looking forward to this since I met you." He reached for the hem of her gray tank top and lifted the garment from her body.

They always said blue flames were among the hottest, and the fires that burned in Ernst's eyes did that saying justice. His gaze took its sweet time moving over her bare chest.

"You are gorgeous," he managed to say as he swallowed repeatedly, trying to get moisture back in his mouth.

Her breasts were full and he knew they were made to suckle him and one day their child. Her stomach was flat but not rigid like his. She was firm, but definitely feminine.

Reaching forward, he brushed her hair back over both shoulders. Not wanting anything to block his view. Then he took two fingers and trailed them down her sternum to her belly button.

"Your skin is like silk," he said as he watched her nipples harden under his gaze. "I can't wait to suck on your breasts." Moving off the bed he stood before her in nothing but jeans and socks. He'd kicked off his shoes as he'd explored her.

"Come here," he said.

Her gaze on his, Kacy moved to stand in front of him. The one lamp lit in the room, casting a glow about them. His large hands settled on her hips only to move upward and cup her breasts. He felt her tremble beneath his touch. His thumbs brushed over the tight nipples, sending more shockwaves through her.

Lowering his head, Ernst took one nipple in his mouth. His tongue laved it while he suckled. Kacy whimpered and gripped his arms for support. Dragging his tongue along her skin, he moved to the second one and showered it with the same attention.

Kacy screamed as her first orgasm in years overtook her body. Eyes a bit fuzzy, she met the gaze of the man totally supporting her weight.

"What are you doing to me?" she muttered.

Ernst swept her up and laid her back on the bed. "Showing you what real pleasure is." He ripped off the bottoms she wore, leaving her totally naked beneath him.

"Ernst," she uttered, embarrassment plain in her low voice, "I just came."

His hand swept over the apex of her thighs and he gritted his teeth as if to control himself. "I know, *schätzchen*. Let's see if we can't set some records."

Kacy shivered at those words. His warm body move away and she whimpered. Then his breath was by her ear. "Don't worry; I'm not going anywhere."

She felt him beside her. Naked this time. Kacy could feel his erection pressing into her side. He would cut her in two. But he didn't shove into her. Instead, his mouth began licking and nibbling around her neck.

"You taste so good, Kacy," he said between caresses.

Kacy felt that burn within her core begin again. Her hips arched in silent invitation as she mewled in pleasure.

"Not yet. You're not ready yet." Ernst began to kiss his way down her body.

Not ready yet? Her body could light the whole city it had so much voltage coursing through it! Her cries were of pleasure and disappointment.

He kissed her breasts and moved down to her belly, his tongue dipping into her navel. He licked across her waist until her body shook from all the tremors coursing through it.

Ernst passed the part of her that called to him with its spicy scent, the damp curls he wanted to touch and taste. He passed her core, just allowing his breath to touch her there. He licked down the inside of one leg to her foot and back up the other.

Kacy squirmed on the bed. "Ernst," she begged.

"What?" His voice was rough with passion. He kissed her as his body settled beside her.

"I want—"

He ran his finger down the bridge of her nose, then caressed her lips. Over her chin and through the valley between her full breasts. Past her belly button and through the patch of wet, sable hair that was at the juncture of her thighs.

His finger moved across the thick nether lips and slipped inside. Kacy came off the bed in another explosive orgasm, screaming his name to the room.

Ernst slid another finger inside her tight body as he felt her juices covering his hand. *Dear God, she is so tight around me.* He just about came right there.

His thumb began to rub her clit, knowing the callused skin brought her even more pleasure. "That's it, baby," he whispered. "Just let it go."

It didn't take long before her body was once again on the brink of an orgasm. Her legs clamped around his wrist to keep him in place.

Ernst latched his mouth onto one taut nipple. Her lower body lifted up as he sucked it at the speed matching the thrust of his fingers. Then he maneuvered his body between her legs, withdrawing his two slick fingers. His thumb stayed on her swollen clit.

Slowly, he guided the head of his unyielding erection to the heat of her body. A small push later, and the tip was in.

Kacy stiffened at the intrusion. Ernst moved his head up to hers so their mouths could meet. "Trust me, *schatzi*." Unhurriedly, he pushed his hips forward, driving himself home into her moist heat.

"Ernst," she panted. She began to arch against him, but he shook his head against her neck.

"Wait. Just hold still." Eyes closed, Ernst prayed for strength. He wanted to pound the hell out of the woman beneath him. Stake his claim on her. Make her understand that no other man would even begin to compare to him.

Drops of sweat fell from his head to her skin. Kacy realized he was holding back his own pleasure to allow her hers. Closing her eyes, she felt his love flow over her.

"Please, Ernst," Kacy said as her hands captured his face, bringing it back up to hers for a kiss. "Make love to me."

"Forever," he promised as his hips began to move back and forth.

Each stroke made her shiver. As another orgasm poured over her, Ernst seemed to lose the thin thread of control he had.

His thrusts grew deeper and faster. Kacy met each one with a cry of pleasure.

Ernst pressed his mouth to hers, his thick tongue matched the pistoning of his hips.

Kacy's legs locked around his waist as he plowed deeper into her. Her eyes had long since rolled back into her head. Nails dug into the tender flesh of his shoulders as he thrust one last time and exploded deep within her.

As his seed covered her womb, their souls intertwined. At that moment, they were one—not a white man and a black woman—but one soul, one person, one entity.

Exhausted, Ernst sagged to the bed, barely avoiding crushing the exquisite woman beneath him. He had nothing left; she had sucked him dry. But in a good way. A very good way.

The chime of his watch told him it was three in the morning. Gathering Kacy in his arms, he tucked her head under his chin and just held her. Ernst wanted to yell it from the top of the world, that he was in love with this woman; but for the moment, he could be content just to hold her.

The same as the night in Hawaii when she had fallen asleep in his arms, he knew the exact moment she was truly asleep. Ernst readjusted them so their bodies were comfortably entangled. Her body caused his to begin to stir. He wanted her again, but he gritted his teeth and let her sleep.

CHAPTER EIGHT

Kacy awoke a five. It never failed; no matter what time she went to bed, she woke at five. At least today was Sunday. Opening her eyes, she saw rain running down the windowpane. Perfect. A rainy Sunday, more reason to lie around.

A gentle smile crossed her face as she thought of Ernst and the tender and gentle way he had made love to her. Slipping out of bed, she grabbed some clothes and headed for the bathroom.

Ernst was awake the second she stirred against him. He watched through lowered lids as she snuck from the room. *Why was she up so damn early?* His body relaxed as he heard the toilet flush. Still tired, he drifted back to sleep to the sound of rain pounding against the glass.

He woke again. Alone. This time he sat up and glanced at his watch. Six-thirty, but no Kacy in bed. Wiping the sleep from his eyes, Ernst slid on his boxers and crept up the hall. She wasn't in the guest room, office, living room, or kitchen. About to get dressed and really search, he noticed the sliding door to her porch open.

Stepping out, he saw her sound asleep on the swing. The rain was coming down hard, but it didn't wake her. Ernst stood over her and looked, really looked at her. Her hair was in disarray. He could see where she had whisker burn on her neck courtesy of him. Thick lashes were resting on her baby soft skin. Her cute little nose and full lips that he loved to kiss made her appear angelic.

Leaning down, he scooped her right out of the swing and carried her back into the bedroom where he put them both back under the covers. Ernst fell easily back to sleep with her in his arms again.

Someone or something was watching her. Copper eyes opened and the first thing they saw was a pair of heart-stopping blue eyes. The man who owned those eyes was propped up on one arm looking down at her.

"Good morning, Kacy," Ernst spoke in a deep voice. It was so comforting to hear his timbre. He reached over and began to trace her lips.

"Morning," she mumbled. "I thought I was on the porch," Kacy said, more to herself.

"You were but you belong in your bed, and my body missed yours." He kissed her before going back to his touching quest.

Kacy put her gaze on him. "Why did you come back?"

His caresses never paused. "Aside from the fact I wanted you and I still do? I came back because it was after midnight, a new day. I came back because I wanted to be with you. I wanted to fall asleep with you in my arms."

His fingertips lightly roamed over her face, as if memorizing every detail. "How are you feeling?" His touch moved down her neck.

"Lazy," she answered with a sigh. His touch was so different; it could stoke her to burning frenzy or offer such comfort and tenderness as it was doing now.

"Hungry?"

"Yes, I am." His touch changed and she began to tremble from the desire she could feel emanating from his fingertips.

His hand stilled. "What do you want to eat?"

Kacy misunderstood. She wanted him to want her again. Since he was asking about breakfast and no longer caressing her, she figured she had been a disappointment, after all.

Feeling her body's reaction, Ernst growled low in his throat and pinned her between him and the mattress. "Sweetheart, I want you so much I hurt." Taking her hand, he placed it on his throbbing erection. "I was thinking of you and how your body is doing." He kissed her briefly. "You didn't disappoint me. Quite to the contrary, I love every response you give me."

Tightening her hand around him, Kacy looked directly into his eyes and murmured, "This is what I want. This is what I need."

Ernst was slipping his penis inside her body in seconds. Soon, they were screaming their releases to the house that shuddered with the force of thunder claps raging outside.

When she awoke a third time, Kacy found one strong, lightly tanned arm holding her down. Running a hand over her face, she turned to look at the clock. Ten. *I never sleep this late.*

Pushing at the arm that kept her there, Kacy groaned as the hold tightened. "Where are you going?" the masculine voice asked as Ernst buried his face into her neck.

"I was going to get up and eat, but…" She shrugged and tapped his arm as she burrowed closer to his naked body.

"I'll take you out for breakfast or brunch." Ernst kissed her behind the ear.

"That's okay." Finding the strength, she wriggled out of his hold. Kacy got out of bed and slipped on her robe saying, "I'm going to go shower."

Ernst flopped on his back and watched as her shimmering gaze moved over his exposed body. "I thought you were hungry." He put his arms behind his head as if allowing her a better view.

"I am but you don't need to buy me a meal." With difficulty, Kacy tore her gaze from his naked chest and began to pick up the scattered clothes.

Rolling his eyes, Ernst climbed out of bed and stepped in front of her. His hands latched onto her wrists as he waited for her to look at him. She did. One eyebrow rose in silent question. It took so much willpower not to look down to his midsection for she knew he was naked.

"I want to buy you breakfast. That is what dating couples do."

Throwing his boxers at his chest, she shook her head. "We aren't a couple." *No matter how nice it sounds.*

His eyes narrowed as he put on his boxers. "What are you saying, this was a one-night stand?"

Kacy heard the menace in his tone and her body instinctively tensed. "I guess so. Look we have nothing in common and I don't —"

"Don't start that shit," he growled. "I want more than that from you, Kacy." His movements were jerky as he pulled on his jeans.

Get rid of him now, girl, before you get any deeper. "But I don't," she lied, nearly breaking down from the pain that flashed across his face.

Ernst clenched his jaw, as if he were struggling to hold onto his control. "Will you have dinner with me tonight?"

"Sure," Kacy said, not looking at him.

"About five at *Fountains*?"

Her dark head nodded. "Sure."

"I'll let myself out." His tone was so formal it killed her.

"Okay." Turning away, Kacy walked up the hall to the bathroom and shut herself inside, not wanting to watch him leave.

The second he heard the bathroom door shut, Ernst sank down on her bed, still rumpled from when they had lain in it and made love. Putting his head in his hands he sighed. "What am I going to do with you, Koali Travis?"

Blinking a few times, Ernst stood up and made the bed. He elected at the last minute to take the picture she had under her pillow and place it on top of the newly made bed, just to let her know he knew how she felt.

"I don't give up that easily, *liebling*." The words were whispered as he kissed two fingers and pressed them to the door she was behind. Making sure the door would lock behind him Ernst walked out her front door and down to his truck. An older woman was on her porch watching him. Ernst nodded at her and waved as he climbed into his vehicle and drove away.

Clean and damp from her shower, Kacy walked out of the bathroom and knew he was no longer there. Her house seemed emptier somehow. Blinking back tears, she headed to her room and saw the bed was made. On top of the pillow lay…

He had found her picture. Ernst knew how she felt. Still in her robe, Kacy crawled into the side of the bed where he'd been. The pillow still held his scent and she buried her face in it. She cuddled the pillow until her doorbell rang. Wiping her eyes, she got out of bed and went to the door. Looking through the peephole, she opened the door with a squeal and jumped into the arms of the person on the other side.

❄ ❄ ❄

"When are you going to get over this hold Kirby has on you?" The question was direct, just like the person asking it.

Kacy swirled her drink. She had changed and was sitting in her living room confronted by a feast and her very good friend Ilanderae Rogue Nycks who'd stopped by for a brief visit. "It's like I told you on the phone, Landi. Every time I think I have gotten past or over him, I see him."

"But, hon, he is still running your life, especially if you let a man like this," she held up one of the pictures they had taken in Hawaii, "walk out of that door." Ilanderae tucked a strand of curly hair behind her ear.

"I know, but my mind is so into self-preservation; it is an instinctive reaction. And Lord knows I wanted him to stay."

Arching a tweezed brow, Ilanderae smirked. "I don't blame you there. How was he, anyway?"

"Landi!" Kacy gasped.

"Girl, please," she scoffed, "tell me all."

So Kacy did. They ate rich food and talked. About men, sex, food, and more sex.

"What are you going to do about Kirby?" Ilanderae asked, suddenly serious.

"I don't see him often," Kacy said.

She leveled one manicured finger at her. "Koali Cynemon, don't you give me that shit. Any second you see him is too much. You need to tell this man of yours about that bastard."

"He's not my man," Kacy protested.

"Any man who rocks your world like that is a keeper. He's your man," Ilanderae insisted.

"I'm doing okay, Landi. Really, I am. I go to the meetings and get support, and I stay busy with work. Really busy," Kacy said, reaching across the coffee table to grab her friend's hand.

"Still live in fear, don't you? When a man raises his voice, you still tense up and cringe. And you will until that bastard is gone from your life forever," Ilanderae swore.

"But I am not giving in and moving my business. I'm established here and I don't want to let him win," Kacy spoke softly as she moved to sit next to her friend.

"You know that man is dangerous. I don't want to get a call saying come down and identify the body. You know you are family to me."

Kacy nodded. "I know. I take precautions, but I haven't seen him around here in a while. It has always been in a public place where I have seen him." Leaning in, she kissed Ilanderae on the cheek. "I love you, too, Landi."

"I know," she said with a smile. "What's not to love?"

They spent the day shopping and catching up. Dropping Ilanderae off at the airport, Kacy sped home to change and get ready for her date. As she was walking through the house toward the garage, her cell phone went off.

"KT Electric," she said as her body automatically turned and headed back to her office. "Evening, Sister," Kacy said as she sat down at her desk.

"The whole thing?" Kacy opened her computer files to the St. Lucia Orphanage. "Don't worry about it; I am looking at the blueprints right now. I will be there within the hour. See you then."

Hanging up, she set her phone down and jogged to her room to change into jeans and a work shirt. Grabbing her briefcase along with her cell phone, she headed out into the garage only to climb into her van instead of her car.

As she drove to the orphanage, she called *Fountains* and left a message for Ernst. That done, she focused on driving in the rain.

Ernst swore as he got the message. *An emergency, huh?* Pissed off and frustrated beyond belief, he went back to his apartment in Suffolk. A knock at the door surprised him and he opened it to see a few of his teammates there.

"What are you three up to?" Ernst asked as he stepped back to let them enter.

Ross answered, "Came to see if you wanted to come out with us."

With a careless shrug, Ernst walked over to his leather couch and sat down. "Thanks anyways, guys, but I am not feeling up to it tonight."

Osten and Dimitri were anxious to get going, so Ross said he would stay and talk to their Chief for a while. When it was just the two of them, Ross sat down across from his senior officer.

"I never really apologized for the incident in Montana, Chief and I am sorry," Ross said in his southern drawl. A while ago, Ross had taken Ernst hostage at knife point before he'd recovered his memory. He'd gotten into a car accident into Montana and while there had met the woman of his dreams, but couldn't even remember his name. When the Megalodon Team had gone up to rescue him, Ross had thought they were threatening the woman he'd come to love. Ernst held no animosity toward him for it; he knew, without a doubt, he'd protect Kacy to the same extent. Ross had only done what'd he been trained to do.

Waving off the apology Ernst said, "There is no need to be formal here. Call me Ernst. Or Ghost. I know you didn't mean to do it and no harm was done." Ernst liked the newest member of the Megalodon Team and his attitude about their work.

"I'm not keeping you from anything, am I, Ghost?" Ross asked as he looked over the nice clothes Ernst wore. Everyone knew he was a jeans and tee shirt–man.

"No, I got stood up."

"Kacy?" Ross asked, unsuccessfully hiding his grin.

Glinting eyes narrowed. "Yes, Kacy."

"What happened?"

"Before or after I slept with her?" Ernst blurted out.

Ross leaned back in his chair and looked at the highest-ranking non-com on the Team. Normally so composed, seeing the raw confusion on Ernst was shocking. Covering his mouth with one hand, Ross asked, "Y'all slept together?" He was struggling to keep the grin off his face.

"Yes," Ernst admitted. "But then she tells me it was only a one-night stand kind of thing. I guess she meant it since she cancelled dinner."

Ross nodded but remained silent, allowing Ernst to continue his explanation.

"Dammit, Ross! There just isn't that kind of passion and emotion between two people if there isn't a deeper connection." Ernst slumped back on the couch. "It wasn't just sex...*damn* good sex. It was more than that. Way more."

Sitting up, he looked directly into the gray eyes of his friend. "And no matter what she says, I know she feels something. She keeps a picture of the two of us under her pillow."

Ross observed and stayed quiet.

"I want to lock her up in the house and keep her to myself. She gets hit on at jobs she does." At Ross's raised brows, Ernst clarified, "She's an electrician."

"An electrician. That's impressive," the Southern drawl said.

"This guy hit on her right in front of me," Ernst snarled. "It was like I didn't exist!"

Fighting a smile, Ross asked, "What are you going to do?"

There was silence in the room as Ernst thought. He rose and grabbed two beers from his fridge. Still silent, he handed one to Ross and retook his seat on the couch. After taking a healthy swig he said in a disgusted tone, "I don't have any idea."

"Do you think she has an issue with the race thing?" Ross wondered as he took a drink.

"She's scared." Ernst told him. "Of what, I'm not sure yet. But there is something in her past that has her spooked."

"Maybe she's scared of her family's reaction," Ross suggested.

Ernst shook his head. "She grew up not knowing them."

"In an orphanage or with foster parents?"

"Jesus, I don't know. Man, I want to ask her so many things, but she is so private. It's like I can see the walls go up and the doors closing around her."

"Well, aren't you a SEAL? You are supposed to be able to go where others can't."

Ernst frowned. "So treat it like an Op?"

"Not exactly," Ross said. "Look, I could be wrong here, but you sound like a man in love. Like Harrier and Cade do when they talk about their wives. Be her support and help her break down those walls."

"So put my experience to use and persevere," Ernst translated.

"Basically. We're stubborn, hardheaded, and sometimes that is what it takes to get the woman we want."

"How'd you get to be so smart about women?" Ernst teased, knowing a lot of the trouble Ross was going through to get Dezarae to be his woman in every sense of the word.

"I'm not. I don't know a damn thing about 'em, except that their rules change all the time."

Chapter Nine

Kacy pulled into her driveway and jumped out of her older model Volkswagen van, entering her house through the front door. Stopping in the kitchen to brew a pot of coffee, she soon was standing under the pounding spray of her shower. Rolling her shoulders, she touched the silver Ankh that she had around her neck, its simple design bringing her comfort.

As much as she'd wanted to see Ernst again last night, fixing the electricity in the orphanage was much more important. They had food that would begin to spoil and children who were scared of the dark.

Having been one of those children, Kacy always put them first. It had taken her a while but she had gotten the electricity back on, but her tired body had taken the nuns who ran the orphanage up on the offer for a free bed. Nevertheless, the cots there were not comfortable at all. She'd slept for a few hours before waking at five, eating with the sisters, and double-checking her work.

The nuns had wanted to pay her for her work, but Kacy would never take money from them. She would pay out of her own pocket first.

Dry, clean, and dressed in another set of clothes for work Kacy, poured herself a cup of coffee in her travel mug and walked into the garage to gather equipment to reload her van. She was going to pick up two generators for the orphanage and take them to them, then she would come home and focus on the other jobs she had.

As the door slid up, Kacy stood in the empty spot her van usually accompanied and watched as a pair of jean-encased legs turned into a hardened torso covered by a black shirt and led to a head that had short-cropped blond hair and eyes that were a supernatural blue. Ernst Zimmermann.

It was seven-thirty in the morning and Kacy was obviously hallucinating. Shaking her head to clear her vision, she took two steps and froze. His truck was parked next to her van in the driveway.

"What are you doing here?" Kacy asked as she hit the automatic lock on her van. "What do you want?" She set her coffee down and began to put things in her van.

"You know what I want," he reminded her in a low tone.

"I have to go pick up a few generators. I'm sorry about last night. Did you get my message?" Kacy shut the van and moved back into the garage to grab her briefcase and coffee.

"Yes," his answering growl reached her. "I got it. An emergency?" His doubt-filled gaze fell upon her.

Kacy answered immediately. "Yes. It was an emergency."

"And I suppose you got hit on?"

"Can't say that I remember, maybe by a guy named Adam." Kacy turned around and waited for him to get out of her garage.

Ernst was beside her in seconds. "I forgot something."

Her brows converged in confusion. "Forgot what?" She didn't see him put anything in the garage.

"This." His mouth was on hers until she sagged against him. Then and only then did he pull away. "Does Adam make you tremble?"

Defiance flared in her gaze. "I don't think that's any of your business. But you can meet him if you want."

Ernst accepted and climbed into the passenger side of her vehicle. "Is he before or after the generator?"

Kacy climbed in the van and looked at the blond next to her. "Do you want your truck in the garage?"

"I think it will be fine. You have a nice neighborhood."

"It's your truck," she replied with a shrug.

Rubbing his hand over the stubble on his chin, he said, "Maybe you're right. Give me a second." Ernst jumped out and got in his truck, moving it into her garage. He smiled widely as he got out, putting his baseball cap on his head.

He walked back to where Kacy sat in her van waiting. Easily, he swung in beside her, "Ready."

"Don't you have to work today?" she asked, backing out of her driveway.

"I just got here, trying to get rid of me already?" he teased.

"No," Kacy said. "Just curious."

"I'm all yours unless I get paged back."

Sipping her coffee, she remained silent as she drove. Pulling into a home improvement warehouse parking lot, she glanced at him. "I see." Grabbing her briefcase and one last gulp of coffee, she got out of the van, setting the alarm she'd installed as she and Ernst walked inside.

Although Ernst wished she would talk, he understood she was working and probably thinking over things. So he watched as they walked, particularly the sway of her hips in the jeans she wore; observed the number of masculine eyes that fell upon her as she passed; noticed the way her hair swung in time with her full strides.

Ernst saw her grab at a flatbed and beat her to it. "I'll get that."

Nodding, she pointed to the left. "Generators are back here."

He walked beside her, glad to be in her presence. She seemed comfortable. Relaxed. At ease.

A masculine voice broke into his musings. "Hey, Chief."

Stopping, Ernst looked and saw another Chief from the base whom he had drinks with on occasion. "Chief Anderson. How are you?" Ernst reached over and shook the man's hand.

"Pretty good. Frustrated. Who's this with you?"

"This is Kacy Travis. Kacy this is Chief Anderson," Ernst said watching, her reaction to the man.

Kacy put out her hand. "Nice to meet you, Chief Anderson." The man was shorter than Ernst but stockier. He had a pair of sparkling brown eyes and dark-brown skin with a shaved head.

"And you," Chief responded with a grin.

"I'm gonna go get the generators," Kacy told Ernst as she grabbed the flatbed.

"I'm coming," he told her.

"No, stay and talk. It will take me a bit. I have to grab some other things as well. I'll meet you by the generators in a while." She patted his arm and began to stride off, not realizing or caring that both men were watching her.

After a brief conversation, Ernst left his friend and sauntered in the direction Kacy had gone. Rounding the end cap, he stopped when he saw Kacy and four other men all talking and laughing. Fighting back his initial jealous reaction, he moved upon the group.

"But, it's better now. That's where I am taking the generators," Kacy's sultry voice was saying.

"Hey, Kacy," Ernst said, standing at the edge of the group and wanting desperately to be a part of it.

Copper eyes smiled as they looked at him. "I'm ready." She turned back to the group, "Hey, guys, this is Ernst. Ernst, meet the guys. Tom, Paul, Bill, and Howard." They all said hello. "I gotta go. Great seeing you again, guys."

"Bye, Kacy," Howard said.

"Don't be late to see Adam," Paul teased.

"I don't plan on it. Bye, y'all." Kacy waved at them and pointed to a full flatbed. "This ones mine."

Ernst took control of it and as they moved down toward the register he asked, "Are they electricians too?"

"Nope. They are independent contractors. Sometimes I wire the houses they work on or build."

The sigh of relief that left him surprised Ernst. They walked past the lighting and fan section when they saw his friend again. He appeared extremely frustrated as he stood in front of the ceiling fans.

"What is he doing now?" Ernst wondered as he pushed the full cart to where his friend stood. "What's going on, Anderson?"

The look on his face was comical. He seemed close to tears. "Ernst, man, I am supposed to be installing fans but you know me. And I like these, but man, I think they are a bit fancy for me."

"What happened to that guy you had doing it?"

"He skipped out with the money," Chief Anderson snapped.

"Man, I'm sorry about that." Ernst said.

"We have that thing tomorrow and she is going to kill me if I don't get them in, so I am going to put them in and just not turn them on," the perturbed man said.

Ernst patted him on the arm. "I don't know what to tell you."

Kacy stepped up and said, "They aren't that hard to install. It looks worse than it is."

"Hon, I am so bad when it comes to electricity it ain't even funny," the Chief said.

"How many are you getting?" Kacy asked.

"Three. Why?"

Kacy looked at Ernst who watched her with a gentle gaze. "Do you know where he lives?"

"I know where he lives," Ernst answered. *Is she really about to offer to do what I think she is?*

"I can install them for you later in the afternoon, say around three to four," Kacy told the bald man before her.

"Are you for real?" the man asked.

"I'm an electrician," Kacy said, not batting an eye.

"What's it gonna cost me?" he asked, Ernst nodding over her shoulder.

"Nothing." She pulled out a card from her briefcase and handed it to him. "If you want to take me up on it, call my cell number. I have to go." Turning around, she began to push the cart again.

Ernst grinned at Chief Anderson's dazed expression before catching up to her and putting his hands beside hers to help move the flatbed along. "That was really nice of you,"

She rolled her shoulders. "He is a friend of yours."

"You do know I know how you feel about me?" Ernst asked in a whisper as they got in the cashier's line.

"Don't read to much into it," Kacy insisted even as she blushed.

"Too late." He reached for her and pulled her to him. "Thank you." The back of one hand ran down her cheek.

It didn't take long to make their purchases and load up the van. "Thanks for the help," Kacy told Ernst, who had lifted the generators for her. "Let's go, I need to get them delivered."

"Who is Adam?" Ernst asked as she drove them towards the outskirts of town.

"A very good friend," Kacy said, turning on her blinker.

Frowning in frustration, Ernst shut his mouth as they pulled up to a large, old building. A small sign sat alongside the road that read *Saint Lucia Orphanage*. Driving around to the back, Kacy pulled up to door with peeling paint.

She was out of the vehicle before the engine had completely shut down. Ernst followed and watched as she knocked on the door. A small black nun answered. "Koali, what are you doing back already?"

"Morning, Sister. I brought the generators," Kacy said.

"You are so kind. Who do you have with you?"

"This is Ernst Zimmermann, a friend of mine." Kacy beckoned him closer. "Ernst, this is one of the sisters who run the orphanage."

The lady smiled and offered Ernst her hand. "I'm Sister Dorothy. You would think she would know all our names. But she insists on calling us all 'Sister'."

"Good morning, ma'am," he said, shaking her hand.

"I will hook one up to each wing of the orphanage just in case," Kacy announced as she moved back to the van.

Ernst followed her with his eyes. "She is an amazing woman," the nun commented.

"Yes, ma'am, she sure is," he agreed, pulling his eyes off his enchantress and putting them on the woman beside him.

Kacy was hooking on her tool belt when the cry came. "Kacy!!!"

She immediately turned around and found the one person she had been waiting to see. Adam. With a huge smile she walked over to him and said, "Adam. Look at you. It is so good to see you." She pulled him into her arms.

Adam was a seven-year-old biracial child who'd been left on the steps of St. Lucia's. Aside from the nuns and monks who ran the orphanage, Kacy was the only constant in his life. His skin was a few shades lighter than Kacy's and his hair was kinky and coarse. He had a smile that rivaled the heavens for brightness and was very active. He loved Kacy.

"Did you come last night, Kacy?" he asked, not willing to let her go.

"I sure did." Her hands tipped up his face so they could be eye to eye.

"I was scared," his voice admitted as his thin body gripped hers.

"But you survived. And when you woke, it was all okay," Kacy assured him.

"Because you came." He squeezed her again and left to stick his head in her van and pull out his own tool belt. As he hooked it on, he turned big, soulful eyes at her and asked, "What are we doing today?"

"Generators. And I…we are going over what I did last night." She ruffled the hair on his head. "Ready to get to work?"

"Yes, ma'am." His small body copied the way she stood. Legs apart and arms crossed.

"Okay, then, let's get to it."

CHAPTER TEN

Kacy and Adam got a dolly and moved the generators. Ernst started to help but the nuns around him stopped him and said, "This is their time. She can do it and he loves to help."

So, Ernst stood back while Kacy and Adam installed the generators. The nun stayed with him the whole time, watching as well. "Where did you two meet?" the kind-looking nun asked.

"In Hawaii," he said with a grin, remembering that first day.

"Were you the one she was supposed to meet last night?" she wondered.

Looking down at her, Ernst questioned, "How do you know about that?"

The nun nodded sagely. "I thought so."

Ernst was totally confused. "You thought so what? Are you saying she was here last night?"

Her covered head moved up and down. "We lost electricity last night in the storm. A bolt of lightning hit so close it fried some of the circuits, so Koali came out and fixed it."

So it really had been an emergency. "Why would you think it was me?"

"Because she's never brought a man here with her. She'd told us she liked the guy she had been going to meet, and she watches you often."

"Does she come here a lot?" Ernst asked, warmed at the knowledge others saw Kacy watching him. *She likes me.*

"Every week to see Adam and the other children, unless she is out of town," she said. "Let's walk around to where everyone is now."

Ernst followed her around the corner of the building. He stopped and stared. About thirty children played in the yard. There were toddlers, teens and every age in between.

He was amazed by the order that seemed present amongst the chaos. A tremor traveled along his spine and he looked around. His blue eyes honed in on Kacy and Adam as they said hello to the other children.

"What started bringing her here?" Ernst asked, wanting to know more about his beautiful electrician.

"She grew up here," the nun stated bluntly.

Ernst wanted to go and gather Kacy in his arms to just hold her. Unable to comprehend what growing up here would be like, he needed to touch her, share his strength with her. Eventually the need grew too much and he said, "Excuse me," going over to Kacy as she talked into her phone.

"Kacy," Ernst said, touching her arm as she clipped her phone back onto her waist.

"Hey, Ernst. I want you to meet a very good friend of mine. This is Adam. Adam, say hi to Ernst."

Dark-brown eyes looked up at him and the child smiled, showing missing teeth. "Hello. I'm going to marry Kacy when I grow up."

Ernst couldn't help but smile at the boy. "I don't blame you. I'd marry her if she'd let me."

"You can't marry her," the young tone whined. "I'm gonna."

"Excuse me," Kacy interrupted. "Let's not discuss my upcoming marriage like I'm not here."

Ultra marine eyes, swirling with emotion, grabbed hers. "Okay, we will talk later on about your imminent marriage." He touched the brim of his cap before turning his attention back to the child.

"What do you do, Mr. Ernst?" Adam smiled at him as he tucked his small, almost frail hand into the strong one of the Navy SEAL and his other into Kacy's softer one.

Slanting a gaze at the sight beside him, Ernst nearly was brought to his knees. *If there was ever a sign that told me this was right, I am looking at it right now.* "I'm in the Navy," he answered the child even as his stare lingered on Kacy.

"I'm gonna be an electric like Kacy," Adam said proudly.

An electric? Well, she is electric all right. "An electrician? That is a good job." Ernst nodded.

Kacy stopped. "Adam, I have to go. I have another few jobs to do today."

A look of abandonment crossed the boy's face before he controlled it. "Okay." He dropped Ernst's hand and wrapped both of his skinny arms around Kacy.

"Hey," she said, kneeling in front of him. "I'll be back next week. I'll come on Sunday and we'll spend more time together, okay?" Ernst moved to stand behind Kacy and he saw the child fighting back tears.

"Okay, Kacy," Adam forced out.

"I can't leave without my smile. Come on, now. Where's my brave little man?" Kacy coaxed.

"What if you don't come back?" The first few tears began to fall.

"Have I never not come back?" she asked as her fingers wiped the tears away.

"No. Promise?"

"I promise," Kacy immediately agreed.

"Him too," Adam insisted.

Ernst met Kacy's shocked gaze and said, "I promise I will come back as soon as I can."

"Okay." Adam took one more hug from Kacy before moving to Ernst and hugging him as well. "Bye," he yelled as he ran off to play on the playground equipment.

Ernst helped Kacy to her feet and said, "He loves you. I didn't know I had competition for your hand in marriage."

A sad smile crossed her face before she got her emotions under control. With farewells to the nuns, soon Kacy and Ernst were back in her van heading for his friend's house to install the fans.

It was six-thirty when she pulled back into her driveway. Parking so Ernst could move his truck, she turned off the vehicle and got out. She picked up her mail that she didn't get the day before on the way to the front door.

Ernst followed and locked her van for her, then he unlocked the door for her. "Thanks," she said as her body brushed past his.

He stopped halfway in the door, blocking her way. "Kacy." His voice had dropped to a seductive purr.

"Yes," she breathed.

"I want to kiss you so bad," he whispered by her mouth.

Her eyelids fluttered. *I want you.*

"I want you, too, sweetheart. I want you too," Ernst breathed.

Kacy's eyes flew open. She met his gaze and he didn't have a smug look, just a passionate one.

"Yes, you said it out loud." His lips brushed hers lightly, teasingly. "But I want more than a one-night stand. More than a fling. I want to be a couple."

Shaking her head, Kacy tried to back up. "No, I don't think that would be a good idea."

Ernst wouldn't let her. Still in the doorway and in view of her neighbors, he held her captive in his arms. "Why not?"

"It…it…it just wouldn't."

"No dice, Kacy. Why not? And you can't tell me you aren't attracted to me. I saw the picture you had under your pillow. And your body wouldn't respond the way it does to mine if you weren't attracted." His gaze bore into hers, not giving an inch.

"I…I…I can't be in a relationship right now," she stammered.

Sliding into the house, Ernst shut the door behind him and steered her towards the living room. "We need to talk about this, because I want one and I know you do too."

"Why are you so determined to date me?" Kacy asked, sitting down on the couch and tossing her mail on the coffee table.

"I want to be a couple with you." Ernst sat down at the other end of the couch and faced her. "You have brought a light into my life that until I met you I didn't know was missing. I don't want to lose that or you."

"You know nothing about me," she said sharply.

"Only because you won't let me. Sweetheart, I want to know every-thing about you. Everything. I want to take you home and introduce you to my family. I want you to come with me to things that my Team goes to." He pulled her across the couch and into his embrace. "I want to know what kind of music you like, what movies you go see, your favorite color. Everything."

Kacy shook her head against the hard planes of his chest. *Get rid of him Kacy. You know what men are like in the end,* her mind screamed. *Give him a chance,* her heart countered. "I don't know." Her voice was tortured. *Think of what a man with his training could do to you,* her brain taunted.

Ernst took a deep breath and caressed her tenderly. "How about this. We do things together on days that we both have time off. Go to dinner, hiking, or whatever." He stroked her hair. "Take it slow."

So slow he would want to find a different woman. "Okay, I'll give it a try," she conceded.

"So, what about dinner tonight?" Ernst closed his eyes and pressed her body closer to his.

"I have some more work to finish up, but we could order delivery. If you don't mind hanging around while I get my work done?" Kacy's voice had dropped to a low whisper as she finished.

"Not a problem. In fact, how about I make dinner for us?"

She drew back and looked up at him. "You know how to cook?"

He flashed a grin. "Yes, I can cook. Does that sound like a plan?"

"Maybe you should look at my kitchen before you decide that. There isn't much there." She moved off his lap.

Standing up also, he followed her into the kitchen. Within moments, Ernst knew he would have to go shopping. "I can do it; I just have to get some groceries." He smiled at her blush.

She turned towards her briefcase. "I will get you some money."

"No." She froze at that word. Gentling his voice, he continued, "I don't have any problem buying groceries."

"But it's —"

"Kacy." He flowed over to her still-frozen body. "Let me do this for you. Trust me, I don't mind at all." His lips brushed over hers tenderly. "Now, you go do your work and I will be back soon. Can I leave the door unlocked or do you want me to ring the doorbell?"

Knees trembling from the soft contact of his mouth, Kacy mumbled, "I will give you a garage door opener so you can just come back in that way."

"Okay," he whispered, stealing one more quick kiss before taking the remote from her and getting in his car.

Kacy stood in the doorway to garage as the big door closed after Ernst. Her fingers ran lightly over her mouth as she remembered his lips pressing against hers so softly. "How can a man who does what he does be so gentle?" Her question was unanswered as she headed to her office.

Ernst pulled into the parking lot of the grocery store. Sitting in the quiet vehicle, he ran over the day's events in his mind. He had known Kacy hadn't had parents growing up, but he hadn't pictured her being raised in an orphanage. Having a nice set of foster parents as what he had envisioned.

It would partially explain her hesitation to make a commitment, however. As her dark beauty swam in front of his eyes, he got out of his truck. There was something more, he knew; something that had her running scared from a serious relationship. Yet even still, Ernst strolled into the store with a smile on his face as he thought about Kacy.

As he directed the man in the meat section to which lobsters he wanted, Ernst wondered about dessert. He knew she loved ice cream, but he wanted to give her something extra.

That grin was still plastered to his face as he went through the check-out line. The girl at the register was flirting heavily with him, but Ernst could see only Kacy and her rich beauty waiting at home for him.

Entering her house through the garage, he put the things away in the kitchen before searching for her. "Kacy?" he called as he moved down her hallway.

There was no answer, but the closer he got to her office door, he heard her talking. Sticking his head in the door, he saw her leaning over a set of large blueprints and wearing her headset.

Her copper gaze found his and she smiled even as she listened to the person on the other end of the phone call. "Just wanted to let you know I was back. I'll be in the kitchen," Ernst whispered as he leaned down and kissed her softly on the cheek.

Kacy touched his cheek in return and mouthed the words "thank you." Then her attention was totally turned back to the blueprints and the conversation at hand.

For a few moments, Ernst stayed in the doorway and watched her work. She was a joy to watch and listen to. Her tone was upbeat and professional at the same time. No words were minced; she shot straight from the hip when she talked to people.

His pale eyes wandered around the room as he was loath to leave her, settling on her bookcases. The top shelf had books of poetry—Lord

Byron, John Keats, Percy Shelley, William Woodsworth, Aleksandr Pushkin, and more. There were some of Shakespeare's works as well.

Slipping out of the room, he began dinner after opening a bottle of water he found in the fridge. Having looked through her music collection he had just pressed play—not finding anything that he would listen to—but as the smooth rhythm and blues filtered through the air, he found it wasn't that bad after all.

It didn't take long to prepare the food and Ernst was at home in her kitchen. The lobsters sat in boiling water on her stove, and now he was finishing the biscuits and about to slip them into the oven. The salad was made and chilling in the refrigerator.

Kacy had known the second his body had filled the doorway to her office. He affected her on so many levels. When he'd kissed her cheek, she'd wanted to end her call and kiss him like their lives depended on it. Despite all her attempts to protect her heart and invariably herself, this man had found a way to get under her skin. If she could just get rid of past memories and find a way to move on.

Setting down her pencil, she rolled her shoulders. Her days were going to be filled, but she still needed to figure out her nights. She wanted to hold onto Ernst and never let him go. He made her feel safe.

The ten million dollar question was would he continue to do so or turn out to be like Kirby.

"Hey, thought you could use this." Ernst's voice broke into her wandering.

Kacy looked up to see him holding out a glass of wine to her. "Thanks," she said, taking the beverage from him.

He sat in the chair beside her. "How's it going?"

"I'm done for the evening. Got a lot of work lined up, so I will be working Saturdays for a while. But that's okay." She took a sip of the wine and added, "This is really good."

Ernst spun her around to face him. "Can I ask you something?"

"Of course." Her eyes were soft as they looked at him, waiting.

"Why did you do what you did for Chief Anderson today?"

True to her word, she'd gone over to Chief Anderson's home after installing the generators to put in his fans. "Like I said before, he was...or is...your friend. It didn't take to long. Why?" Her gaze dropped to the wine she swirled around in her glass.

"You are a unique woman, Kacy. Come on; dinner is almost ready." He touched the tip of her nose and stood.

"You didn't answer my question, Ernst," she said, standing and following him up the hall to the kitchen that smelled heavenly.

"I'll tell you once you agree to date me." He put his wineglass on the counter and pulled out her chair for her. "Your seat, my dear," Ernst said with a nod.

CHAPTER ELEVEN

Lobster Newburg, fresh salad greens, cheesy biscuits, a perfect wine, and dark chocolate Pavé with raspberry sauce. Kacy was stuffed. Happy, but stuffed.

"You can cook a mean meal, Ernst. Thank you," she complimented over her shoulder as she loaded her dishwasher.

"I learned a few things in my travels," he responded as she felt his gaze admire her body bent over the dishwasher.

"Well that one you definitely learned well." Sneaking a look at him over her shoulder, she smiled. "I'm full." She put in the soap packet and closed the door to turn the knob and begin the cycle. Kacy reached for the dishrag only to find Ernst was already wiping down the table. "I was going to do that; you cooked."

"*Schätzchen*, I like working beside you. And I don't mind wiping off a table." He winked at her.

"You are very pushy." *I wish I knew what he was calling me.*

"You've told me that already. But you're right. I am especially about things I want." His eyes burned with a heat that should have warned her of things to come. "And I want you."

Goosebumps broke out over her skin. "Pushy," she said with a half smile. *Dangerous. This man is dangerous.*

He shrugged. "You say pushy; I say determined. Now, come tell me about you." Ernst took her by the hand and led her outside to sit on the porch swing.

Tucking her feet under her, Kacy leaned against the man beside her and watched as night fell over the city. "What do you want to know?"

"Why didn't you tell me you were raised in an orphanage? St. Lucia's to be specific."

"I don't know. But you know now." Her eyes fluttered closed as his arm settled around her shoulder.

"But you didn't tell me. Tell me about Adam."

"Adam is the sweetest child I know. I was out there the night he was dropped off. Five weeks old and they left him. Because he was mixed." Her tone betrayed her pain at the child's treatment.

Readjusting himself so he could hold her better, Ernst tucked her head under his chin. The night air thick was with humidity and the promise of more rain. "Go on," he encouraged.

"I have been to see him at least once a week since then. He is like family to me." Her voice broke.

"And he idolizes you. Not to mention being in love with you. I think it's great he wants to be an electrician."

Rubbing her back, he waited until she said something else. "It is great. But we also do other things, so this coming Sunday, I'm going to take him horseback riding. He has a horse that he loves to ride."

"Want another body along on the trip?" Ernst asked,

"He'd like that," Kacy said.

"What about you?" he asked on a whisper.

"I'd like it too," she admitted. "A lot."

"Well consider me there...unless..."

"Unless you are off saving the world. Don't worry, I won't say anything to Adam about you coming, that way he won't be disappointed if you can't." The sound of light rain on the roof of her porch made her open her eyes.

"I don't want to let down either of you," he swore.

"I understand that you get called away at a moments notice. I'll be saddened but not angry." Kacy didn't fight it when he tugged her back down to his side.

"Where should I meet you?" he asked as his hands created havoc in her lower body.

"Here is fine. I am out to St. Lucia's by seven and it takes about thirty minutes to get there. Well, less when I drive my car," she said and chuckled.

"It's a date." He kissed the top of her head. "I should get going. Thank you for such a lovely night, Kacy Travis."

Saddened, Kacy stood and accompanied him into the kitchen where she looked over his hardened physique. There really was nothing soft about him at all until he glanced at her with those eyes. They were so emotional; they hid nothing from her. But for all his strength, all she had seen from him was gentleness and kindness. "Thank you for dinner."

Picking up his truck keys, he opened her front door. "It was my pleasure. Goodnight, Kacy."

Taking a bold step she offered, "You don't have to go."

Ernst swallowed hard and she saw desire rage like a squall in his eyes. "Yes, I do. I told you I want more than a one-night stand. When you are ready for that, then I will stay." Inhaling deeply, he raked his gaze over her once more. "Come give me a kiss."

I want more than a one-night stand. Stay with me forever, Ernst. Kacy stepped in closer and slid her arms around his neck, telling him with her kiss what she wasn't strong enough to voice out loud yet.

Reluctantly pulling away, he muttered, "Good night, *schätzchen*. Sleep well." One more fast kiss and he was out the door heading to his truck.

❀ ❀ ❀

Kacy had dreams full of Ernst. Her free times during the next day were centered on him. Every time she closed her eyes, she saw his eyes staring at her, boring into her soul, seeing more than she wanted to reveal.

Shutting the door behind her, she headed for the shower. She had a meeting tonight and would just make it if she hurried. Her last job had taken much longer than she had anticipated. She dressed in blue jeans and a white tee shirt and clipped her phone on her belt. Jumping into her car, she backed out of the garage and made sure the door shut all the way before tearing off down the street. Kacy didn't even notice the truck that she blew past.

Her phone rang and as she whipped around a corner, she answered it. "Travis."

"Evening, *liebling*," Ernst's voice thrummed through her body.

"Evening, Ernst." Kacy sat impatiently at the red light. "What are you doing?"

"Wanted to see if you wanted to grab a bite to eat with me tonight." He chuckled slightly. "But you drove right past me like a bat out of hell!"

Green. She shifted her car into gear and drove on. "Sorry, I have a meeting."

Silence for a moment and then he said, "What about after? Meet me for a drink?"

"I don't think that would be a good idea tonight," she said. "What about tomorrow?"

"Is everything okay?" He hadn't liked how fast she had driven past him.

"Sure," her voice wobbled a bit. "Look, I really have to go. Talk to you soon? Bye." She hung up.

Blue eyes narrowed in concentration as he decided what to do.

Kacy ran up the steps into the Baptist church and down the hall to the room that was full of women. The meeting was a double-edged sword. It was fortunate they were there and extremely unfortunate they had reason to be.

"Hey, y'all. Sorry, work was a bit longer than I anticipated," Kacy said with a smile as she slid into her usual seat.

"Evening, Kacy." A tall woman stood and looked over them. "Don't worry about it. At least you made it. Okay, ladies, another month has gone by. How are we all doing?"

For the next three hours, Kacy sat, listened to, and shared her feelings with the Battered Women's Support Group. "Well," she said when it was her turn. "I did meet this really wonderful guy." She smiled as the women encouraged her with nods. "But I am *so* scared. I still see Kirby around town. It's rare and he never speaks to me, but all it takes is a single look."

Kacy took a deep breath and continued as one of the women next to her grabbed her hand in support. "This new guy wants a relationship and my heart tells me to give him a chance but my brain can't get beyond my past. I don't want to lose this guy because I can't let go." She frowned. "I guess I don't know how to let go of the past."

One of the women asked, "Do you get any bad feelings from him? This new man?"

"Not a single one. He is so kind and so gentle I almost don't believe it's real." Kacy grinned. "He cooked me a lobster dinner last night. I took him with me to see Adam." The women were amazed by that for they knew about Adam. "But the second I begin to believe that maybe it will be okay this time, I panic."

"Not all men are abusers. That is the main thing we need to remember. There are good men out there," the meeting coordinator said. "My husband is one of them. Lots of us are married now. If you let Kirby keep you from him, then he still wins. And we don't want that."

"No. So I should give him a chance, then," Kacy stated.

"We all know the signs of abuse and if you see them, get out. Call anyone of us, but just get out. Who knows, though, maybe he is 'the one' for you." The woman looked at everyone there.

"And if he is, we want to be invited to the wedding!" Another woman said, only to be echoed by the others in the room.

"I am blessed to have such wonderful, supportive friends," Kacy said.

"We all are. Well, ladies, I think that is a wonderful note to end on. Group hug!" The fifteen women stood in a circle, hugged, and prayed for their continued safety and for the other women who hadn't yet found a way out from under their abusers.

Kacy walked out with one of the newer women. "Let us know how it goes with this guy, Kacy," she said with a wink before climbing into her car.

"I'll do that," she responded, waving as she unlocked her car and slid behind the wheel.

Sitting behind the wheel, she picked up her cell phone and stared at it for a moment. Quickly, before she could change her mind, she dialed a number and pressed call.

"Hello?" the deep, masculine voice said.

"Is it too late to change my mind about drinks?" Kacy asked as she shook her head over the heavy metal music she heard in the background.

"Never," he promised. "Where do you want to meet?"

"Well, I'm in Suffolk, so I can come to your place," she said.

"Here?"

"Maybe not; why don't you suggest a place." Closing her eyes, she prayed she wouldn't be too embarrassed to look at him when she got there. It was obvious he didn't want her at his place.

"No, no, here is fine. I want to show you my place. Just keep in mind I am a man living alone," he said.

"I don't want to impose."

"*Liebling*, I want you in my place. Where are you? I will give you directions."

Kacy told him and he relayed how to get to his place. Shutting her phone, Kacy started her car. She knew exactly where he lived. It was a few blocks from where she had done some electrical work. Twenty minutes later, since she'd stopped off at the store to get some ice cream and toppings, she pulled into a parking space at his apartment complex.

Ernst was outside waiting for her. The second she got out of her vehicle, he was moving towards her. "What took you so long? I was getting worried." He pulled her into his arms and kissed her like she was his only chance for life.

"I stopped at the store," she rasped when he backed off her mouth. "Ice cream and toppings." Kacy grinned.

"Of course," Ernst said. "Well, come on up." He took the bag from her and peered inside. "Looks like there are more toppings than ice cream!"

"Well, I like my toppings." Kacy locked her car and fell into step beside him.

"Stairs or elevator?" he asked.

"What floor do you live on?"

"Top floor." His eyes moved over her drawn face. Her happiness was forced. "Let's take the elevator.'

"Okay." Kacy stepped in beside him and remained silent as it went up to the eighth floor.

Ernst watched her as the elevator rose. "What made you change your mind?"

"I'm not entirely sure, but I wanted to see you." The doors slid open and he gestured for her to step out first.

"I wanted to see you too. And I'm glad you called." He opened the door to his apartment and allowed her to enter before following.

Kacy took in Ernst Zimmermann's apartment: big screen television, leather furniture, a game console. "Very nice," she said.

"Let me put this in the freezer and I will give you a grand tour." Ernst walked past her, touching her gently on the small of her back briefly.

She slipped off her shoes and waited for him on the hardwood floor. He was wearing a pair of jeans and a button-down brown shirt that was completely undone, showing off glimpses of the chiseled muscles of his chest. Her throat was dry from her desire for him.

"Come on." He beckoned to her. "This is my living area." His shirt opened as he turned a circle to show off the room.

"I gathered that," Kacy quipped.

"Let me show you the kitchen." Ernst led her to a room that was the total opposite of her kitchen. Appliances of all kinds were on his countertops. Copper pots were hung from the walls and they were spotless.

"You cook a lot."

"I like a good meal when I am home. I don't always get good things when we are deployed." He took her by the arm and led her down a narrow hall. "Bathroom is right here." The door was open.

Kacy looked inside. Clean again, but definitely masculine — not a bit of color or softness in it. "Looks like a bathroom."

"Well, that's good. This is my workout room," he said, opening another door.

Kacy stuck her head inside. Lots of bars — there was even one in the doorway. A home gym was in a corner. A heavy bag, free weights, and tons of things she had no idea what they were also filled the room. "Wow! Do I want to know what this bar in the door is for?"

"Chin ups, pull-ups, among other things," Ernst said, watching her.

"I don't think I could do one. How many do you do?"

"A lot. You can do one; go on, give it a try."

"Give it a try?" Kacy shook her head. "I couldn't even reach that bar."

"Come on, Kacy, I'll help you," he coaxed.

"You won't let me fall?"

"Never," he vowed. "And I'll even help you up."

"What? You gonna lift me up there?" She looked up and then said, "Bring me a chair or something."

Ernst chuckled. "It's not that high."

"Not for you," she complained. Suddenly there was only air beneath her feet. Ernst had lifted her right off the ground.

"Grab on," he instructed.

Kacy did. "I can't do this, Ernst." She kept looking up.

"Of course you can." She glanced down and he grinned. "But take your time; I've got a great view right here.

She trembled from the feel of his warm breath on her belly. "I can't."

"Yes, you can. Pull yourself up. Just once. Come on."

Kacy swallowed, swallowed again, and pulled. She got her chin above the bar and yelled, "I did it!"

Leaning against the wall close enough so he could grab her if she needed it, Ernst was eagerly watching her. "Yes, you did. Can you do it again?"

"No, my arms are trembling." Kacy turned her killer eyes on him. "Help me down?"

"Give me one more. I'll let you have first take of toppings," he bribed.

She watched him. "Once more and then you will help me down?"

"Just one."

"Okay." Kacy pulled herself up so her chin was over the bar one more time. "There," she panted. Lowering herself so her arms were fully extended she said, "Help me."

"I'm right here. Let go."

"I can't feel you," Kacy said.

"Trust me, Kacy. I'm not going to let you fall."

She let go and found herself in his strong embrace. "You caught me." Kacy said as he slowly set her on her feet.

"And I always will. Now, I believe you have first choice of toppings."

"Don't I get to see your bedroom?" Kacy blurted out. "I showed you mine."

CHAPTER TWELVE

Pure fire raged in his eyes. "I will show you whatever of mine you want to see."

"I'll start with your room," Kacy said.

You'll end there, too, if I have any say in it. "Very well, it's right down here." Ernst placed his hand at the bottom of her spine and propelled her towards his room.

"I've always wanted to see what a den of sin looked like," she teased as he opened the door.

He chuckled. "No den of sin here, unless you want to help me commit some sins," Ernst offered.

"Pushy," was all she said as her copper gaze took in the bedroom.

A platform bed with a dark-brown comforter and matching pillowcases on it rested along one wall. An armless chair was in the corner by a table and lamp. The room was sparse aside from basic furniture.

"Not what you were expecting was it?" Ernst whispered beside her.

"No," Kacy admitted. "Not at all. Do you not want to decorate?"

"I desperately want a woman's touch in my place, but until now, I hadn't found the right woman." He wrapped his hands around her waist, bringing her to rest against his chest. "Although, I am not here enough to really enjoy anything. So I guess it works out."

She pointed to some frames on his dresser. "Are those pictures of your family?"

"Yep." He went with her to the frames.

Kacy picked up the one with four people in it. "Mom, Dad, a brother, and you."

"I'm the baby. My mother's name is Nonnie. My father is Otto, and my brother's name is Adolf."

A smile cracked Kacy's lips as she looked up at the man beside her. "As in Adolf Hitler?"

Ernst shook his head as he remembered their exchange in Hawaii. "Adolf is a very common German name."

"So he could give me some German, then." Her fingers traced lightly over his brother's face. He was classically handsome but nothing close to the man beside her.

"Over my dead body," Ernst growled.

Kacy shoved him with her shoulder. "Hey, I seem to be having enough trouble with this German in my life now. The last thing I want to do is add another one in the mix."

"There wouldn't be trouble if you would just agree to date him," he purred.

"I have some things to tell him before I can do that." Her fingers kept busy tracing the designs on the frame.

Taking the picture from her, Ernst tipped her face up toward him with one fingertip. "I'm all ears." He regarded her intently.

"Can I get some ice cream first?"

"How do you eat so much and not get fat?" he asked as his mouth snuck up in an amused grin.

"I am fat," Kacy said, "I'm just too addicted to ice cream to care. And toppings."

He laughed out loud. "Can't forget your toppings." Lifting her up off the floor, he spun them around in a circle. "Okay, let's get you some ice cream." He kissed her and shooed her out his bedroom door, vowing before long her dark body would be spread out on his mattress. "And you're not fat."

Dishing up the chocolate ice cream, Kacy flipped a bunch on her white shirt. "Damn it," she swore as she tried to get it off.

"Just take it off and wear mine," Ernst said, watching her blot water on her chest, slowly exposing one lace-covered breast to his eyes.

"I'll be fine."

"I won't. There isn't much hidden with a wet white shirt, Kacy." His voice was deepened by desire.

"I see your point."

Not yet you don't. "Here." He slipped off his button-down and handed it to her, then turned his back so she could slip into it.

When he thought enough time had passed, he faced her again. "My shirt never looked so good." His sexy voice made her open her closed eyes and pull down the collar of his shirt she'd been inhaling.

Ernst wanted to drop to his knees and bury his face in her stomach. She was so frickin' beautiful standing there in her blue jeans, socks, and his brown shirt. Feral flames burned in his eyes as he reached for his bowl of ice cream and sat down at the table waiting for her to join him. She did, and soon they were eating ice cream.

"What did you want to tell me?" Ernst asked as he ate a spoonful of caramel sauce.

"I need to tell you something before you decide whether you want to have a relationship with me. Or attempt one."

"Sweetheart, unless you are telling me that you are married, there is nothing," he put down his spoon and stared at her, "and I mean *nothing* you can tell me that would change my mind about having a relationship with you."

Kacy couldn't hold his gaze. Messing with her ice cream she said, "You know my meeting I had this evening?"

He laced his fingers under his chin and watched her toy with her bowl. Her hands never stopped moving.

"I go once a month." Her eyes were full of indecision as they looked at him. Shaking her head, she stopped.

Ernst fought back his need to touch her, offer her strength. The amount of torment on her face made him want to weep. Tense moments passed as she tried to find a way to keep talking.

Standing, he walked around the table, took the spoon from her hands, and led her to the couch. "Don't shut me out, Kacy, please let me in," Ernst whispered as he rubbed her back. "I can't help if you don't tell."

"It's a battered women's group." Her words were mumbled into his bare chest.

Ernst's eyes were harder than permafrost and colder than absolute zero in seconds. His body surged with bloodlust. "Who?" he gritted out.

"A guy I used to date. Used to be in a relationship with." She kept her face buried in his chest, refusing to look at him.

Well, that explains the hesitation she has. God damn it! I want to hurt something! "This is why you are hesitant about us," he stated.

"Yes." Her response was so low, he almost didn't hear it.

"Kacy," he breathed into her ear. "I would never raise a hand to you. I swear it. I know we will disagree and argue, but I would never, *ever*, hurt you." Those arms of steel held her close.

"I want to believe that, and I'm trying, but I can't get him out of my head!" She sat up away from Ernst and began hitting the heels of her hands on her temples. "I can't forget him!" she cried.

Immediately, he grabbed her hands. "Stop that," Ernst ordered as he tucked her back tight to his chest. "Let me help. Make it so I'm the one you see when you close your eyes. Make it my voice you hear." *I am going to kill that bastard!* "Trust me, Kacy."

Wiping away her tears, she said, "I'm sorry. I just relive the past more when I go to the meetings. Some nights are worse than others."

His lips brushed her forehead. "Thank you for trusting me enough to tell me."

"Ernst?"

He could hear the exhaustion in her voice. "Yes, *liebling*?"

"Could you just hold me for a while?" Kacy asked in a shy voice.

"For as long as you want, *schätzchen*. Are you comfortable?"

Kacy pushed him so he was lying down on the couch and she tucked herself between the back of his couch and him. Her face buried in his neck, her hand resting on his bare chest, she sighed as he locked his arms around her. "Perfect. Don't let go." She yawned a bit. "What does it mean? Those words you keep saying to me?"

I don't plan on ever letting you go. "I won't. *Liebling* means beloved or darling, and *schätzchen* and *schatzi* mean 'little treasure'," he said, glad the only light on was the one in the kitchen. He closed his eyes and fell asleep, listening to her deep even breaths.

Hours later, Ernst awoke with unoccupied arms. "Kacy?" his sleep-laden voice asked. "Where are you?" No response.

Climbing off the couch, he padded throughout his apartment only to come up empty. She was gone.

The dishes in his kitchen were clean and he saw a sheet of paper taped to his coffee pot. Immediately he pulled it off, opened it, and read:

Ernst:

Thanks for the drinks…well the ice cream.

Thanks most for listening. If you're still around

Sunday the offer is still open for the ride.

I'd love to have you join us.

Thanks for last nite.

You have no idea what that meant to me.

~Kacy

Looking around his kitchen, he had no clue how she'd left without alerting him. "You have no idea what it meant to me, either, *liebling*." Ernst made his way to his room and changed into running clothes.

When Ernst got back from his run, he wanted to call her, make sure she was okay. All day that feeling was with him. As he went to the base and worked out, her image was foremost on his mind.

"Hey, Chief," a voice reached him.

His artic eyes swung over to meet the dark-brown ones of his team-mate, Osten Scoleri, better known as "Baby Boy." "Scoleri," he responded with a smile.

"Wanna spar?" The men kept in top fighting shape.

"Sure," Ernst said, following him inside the ring not and paying attention to the other teammates who settled around the ring. *Lord knows I'm still spoiling to hit someone.*

"How's things?" Osten asked as he threw the first punch.

Dodging it easily, Ernst tossed a jab back and said, "Shitty."

"Why do you say that, Ghost?" A few more quick thrusts were tossed his way.

"Just found out some bastard's been beating up my woman." All the men there got wide eyed at Ernst's words. Osten was so stunned he didn't put up his hands and so took an uppercut to the chin knocking him back onto the mat. "Hell, you okay man?" Ernst asked, crouching beside him.

Osten sat up, his dark eyes still wide. "Kacy is in an abusive relationship?" he asked, totally disregarding Ernst's question as the blond helped him out the ring. Ernst knew he would be answering questions for a while.

The rest of the team circled around to hear his response. "Yes, damn it. Well, not any more, but she was. She goes to a battered women's group for meetings once a month." Ernst did a spinning back kick at the heavy bag he passed. "I just want five minutes with that motherfucker," he swore as he began to pound the bag.

His teammates looked at one another. All of them wanted to hurt this person. They might not know Kacy well, but they loved how she affected Ernst; and when he'd told them what she'd done for another chief on base, they liked her even more.

"What does that mean for the two of you?" Tyson asked.

"I don't know. She wanted to tell me before I decided if I wanted a relationship with her or not."

The men laughed, for they all knew he had decided that after that first date in Hawaii. Perhaps after he had run into her on the street that first day. Kacy Travis didn't stand a chance.

"I found out she grew up in an orphanage—St. Lucia's here, but she was born in Hawaii. There is a little boy at the orphanage that she goes to see every week, and I am going riding with them on Sunday unless we are elsewhere." Ernst wiped the sweat off his face and looked around the gym at his close friends.

"I'm in love." Ernst threw a glove at Maverick who groaned in dismay. "I am. I want to be with her all the time." He took off the other glove. "Get this—I sleep so well with her I didn't even hear her leave this morning."

"At the risk of having you shoot me, when did y'all start sleeping together?" Scott asked, barely keeping the smirk of his face. The rest of the men openly laughed.

"A hell of a lot sooner than you and Lex did!" Ernst snapped back playfully.

"Well, it would have been sooner if she would have stopped tossing those damn rules and regulations in my face," Scott growled, remembering his obstacle filled path to get to his woman who was also Navy.

"Oh, hell, you are going to make me sick," Maverick groaned again. "Who wants to spar with me?" Hondo took him up on it and soon they were in the ring fighting. Ernst stayed near Scott and Tyson.

"What are you going to do?" Tyson asked as he watched the two men in the ring.

"Be there for her. Support her and try my best not to kill the man who dared lay a hand on her," Ernst said honestly.

"We should have a get-together, the whole team. You bring Kacy and she can meet our wives and girlfriends," Scott said.

"I will run it past her," Ernst said. "Hey…thanks." One side of his mouth quirked up in a smile.

"Well, it sounds to me like she is about to be family," Scott said with a grin.

Ernst nodded. "That is my intention."

"We should make her feel at home then. Talk to her and get back to us on it." Scott slapped him on the back.

"I have to get going," Ernst said.

"Hot date?" Tyson teased.

"God, I hope so," Ernst replied even as a soft grin stretched his face.

Ernst showered, changed, and left to the hooting and hollering that his team sent his way. Waving over his shoulder and simultaneously giving them the finger, he strolled out of the gym and headed towards his truck. It was after five. He waited until he was all the way home before he called her, not wanting to be distracted by traffic.

She should be home or on her way there. Dialing her home phone first, he got the machine and hung up without leaving a message. Then he called her cell.

CHAPTER THIRTEEN

Kacy had an extremely busy day. As she was finishing up her last job of the day, her cell phone rang. "KT Electric."

"Kacy, you got a minute?" the masculine voice asked.

"Sure, Brett," she replied easily, recognizing his voice. "What's up?" Kacy quickly reattached the faceplate and stepped back to view her work.

"I'm at a job and it is a fuckin' mess. Can you give me a hand?"

Slipping her cordless drill back in its holder, she asked, "Where are you?" She and Brett often referred people to each other if they were overloaded.

Brett sighed with relief and gave her directions. "Thanks so much, Kacy."

"Hey, no worries. I'll be there as soon as I clean up here."

"I owe you for this. I'll give you half."

With a smile Kacy said, "See you in a few." She hung up the phone, gathered all her equipment, and put it in the van. The house was ready for the inspection. With a groan, she locked up behind her and climbed into her van. "I'm so hungry. Oh, well, I'll get something after."

Kacy drove listening to the radio, and just as she was almost to Brett's site, her phone rang. Not even looking at the number she answered, "KT Electric."

"Hello, *liebling*." His words thrummed through her body.

"Ernst," she mumbled. "How are you?"

"Wondering why you snuck out on me last night? Missing you."

"I had to get home; my day started pretty early. I left you a note."

"I know I got it. I wanted to wake up with you," Ernst admitted.

He sounds like he is pouting. "Sorry," she said lightly. Kacy turned off her van and climbed out. She waved at Brett as he walked towards her.

"What about dinner?" Ernst asked, stretching out on his couch.

I am so frickin' hungry. "I can't. I'm at another job." She paused. "Hey, Brett, be with you in a sec," Kacy said before speaking to Ernst again. "And I don't know how long I'll be."

"Brett?"

"Yep. He called and asked for my help. I'm really sorry about dinner. Maybe tomorrow?"

"Sure," he said with forced lightheartedness. "Tomorrow."

"Good." She smiled wistfully. "I gotta go, I'll talk to you later." Kacy hung up the phone to meet Brett's amused gaze.

Brett arched a black brow. "Who was that?"

Kacy blushed. "The guy from Hawaii."

"Hawaii? That white guy on the pier?" he questioned.

"That's the one. He lives in Suffolk."

"And you're dating?" Brett helped her grab some things he knew she would need. There was brotherly mischief in his eyes.

Were they? He hadn't asked again after she told, but considering what he said previously...maybe they were.

"Kacy?" Brett was waving a hand filled with conduit in front of her.

"Huh?"

"Are you two dating?" He cocked his head at her. "I lost you for a sec there."

"Sorry, yes, we're dating." Kacy hooked on her tool belt. "Let's go; fill me in."

They walked into the old building and Brett showed her to the breaker box. "Okay, see the main is off but..."

"But there's still power," she finished for him. Pulling a device off her belt she said, "Well, get your signal tracer and let's go find where someone rerouted some power."

"I'll go this way," Brett said, pointing upstairs.

"Okay, I'll start basement and work up."

"Great." They each headed off to their designated areas.

For a while they worked in silence until Kacy hit a signal. Pressing the button on her phone she used the walkie-talkie feature to contact Brett. "Found one, Brett. Here in the basement, there is another small room."

"Sweet. On my way," he responded. Moments later, he appeared in the dark and semi-damp basement; they could hear the water dripping somewhere. Brett whistled. "They didn't say anything about this room and I didn't see it. How'd you find it?"

"Don't know for sure," Kacy said as they both moved into the small room.

"I think this is it," Brett said, following the signal he was receiving.

Kacy glanced around and tried to contain a shiver. The lone light bulb only added to the eerie feel she got.

"You okay there, Kacy?" Brett asked, looking at her over his shoulder as he removed the faceplate he knelt before.

"Sure. I just don't like the feel of this room."

Brett sent her a wry smile. "You wanna go and see if there is no long-er a signal at the breaker box?"

"Hell, yeah." Kacy turned around and froze.

"What, Kacy?"

"Be careful, Brett. Just be extra careful down here." Her words were full of concern.

Half past eight they were done. The house had been a nightmare — bad switches, wild wiring. It was floating, which meant there was no ground on the service.

At least it was set so Brett could now rewire safely. Handing Brett a list of what she used, since he'd insisted on replacing those items, she slammed the door of her van shut. "I am so frickin' hungry I could eat an elephant," Kacy complained.

"Wanna grab dinner?" Brett asked.

"Yeah, that would be great. Where do you want to go?" Kacy opened the driver's door and looked at Brett over her shoulder.

"There is that little Italian place just off of Twenty-First that looks good."

"Pasta sounds excellent. Meet you there." She slid behind the wheel and shut the door, driving off and waving over her shoulder.

Brett pulled in moments behind her at the restaurant and they walked in together. It was a quiet place that wasn't too busy. A warm welcome greeted them as they were shown to a nice table.

"Thanks for this idea, Brett," Kacy said as her copper gaze looked over the menu.

He smiled in return. "Hey, I owe you so much for coming out to help me."

They placed their order and sat back to wait for the appetizers. "Tell me, Brett, how is Lisa?"

Lisa was Brett's girlfriend. "She is doing okay; comes back to town next week."

"When are you gonna marry that woman?" Kacy asked with a smile.

A faint blush crept over his cheeks. "Actually, I am going to ask her when she gets home."

"For real?" Kacy squealed.

"Yes. It's about time she made an honest man of me."

Kacy touched him gently on the arm. "Congratulations, Brett. You two make a wonderful couple."

The two friends had a light-hearted dinner. It was after ten when they parted ways in the restaurant parking lot. Kacy finally drove home with a full stomach. The one thing that would have made the night better was having Ernst with her.

Shaking her head, she grinned at how pathetic she was. Easing into her garage, she shut the door behind her as she walked into her home. Kacy stopped off at her fish tank to feed her babies before going to her room to shower and change.

Padding in boxer shorts and a tank top to the kitchen, she went to the freezer. Ice cream time. Noticing the light blinking on her machine, she pressed play as she grabbed a bowl for her nighttime snack.

The first few messages she knew were for work. As she dished up the chocolate treat she heard two hang-ups. Shrugging them off, she reached for her toppings and began to add them liberally.

The patter of rain on her windows made her look up. *I didn't know it was supposed to rain.* Soon her attention was back on the toppings as another person asked for a bid on her answering machine. Leaning against her counter, she began to eat the ice cream when the next message began to play.

The bowl fell to the floor and shattered as Kacy bolted toward the garage.

❀ ❀ ❀

Ernst had set the phone back in its charger after hanging up with Kacy. Turning on some AC/DC, he'd begun making himself some dinner. After his dinner had finished cooking, he sat down on his couch and turned off the music and to watch a baseball game.

His phone rang, jolting him out of his trance. "Hello?" He hoped it was Kacy.

Nope.

"Hello, Son," Nonnie Zimmermann said.

"Hello, Mother." Ernst shut off the television and ambled back into his kitchen. "What's going on?" It was nine o'clock.

"Calling to check on you. You haven't called or come home in a while," she reprimanded.

"Been busy, Mom, sorry."

"We are having a gathering on Sunday. Come."

Images of Kacy and Adam on horseback flashed through his head. "Sorry, Mom, I have plans if we are still here."

"Doing what?" the dubious voice asked.

"I am spending time with my girlfriend and a child from an orphanage," Ernst claimed, happy as hell he could actually call Kacy his girlfriend.

There was a moment of silence on the line. "Well, what is she like?"

"Beautiful, smart, and sexy," Ernst replied immediately.

"Do we know her? Her family? Anything about her?"

"Mother, you don't know her or her family. I promise I will bring her out there to meet you but not this Sunday. I'm sorry."

"I guess I understand. You don't want to see your family," she bemoaned.

Ernst rolled his eyes and put his dishes in the dishwasher. "I want to see my family. But we have plans for this Sunday and I am not going to ask her to change them."

Nonnie sighed heavily. "If I can't change your mind, then fine. But I'm not the only one who hasn't seen you in a while, you know."

"I will come out as soon as I can mother. Please stop trying to make me feel guilty," Ernst begged as he saw the toppings Kacy had brought over last night.

She put in one more dig. "You know Adolf is here."

"Yes, Mother, but he lives at home. I don't." Ernst shook his head. Their conversations were always like this. His mother wanted him at home living under her roof so she could run his life.

"He is home with his mother; there is nothing wrong with that," she snapped.

"He is a thirty-eight-year-old man. Adolf should be married and raising his own family."

"Your brother just hasn't met the right woman yet," she insisted.

For you, Mother, he hasn't met the right woman for you. "Okay, Mother. I have to go. I will be home soon and I will bring Kacy with me."

"Kacy? Is that her name?"

"Yes. Now goodnight, Mother." Ernst hung up the phone, only slightly exasperated with his parent. She hated what he did for a living and always tried to get him to stop and work with their father in the warehouse. But manufacturing machine parts wasn't Ernst's idea of a fun job.

Ernst worked out again and showered before heading to bed. It was eleven-thirty and he was getting up early to go running. Not to mention, dealing with his mother made him tired.

Sliding between the sheets nude, he closed his eyes and dreamt of Kacy Travis in his arms, in his bed and in his life.

BAM! BAM! BAM! BAM! The fierce pounding had Ernst bolting out of bed. Drawing on his pajama bottoms, he ran to his door.

BAM! BAM! BAM! BAM! "What the hell?" he swore as he wrenched the door open.

Kacy stood there drenched to the bone in boxers and a white tank top that was plastered to her body. She wore no bra, a fact he couldn't help but notice. Her hair was flattened to her head, but it was her eyes that caused him great concern. They were so full of fear and hopelessness.

"Kacy? Jesus, sweetheart, get in here. What's wrong?" Ernst reached for her only to have her launch herself into his arms, pressing her wet body to his dry one.

Backing up into his apartment, he carried her now sobbing body straight to the bathroom. She was shivering. Setting her down on the floor, he had to pry her hands off him. "*Liebling*? Sweetheart, what happened?"

Kacy just climbed closer to him again. Her teeth chattered so much Ernst wouldn't have been able to understand her if she had been talking. Reaching around her, he turned on the shower and walked them both into it when it was warm enough.

The spray soon began to sink into her bones and the chattering slowed down. Ernst held her, allowing her to cry out whatever was bothering her. Finally, she moved back from his embrace and looked up at him.

"Kacy, what the hell happened for you to come out in the rain in this little bit of clothing?"

Wiping away the water that ran down her face, her eyes met and held his. "I'm sorry for barging in on you."

"What happened?" *Trust me, please, Kacy.*

"After work, Brett and I went to dinner. I got home about eleven. I took a shower and changed. I went into the kitchen for..." she paused and gave him a tremulous smile, "...for ice cream. Anyway, I hit the playback on my machine and *he* was on there. Threatening me."

A switch flipped in Ernst. Gone was the lighthearted and carefree man; a battle-hardened warrior took his place — one who wanted blood. His eyes were blank and deadly as he looked at the frightened woman in his shower.

"I didn't know where else to go," Kacy babbled on.

It took a great deal of effort for Ernst to control himself. Forcibly calming himself, he tipped Kacy's face towards his. "First thing is we get out of this shower and into some dry clothes." His mouth quirked. "No matter how long I have wanted to get you in the shower." *And I am not even going to think why she was at dinner with Brett.*

Kacy smiled, but it didn't reach her eyes. "Let's get out and get you dry," he said as he shut off the water.

It was like dressing a puppet. Kacy stood on her own, but she seemed vacant. Ernst stripped her clothes off and wrapped her in a big, fluffy towel. Putting another towel around his waist, he left her in the bathroom to get her something to wear.

She remained in the exact spot he'd left her, fingers clutching the towel like it would run away if she loosened her grip. "Here," he said. "Put this on." Ernst handed her a tee shirt and a pair of boxers. He had changed into another pair of pajama bottoms.

Kacy dropped the towel and put them on in record time. His pale eyes moved over her standing before him in his clothing. A gray shirt and blue boxers, she had never looked so enticing.

The second he saw that haunted look on her face, his lustful thoughts took a backseat to finding out exactly what had happened. He made sure their wet clothes were hanging so they would dry. Holding out his hand he said, "Come to bed and tell me what happened."

Obediently, Kacy put her hand in his and allowed him to walk her down the hall to his room. She stood like a statue as he pulled back the covers on one side for her. "Kacy," he said.

It was like she blinked and was back in his time and place. "Coming," her low voice said.

In seconds, Ernst was in bed with Kacy. Her body curled up to his immediately and she shook for a bit until she got her emotions under control. Her bare legs brushed against his cotton-covered ones.

"Tell me what happened," he ordered as his hands locked around her, securing her to his body.

Chapter Fourteen

"He said he was coming for me. That his face would be the last thing I saw." Kacy's body shuddered. "I don't know what else because I ran."

Ernst's eyes closed in prayer to have five seconds with that man. They opened when she said, "I ran to the garage to hide like I had in the past, but it didn't make me feel safe."

Like I had in the past. Ernst wanted to kill this guy. It was obvious someone wasn't doing his or her job to protect her. Now it was his job, and he would do it correctly. "Then what?" he prompted.

"I jumped in my car and came here." It was on the tip of his tongue to ask why, but she continued. "You were the only thing that came to my mind when I tried to figure out a safe place."

A warm feeling began to thaw the coldness that had filled him at her revelation. "I'm glad," his honest admission came. "I didn't think it was raining so hard out."

"I paced outside deciding if I should come up or not," she breathed into his neck.

"My door is always open for you," he whispered. "I want you to go to sleep now."

Kacy nodded and did just that.

Ernst stayed in that same position until he knew for certain she was in a deep sleep. After that, he carefully removed his body from bed and went to workout.

Pounding the heavy bag, he imagined it was the man who did this to her. He wanted to go to her house and listen to the message, but didn't want her to wake up alone.

"Ernst?" Kacy's sleepy voice asked from the doorway a few hours later.

Spinning around, he flowed towards her like a ghost, one reason why he had his nickname. "Did I wake you?" His eyes were once again gentle as he looked over her exhausted body.

"No, I got up to use your bathroom." Kacy yawned. "What are you doing up?"

Ernst trailed one hand down the side of her face. "Just getting rid of some extra energy." He winked roguishly. "I didn't want to wake you."

"I'm awake now," Kacy answered in return. She stepped in close and slid her arms around his naked and sweaty torso.

Ernst had an instant erection at her words. "Kacy," he groaned, pulling her tighter to him as he moved his hands under her...well...his shirt. "Tell me to stop," he rasped as his hands tugged the shirt completely off her body.

"Stop," Kacy ordered, "stop talking."

Ernst struggled to rein in his control. The second her tongue swiped across his nipple, it vanished like mist under the sun.

Closing her eyes, Kacy took a deep breath and allowed his scent to wash over her. *How I long to be truly loved by this man.* Her tongue tasted him; her nose smelled him; and her body absorbed him. Pure man, sweat and all.

Ernst picked her up and carried her over to the floor mat, her shirt still by the door, forgotten. Laying them both down he whispered in her ear, "You are so beautiful, Kacy."

She felt it.

His large hand cupped one breast and she arched her back, a purr emerging from her throat. Ernst's erection throbbed painfully. "I want you, Kacy," he said, dipping his head down to suckle on her other wanting breast.

"Yes," she whimpered as her fingers grabbed at the mat.

"'Yes' what?" he murmured against her pebbled nipple. "Tell me you want me."

"I want you," Kacy spoke heavily as her body tried to press closer to his.

"No, tell me you want *me*," Ernst demanded. He flicked his tongue over her nipple before grazing it with his teeth.

"I want you, Ernst." Kacy touched his face so he would look up at her. When he met her desire-filled eyes she continued, "I want you to make love to me."

There was no more holding back after that. Ernst covered her body with his as he kissed her. He put his forearms under her shoulders and held her head in his strong hands.

His tongue slid eagerly into her waiting mouth. Kacy's tongue began to stroke along it before she began to suck on his tongue. Ernst moaned as his penis twitched in the confines of his pants. They were removed quickly and followed by his boxers flying off her body. His skin felt as if live electricity danced upon it. This man charged her system like no other. Settling back over her, he pressed their mouths together as he thrust fully into her with one stroke. The warm heat of her body cocooned him as if they were perfectly tailored for one another.

Kacy released a hiss of pleasure as he drove deep within her. Her bare feet stuck to the floor mat as she braced herself for his thrusts. Copper eyes were hooded as they lingered on the man above her.

Ernst began to move slowly as his lips nibbled around her full mouth. "Kacy," he mumbled between love bites.

"What?" her panted response came.

"Are you..." His hips thrust deep. "On any protection?"

"No," she shuddered, raising her hips to allow him deeper penetration.

He focused his eyes on her. "Do you trust me?"

Do you, Kacy? Do you trust this man? Her molten eyes widened as he slowed, lifting his upper body to look at her even more closely. "Yes," she said simply.

She saw his eyes brighten at her confession. "Okay, then." Ernst gently moved her legs so her calves rested on his shoulders.

Driving his pelvis faster, he watched as he sank between her dark, sexy thighs. Kacy felt him grow even harder inside her.

Kacy's eyes rolled back into her head as she began moaning louder with each deliberate stroke he gave her willing body.

"More," she begged, her hips undulating even more.

"Yes, ma'am." His fingers gripped the flesh of her hips, holding her at the angle that sent shivers through them both with each thrust.

"Harder, Ernst," Kacy pled. She was so close to that edge she could taste it.

He gave her what she wanted. The sound of her sweaty skin skidding on his mat as he pounded into her filled the room. Her fingers dug into his wrists as he held her.

Flushed bodies united as a storm raged outside, its fury and tempo matching the raging emotions in the room. He watched her body with his ghostly eyes. It writhed on the mat, covered in a sheen of sweat that made her glow. Her full breasts jiggled each time he buried himself in her. Her thick hair sprawled about her with some strands sticking to her face. Full lips parted, swollen from his kisses.

She was beautiful.

Feeling her tighten around him Ernst increased his speed. Moments later she came...hard, screaming her release to the room and whole apartment. Seconds later Ernst came deep within her, covering her womb with his sperm. Totally spent in more ways than one, he withdrew from her and collapsed beside her, tucking their sweating bodies together.

"Did I hurt you?" he asked a bit later, running his fingers over one hip.

"No, every ache is a good ache," Kacy said contentedly. "The room's really bright," she observed, burrowing her head into his chest.

"Well, I can't say I'm sorry about that. I love watching you when we make love." Ernst brushed some hair off her shoulder.

"Quiet." Kacy smacked him on the arm. Then, she yawned.

"Ready for bed?"

"Yep. But we should clean up the mat first." She could feel the wetness beneath her.

Ernst rolled onto his back, keeping her on his chest. His erection easily felt between them as he lifted her into a sitting position. "How about we add to it first."

Eagerly, Kacy rose up higher and slid down over his pulsating member. "Oh, yeah," she muttered as he again stretched her body.

"Ride me," he whispered, his hands reaching for her breasts.

A rare heat filled her copper gaze. "I like to ride."

And so she did. Ernst was in agony as she rode his body at her own pace. Sometimes fast. Sometimes slow. But it was always one hundred percent enticing, erotic, and torturous to the man beneath her.

After her third explosive orgasm, Ernst took matters into his own hands. Literally. He pounded up into her, gripping her full hips. Watching as she sucked her lower lip into mouth. Tugging her down to him for a passionate kiss, Ernst unloaded another batch of sperm deep within her responsive body. This time it was Kacy who collapsed. Her form shook with the extra twinges of pleasure that raced through her.

Ernst kept kissing her. He couldn't get enough. When his mouth left her tender one he said, "Bed now?"

"Well, I guess it would be nice to try your bed," Kacy teased as she moved to his side, only to curl up on him.

"We could just try all the rooms and see which ones we like best," Ernst said with an easy shrug.

"Sounds good to me. But later, I'm not used to all this sex." Her words were slurred. "That many intense orgasms are tiring for me."

Ernst had a smile on his face wider than the ocean. "Love, *liebling*. Not sex, love." His whispered words were the last she heard before falling into a very deep, very sated sleep.

When Kacy awoke at five, her body was sore but she couldn't care less. Strong arms held her in their protective embrace. Although tender and probably raw, Kacy felt her body respond to the semi-hard erection pressing into her torso. She reached down and wrapped her hand around it. Ernst moaned as his hips bucked against her. Within seconds, he was fully erect and throbbing beneath her palm. It was like holding velvet over iron.

Kacy began caressing him nice and slow. She watched her hand moved back and forth along his rigid penis. The tip had a few drops of precum and her thumb wiped it away before continuing her up and down action.

"You trying to kill me?" His voice deepened by sleep and desire brought her attention back to his eyes. They were so magnetic; she loved their ethereal beauty.

Her fingers tightened around him. "Want me to stop?"

"Hell, no!" he groaned, flopping over onto his back and allowing her easier access to his body.

Free to move more, Kacy used her other hand to cup his scrotum. She kept him at a fevered pitch. His hands clutched the bed covers repeatedly.

Slithering down his body, Kacy took the head of his erection in her mouth. "Kacy," he hissed. She took in more and more of him until her lips met her hand at the base of his penis. Up and down she bobbed her head. Letting go of him with her hands, she took his full length in her mouth.

His hands dug into her hair, guiding her to the speed he wanted. His hips bucked as his body grew closer to release. Kacy allowed him to set his desired pace.

"I'm gonna come, sweetheart," he said in a gravely voice.

She increased the suction she had on his thick penis. One hand moved back around to play with his scrotum, lightly running her nails over it.

"Jesus," he moaned as his hips jerked once and he came deep in her throat. Her luscious mouth slurped along his length as she made sure to milk him clean.

Ernst reluctantly pulled away from her mouth and readjusted her so he could slide into her with one stroke. It didn't take long before she was screaming to the room herself.

Leaving her body for a moment, he flipped her over on her belly, slid his arm under her pelvis, and lifted her. Then he was back in her heat.

"Shit," she wailed as her body surged forward with every thrust he delivered. "That feels good." Her hips began to move back toward him each time.

Her fingers dug into his bedding and her body moved beneath him. Reaching around her, he played with her clit, sending her spiraling over the edge and taking him with her.

She collapsed face first into the mattress. Her body still shook with aftershocks. His warm body covered hers as his stubble-roughened cheek rubbed her smooth one. "Thank you for that," he muttered in her ear.

"Thank *you*," she spoke softly.

Rolling off her, he pulled her in closer to his body. "How are you feeling this morning?"

"Satisfied. Almost totally," she teased.

"Almost?" he growled.

"Well, I would like more, but I have to get home." She looked up at him in time to see the humor leave his eyes.

"Not alone. I'm going with you." It was an order, not a request.

"Okay," Kacy said as she made to get out of bed. *I want you with me, anyway.*

"And you are wearing another one of my shirts. I don't want you going out in public without a bra on and just a tank top," Ernst added, sliding her back across the bed and into his arms.

"Are we dating now?" Kacy asked as she touched his face.

"Yes," he said immediately. "I am your boyfriend, you are my girlfriend, and we are most definitely a couple."

"I have to get home," she insisted. His words, although extremely sweet, didn't seem real in a way, and so she ignored them for the moment. The fear of going into her house nearly overwhelmed her.

He nibbled on her neck. "Let's shower and get going."

❄ ❄ ❄

Ernst kept Kacy behind him as he went in her house. His body was alert for anything. She remained silent while entering her home. He made a swift and thorough check of her domicile before he spoke. "We are the only ones here."

"Thank you for coming with me." She looked into the kitchen and saw the broken dish and dried mess on her floor. "I have to clean that up."

"I want to hear your message." He noticed how her relaxed body tensed up immediately.

One finger pointed to the machine. "There it is." Kacy headed for the kitchen.

Ernst pressed play and listened to all the messages. His physique grew rigid the second he heard the malevolent voice. The man who had loved Kacy that very morning had been replaced by the SEAL who was ready for battle.

Giving himself time to calm down, he went to the kitchen where Kacy sat on the floor scrubbing the mess she had made last night. "Why don't you have a restraining order against him?"

The scrubbing became more intense. "I do," she said. "It just doesn't matter."

Ernst ran a frustrated hand over his face. "I don't want you here alone."

Looking over her shoulder, Kacy sent him a kind but fearful smile. "I live here and work here. I'm not moving."

Crouching down beside her, he grabbed her hand, halting her motion and bringing her eyes back to him. "This man is a danger to you."

"I know," she said quietly.

There was loud pounding on the front door, startling them both. Kacy rose to answer it but Ernst shook his head and said, "I'll get it." He prowled towards the door, his body deceptively relaxed. Opening it, he said, "Yes?"

"Who the hell are you?" a voice asked. "Where's Kacy?"

"I'm here Landi. Come on in," Kacy beckoned.

Ernst barely got out of the way before the woman barreled past him and grabbed Kacy in a big hug. "Are you okay? I've been calling you nonstop since your meeting yesterday!"

Hugging her back, Kacy nodded. "I'm sorry. You-know-who called and I got the message when I got home from the meeting."

"That bastard called you?!" Her small body shook with rage.

"I'm okay. I went to stay with Ernst," Kacy said, pulling back from her friend.

"Ernst?" A huge smile crossed her face as she spun around to look at the man standing there in Kacy's entryway. "You're the guy from Hawaii. The Navy man, I recognize you from the pictures."

Ernst looked at the woman standing beside Kacy. She was dressed in pink pants, a white shirt, and shoes. Her dark skin looked good with that color. Her eyes were a rich brown and her wavy hair was held up with a pink ribbon. She was short about five-two or so, and not very big. "I'm Ernst." He held out his hand.

"I'm Ilanderae; you can call me Landi." She winked at him. "You were right, Kacy, he is hot."

"Landi," Kacy protested as a blush ran over her face.

"Well, he is." Her sweet face grew serious. "Are you going to kick the shit out of this man who is bothering my Kacy?" Ilanderae asked Ernst.

"I just got done telling her she shouldn't be here alone," Ernst said, realizing he had an ally in Ilanderae.

CHAPTER FIFTEEN

Kacy drove to her first job site of the day. She was almost running late. Ernst and Ilanderae had been formidable together, but she had stood her ground, she was *not* moving.

She did call the police and gave them the message on her machine. Since the caller had never identified himself, they couldn't do anything, news that didn't surprise Kacy at all but pissed off Ernst and Ilanderae even more.

After promising to call him once she had returned home for the day, Ernst had left to go to the base, leaving her breathless from his kiss. Soon after, Ilanderae left to get to work.

✺ ✺ ✺

"He said his face would be the last thing she ever saw. That there was nowhere she would be safe from him. He was coming for her. He said she would pay for going with another man. Told her how worthless she was and pathetic," Ernst relayed his teammates as they sat around a briefing table. "There was a lot more but that's the overview."

The room was silent before Maverick spoke up, "So when do we find him and teach him a lesson?"

Pale eyes were grateful as Ernst looked at Maverick. "Thanks, man. Believe me I want to kill him, but I don't want Kacy to view me in that same way."

The men nodded. "What about the police?" Osten asked.

"To them it was a crank call. The number was from a pay phone and he never left his name." Ernst paused. "I still don't know that bastard's name."

"But she came to you, so that must mean she trusts you. Even after being warned about dating someone else," Aidrian said in his Irish lilt.

Ernst shook his head. "That was at the end of the message. She ran before she heard it all. She used to hide in the garage. Kacy told me that's where she hid in the past." He smacked the table in frustration. "I hate that I can't help her."

"Seems to me like you did," Scott's deep voice added.

"I can't protect her in Suffolk, unless I kidnap her and move her in with me."

"So move in with her," Dimitri suggested.

"I don't want this guy to see that and come after her the next time we are on a mission. Trust me; I thought about that." Ernst looked around the room at his friends. His teammates. His family. "Thanks, guys."

"Okay," Tyson interrupted. "I have a bit of business that just came down the wire." All eyes turned to the Team's second-in-command. "We need to do some PR. You know, go to schools and talk with the kids. Volunteer?"

For the second time that morning the room fell silent, this time for a different reason.

"Well, don't everyone volunteer at once," Tyson joked. "Come on; it's a few days of sitting behind a booth, answering questions."

Osten "Baby Boy" Scoleri said, "I'll do it."

"Thanks," Scott said. "Good news, now, we are all coming up on two weeks down time. Apparently, we were a bit rough our last time out and we need to rest. Scoleri, the PR thing is next month. I'll get you the details later."

"Okay, Commander." Osten replied.

"Oh," Ross spoke up. "I forgot; there is a classic car show just over the state line in North Carolina tomorrow. I'm gonna go see Dezarae since she has been avoiding me, if anyone cares to come along."

"Need backup, man?" Ernst teased.

"Hell, yeah," Ross drawled. "That woman is something else."

They were all in. Each man loved classic cars and was more than willing to support Ross.

"That's all, men. See everyone tomorrow." Scott said closing his file, showing the room his wedding ring as the sun glinted off the gold.

One day, Ernst thought, *my ring will do the same.* Walking to his truck, Ernst realized that he still didn't know much about Kacy.

He spent the day at the base, but it wasn't until seven that his cell phone rang. "Chief Zimmermann," Ernst said automatically.

"You're a Chief, huh?" Kacy's sexy voice asked.

A grin spread across his face as he sat down on the couch, turning down the music. "Yes, ma'am, I am."

"See there, I learned something new."

"Come on over and I'll teach you something else as well."

She laughed. "Sorry, I'm at home. You said to call, so I am."

"I wanted to make sure you were okay; it wasn't a command," he said frowning over her choice of words.

"I know. And I thank you for your concern. Also, I wanted to hear your voice."

"That's better," he granted. "What are you wearing?"

"Oh, some small, silky, and exposing thing."

His body responded instantly. "Teasing me, *schatzi*?"

"Yep. I *just* got home. Actually just wearing torn jeans and a sleeveless shirt. I'm feeding my fish and am about to order pizza."

"You haven't had dinner yet?" Ernst questioned.

"Nope. Long day. So I am going to eat pizza and watch the Braves."

He sat up. "You like baseball?"

"Love it," she vowed heading to her bedroom to change.

"Want some company?"

"Sure. What do you want on your pizza?"

"Anything except sardines. Can I bring anything?"

"Beer," Kacy answered. "Can't watch baseball without beer."

"Got it. Be there soon. Bye, sweets." Ernst hung up.

Kacy ordered the pizza and turned on her television. She loved sports, but that was about the extent of what she watched. If there was a history thing on a poet she would watch that, too; otherwise, she wasn't a television person.

Flipping through her mail, she straightened up her spotless home. She put down fine china: paper plates, plastic silverware, and paper towels for napkins. The order consisted of pizza, breadsticks, and wings, so she figured they would be fine.

Padding through the house in Braves socks, she moved to the door when the doorbell chimed. Opening it, the pizza guy stood holding her order.

She grinned at the familiar face. "Evening, Randy."

"Evening, Kacy. Ordered more tonight," he observed.

"Watching the game with a friend," Kacy said, stepping back to let him inside. Randy had been delivering pizzas to her for over two years. He put the order down on the coffee table.

Handing him a check, she followed him back to the door. "Thanks, Randy," she called as he went back to his car.

"My pleasure. It's always good to see you. Bye, Kacy."

"Bye, Randy." Kacy closed the door and went back to her coffee table. She arranged the food on the table and watched the television as they went through the Braves lineup.

The doorbell rang again and her stomach flipped as she knew who it was. Ernst. Running a hand down her jersey, she strolled to the door, appearing much calmer than she really was.

Ernst stood there holding a case of beer in one hand and a dozen purple lilies in the other. "Evening, *liebling*," he said, leaning in for his kiss.

"Evening," she drew out as their lips separated.

His gaze took in her black pants and Braves jersey. "You look hot."

"Come on. Food is here and the game has started," she said with a blush.

He offered her the flowers. "These are for you."

A stunning smile crossed her face. "They're beautiful, thank you." Taking them, she walked inside, leaving him to follow.

"So, do I want to know," he began, trailing her after shutting the door behind him, "why you are wearing number ten?" Ernst put the beer in her fridge.

Filling a crystal vase she responded, "'Cause he is my favorite player." Cutting the ends off the lilies, she put them in the vase and set it on the table. "That looks wonderful. Thanks."

A roar from the television grabbed their attention. Taking his hand, she dragged him back into the living room. Soon, they had food on their plates and beer to drink.

Side by side on her couch they sat. Kacy really got into the game, yelling at the television, voicing her opinion. She drank her beer and complained about the umpire's call.

"I think it was a good call," Ernst commented matter-of-factly.

"What?!" she screeched. "That pitch was nowhere near the strike zone! It was a ball. That ump is blind!"

His robust laughter reached her ears. "You are so passionate about this game, aren't you?"

Her copper eyes swung to his face and narrowed at the glee she observed. "You just picking on me, aren't you?"

Ernst nodded and tapped her on the end of her nose. "Pretty much." Rolling her eyes, she got up to grab them each another beer.

The end of the game had her at the edge of her chair. In the end the Braves won, but it was nail-bitingly close.

Chatting about the game they began to clean up. Ernst carried the boxes into the kitchen while Kacy searched for a container for leftovers.

"How long have you liked baseball?" Ernst asked, putting away the wings in the tub she provided.

"For about as long as I can remember. Baseball, football, and hockey. Mostly baseball and football," she answered, snapping the lid on the container holding the pizza.

"And the Braves?"

"It seemed right. The Braves and the Panthers, those are my teams. Rangers for hockey." She placed the recycling on one side of the sink before putting the leftovers in the fridge. "Did you want any of the pizza or wings?"

"I'm good," Ernst said, admiring just how damn cute she was.

"I'll be right back; I have to put this in the recycling bin." She grabbed the empty beer bottles and boxes from dinner and went into her backyard.

Ernst wiped down her coffee table and made sure the place was clean. He'd not dated a woman who loved sports as he did. They *were* perfect for one another.

He was still straightening up when Kacy came back inside. "You didn't have to do that."

"I don't mind," he told her, going back into the kitchen to wash and ring out the rag.

Kacy turned on some slow music and joined him in the kitchen. "Thanks for coming over."

Ernst leaned against the counter and drew her into his body. "Thanks for having me."

The only lights on were the two over the sink and they were dimmed. Kacy wrapped her arms around his waist and let him just hold her.

His cheek rested along her temple and he closed his eyes, perfectly content. "When is your birthday?" he asked after a few moments.

"Want to see if we are compatible for one another?" she queried.

"*Schätzchen*, I already know we are. I just want to know more about you."

"Let's go sit on the swing."

Ernst and Kacy cuddled up on the swing, talked, and made love into the wee hours of the morning. As he tucked her into bed, he smiled as he memorized her beauty. "I will see you on Sunday, *schätzchen*."

"Have fun at the show," she murmured, exhausted from her long day and making love on her porch swing.

"*I love you.*" He mouthed the words as he left the room, leaving her to her slumber. "I will."

Chapter Sixteen

Six in the morning Sunday, Kacy's doorbell chimed. Drinking her coffee, she ambled over to the door and swung it open. Ernst stood there dressed in a tight Navy shirt and blue jeans. He had hiking boots on his feet.

"Morning, sweetheart," he said as his eyes raked over her tight jeans and tank top.

"Hey, Ernst, come on in. I just made a pot of coffee." Kacy stepped back to allow him entrance.

His tall body followed hers and he kissed her. "Can't forget that." She knew she tasted like coffee and mint. "I brought bagels," he said holding up the box.

"Good, I'm hungry." They entered the kitchen where she got plates down and he reached for a mug to get himself a cup of coffee. "How was your show?" she asked as she grabbed knives and cream cheese.

"It was really nice. Ross got his woman to agree to marry him." Ernst said, pulling two glasses down for juice.

Kacy set the pitcher of orange juice on the table and sat. Ernst followed moments later. "Well good for him…them." She took a plain bagel and cut it open to put some whipped cream cheese on it. "So three of y'all are married or going to be; who's next?"

He looked at her intently even while shruggin' his shoulders. "Who knows? I am pretty sure it won't be Aidrian or Maverick."

So he isn't planning on getting married soon. Why that bothered her, she didn't know. "They have something against marriage?"

"So they claim," Ernst said as he bit into his bagel.

Kacy shrugged and concentrated on her breakfast. "Well to each his own."

"Where is this stable?" Ernst changed the subject after a few quiet seconds passed.

"About forty-five minutes from St. Lucia's. Why?"

"Just wondering. We should be going." He nodded toward the digital readout on the microwave. Almost six-thirty.

Standing, Kacy drained the rest of her orange juice and grabbed two travel mugs. Handing one to Ernst she said, "For your coffee." Her kitchen was once again spotless after a swift cleaning.

"Ready?" he asked.

"Just let me grab another shirt." Kacy went to her room and came back slipping on a button down–short sleeve shirt over her tank top. He noticed she had also put on her boots.

"I am going to be the envy of all." He kissed her again, this time lingering on her lips.

"We need to go. I don't want to keep Adam waiting," she said, breathless when they broke apart.

"As you wish." His hand stroked the side of her face. "I'm all yours." Kacy's eyes flared hot passion before she gathered her control, but he'd already seen it. "Later, sweetheart, I promise." He kissed her again and grabbed his coffee.

Kacy grabbed her mug, wallet, and keys, then went into the garage after locking the front door. "Do you want to put your truck in the garage?"

"If you don't mind," he said.

"Not at all." Unlocking her car, she put in her coffee and reached for his. "Go get in and I will back out."

The exchange of vehicles didn't take long and soon Ernst was sliding into the leather interior of her car as the door of her garage closed, locking in her van and his truck. "You have a sweet ride," he praised.

"Thanks." She put them on the road and within minutes they were flying toward the orphanage.

"How long have you been riding?" Ernst asked after they had driven in companionable silence for a while.

"About fifteen years. I love outdoor activities; and when a friend suggested I try it, I found I loved it." Kacy said, expertly maneuvering the car around the curves that led to where a seven-year-old waited for them.

"Is there anything you can't do?" he wondered as she slowed down to turn into the orphanage.

"Besides cook?" She laughed. "Yes, there are a lot of things I can't do." Kacy stopped the car by the front and got out. Adam was waiting on the step along with one of the nuns.

"Nice to know," he muttered as he too got out of the vehicle.

"Kacy!" Adam shouted as he bolted down the steps into her arms.

She hugged him back. "Hey, Adam. Are you ready?"

He began to cough. "Ready," he said when he finished.

"See who came with." Kacy pointed towards Ernst. "Go say hi to him."

Adam ran over to Ernst and hugged him as well. As the two males began to talk, Kacy walked up to the Sister waiting there. "Is he okay?" she asked, concerned.

Kind eyes looked back at Kacy. "He has been coughing more, but he is okay. Just take it easy."

"Okay." Kacy blinked back tears. "Thanks for letting me take him."

"You are the thing that makes him happy, my dear. Now, go and have fun," the nun said, kissing her on the cheek.

"I...we will. See you later today." Kacy returned the kiss and turned around to see Ernst crouched down listening intently to Adam.

Walking over to the men she was going to spend the day with, Kacy put forth the question, "Everyone ready?"

Two pairs of eyes looked up at her, one dark-brown and the other a pale, icy blue; both affected her heart. "Yes," they said together.

Parking the car in the empty lot, Kacy shut down the engine and got out. Ernst climbed out of the other side and tipped the seat up to let Adam out as well. The trio walked up to the stable.

"Patch!" Kacy called. "You in here?"

A tall burly man stepped out of the barn. "Kacy, good to see you. And you brought my favorite little rider! How are you Adam?" Patch knelt down to shake Adam's hand.

"Good," Adam said with a smile.

Standing, Patch looked over at Ernst who had taken up a position by Kacy. "Name's Patch. Who are you?" He offered his hand.

"Ernst," came the reply along with a hand.

Both men sized each other up in seconds. Patch turned to Kacy and said, "I'll take Adam and we will get his horse ready. Kacy, yours is waiting for you in his stall." He put his blue eyes on Ernst and asked, "Are you a good rider?"

"Passable. No cowboy, but I can sit a horse," Ernst said.

"Okay, Kacy, why don't you get him on Rex?" Patch suggested as he took Adam's hand and led him into the barn.

Kacy smiled at the retreating duo before she looked at Ernst. "Ready?"

"Absolutely." Ernst winked at her and leaned down to kiss her briefly.

Holding hands, they walked down the aisle of the barn. She stopped by a stall and said, "Here you are. This is Rex."

Ernst looked in at a nice roan gelding. The horse snuffed him and nudged his outstretched hand. "He's a beaut."

"His stuff is here. When you are done, meet us out front, okay?" Kacy pointed to the equipment on a hay bale and waited for an answer.

Ernst nodded and slipped into the stall to put his tack on. "Got it. See you in a few."

Kacy disappeared. She went to the stall that housed the horse she always rode, a large bay Morgan gelding named, Bonfire.

Soon, all of them were out front. Adam was already in the saddle of his small paint gelding named Cyclone. Kacy had her horse tied to a hitching post as she walked over to Adam. "All ready?"

"I'm ready," he said full of excitement.

"Good. We are just going to take it easy today, okay?"

"I know," he said. "Ernst is on; let's go." Adam picked up his reins.

"You two go ahead; you know where to go, Adam. I want to talk to Patch for a moment, but I will catch up," Kacy ordered.

"Bye, Kacy," Adam said, nudging Cyclone and walking off. "Come on, Ernst. Follow me."

Ernst did after casting a look towards Kacy who nodded. Rex stepped out easily and soon the two of them were out of sight.

"Thanks, Patch. I know how much this means to him," Kacy told the large man standing with her.

He smiled at Kacy. "I love that little boy. This is on the house. Now, go on and have fun. Just be back by dinner."

She hugged Patch and blinked back the tears that threatened to fall. "And we love you. Sure you don't want to come?" she asked as she drew back.

"I have work to do on some tack. Go on, now, get outta here," he ordered gruffly, trying not to show any more emotion.

"I'm going." Walking over to Bonfire, she untied him and swung up. As he began to walk off, she urged him to a gallop, and she was soon on the heels of Ernst and Adam.

Ernst turned his head at the sound of approaching hoof beats. He stared as Kacy and her horse came into view. She sat him like she had been riding forever, her body moving fluidly with his gallop as they cut the distance down.

"Hey, guys," she said as she pulled the gelding back to a walk. "Sorry about that. So Adam, where are we going today?"

"Let's take him to the river," Adam answered.

"Okay, with or without the switchback?" Kacy questioned.

"With. I like that part," Adam responded with a grin.

"Sounds like a plan." They were moving across a field, so each adult sandwiched Adam and the trio walked side by side.

The little boy chatted nonstop as they moved along and Ernst answered every question put to him. The child was amazing, full of questions and his own theories on things. Kacy stayed quiet, but he could feel her eyes on him over Adam's head. When he looked, she was watching him with a longing expression on her face.

Winking at her, he smiled when she blushed and then looked away. At the river, they trotted through the water and allowed the horses to get a drink. They had been riding for about an hour.

Adam wanted to go down the switchback, so Kacy took them around there. In the open field, she allowed Adam to gallop, but only for a little bit. Ernst kept pace with him and again was amazed at the boy's ability.

When Adam wanted to stop and just sit at the top of the switchback for a while, he sat beside Ernst. Kacy smiled over the decision and sat opposite them both, listening to the chatter.

After a while, Ernst helped Adam back up on the horse; it was time to go down the switchback. "How do you usually do this Kacy?" Ernst asked.

"Well, I usually go first, but you can if you want," she offered.

"No, I'll bring up the rear," Ernst said.

She shrugged easily. "If you want. Ready, Adam?"

"Ready," his voice came.

Kacy led the way. Bonfire picked his way carefully and navigated with ease. Adam did beautifully and Ernst found himself watching Kacy as she sat on her horse. She was all he could ever want.

As the horses left the switchback and reentered the river, Ernst realized what he wanted. A family. Kacy and Adam would be a great start.

"You doing okay back there?" Kacy asked as she allowed Adam to go on ahead.

"Just thinking," Ernst said with a smile.

"About?" she prompted.

"The future," he stated, looking her directly in the eyes.

"I see." Kacy put her gaze on Adam who was looking at the wildlife and scenery. The child seemed so happy.

"Can I ask you something?"

Copper eyes swung back to Ernst. "Go ahead."

"Why don't you adopt Adam? It's obvious you two love each other." Ernst saw the pain flash across her face.

"I tried. But I wasn't good enough according to the state. Since I was still relatively new in the work I do, they didn't think I'd be able to give him what he needed." Kacy's voice.

He reached for her hand to squeeze. "I'm so sorry."

"Not your fault. Adam," she said loudly, "stay closer." Her voice lowered. "So that's why I see him when I can."

Ernst didn't know what to say. "For what it's worth, I think you'll make a great mom."

"Maybe," she replied softly.

"I'm sure of it." Ernst dropped it since Adam was waiting for them.

"Do you think the hawk will be there Kacy?" Adam's young voice asked.

"Could be. Keep your eyes peeled for him." Turning toward Ernst she explained, "There is usually a hawk sitting on a fencepost that we pass right before the barn."

"I call him Raja," Adam announced proudly.

"That's a very good name," Ernst agreed.

Adam once again dominated the conversation, pointing out trees, plants, and flowers to Ernst.

Back at the barn, Adam stuck to Ernst and told him about the first time they had seen Raja. The hawk had been there today again.

Kacy watched them, hovering in the background with tears in her luminous eyes. The horses were put away and they said goodbye to Patch before walking to the car. She had pictures of the three of them together both with and without the horses.

Adam began coughing again. Kacy immediately gathered him to her and rubbed his back until he stopped. His big brown eyes seemed tired. "You okay now?" she asked, hiding her concern.

He nodded. "Kacy?" Adam stopped her with a touch.

She met his gaze. "What is it Adam?"

"Can I see Cyclone one more time? I forgot to say goodbye."

Kacy looked at Patch who stood there. He nodded. "Sure. Come on."

His tiny hand slipped into hers and they went back in the barn. Cyclone leaned down and nuzzled Adam as the child said his goodbyes. "See ya, Cyclone," he spoke gently. "Okay, I'm ready."

"Let's go, then. Are you hungry?" Kacy questioned as they walked hand in hand out of the barn.

"Sure am."

Ernst was waiting by the car. His eyes lingered over Kacy and the boy with her. "What now?" he asked as they got close enough.

"Food," Kacy stated bluntly. "This little man is hungry."

"Me too," Ernst said with an easy grin. His eyes however burned a different message for Kacy. Her body was on his menu.

Trembling, Kacy got behind the wheel as Ernst buckled up Adam in the back before sitting in the front passenger's eat. Driving them to a family restaurant, she kept one eye on Adam who looked like he was dozing.

Ernst reached across the middle console and held her hand. He sent her a gentle smile when she met his gaze.

Adam walked between them as they entered the restaurant. Kacy watched as Ernst took over. He asked Adam which seat he preferred. Then men were side by side in the booth and Ernst helped Adam decide what he was going to have.

Kacy handed Ernst her keys after their meal so he could drive. As they were on the road back to the orphanage, Adam had fallen asleep, jarred only by coughing spells.

Back at St. Lucia's, Kacy woke up the little boy. "Come on, Adam. Time to get up."

Sluggish still, Adam climbed out of the car. "I had a great time, thanks." His young voice was raspy from all his coughing.

"Me, too, sweetie, me too." Kacy said, trying hard to smile.

Adam looked at Ernst and went for a hug. His skinny arms slid around Ernst's neck as the man bent down level to the child. "Thanks, Ernst."

"You are so very welcome. I had a great time." Ernst said, smiling as he hugged Adam back.

Adam pulled away and walked to Kacy, holding out his arms. Kacy dropped to her knees and pulled him in. "I love you, Adam," she whispered.

"Love you, too, Kacy." He kissed her cheek. "Thank you."

"See you soon," Kacy said in a quiet voice. She pulled back when he didn't respond. His eyes were sad, but he smiled when she looked at him.

"Yeah," he responded faintly. "I'm kinda tired; I'm gonna go lay down."

"Okay, baby." Kacy stole one more kiss and released him. Adam moved towards the nun waiting for him, looking exhausted and frail.

Ernst stood by Kacy as they waved to Adam, his arm around her shoulders. "Let's go, sweetheart." He put her solemn body in the passenger side and slid behind the wheel and drove.

He took them to a park. Getting out, he held out his hand for her to hold. "Come take a walk with me."

For a while, they strolled in silence. Holding hands, he led them down a path that followed a winding stream.

CHAPTER SEVENTEEN

"Thanks for letting me come along today," Ernst broke the silence.

"I know it meant a lot to Adam to have you with him today," Kacy responded. At the arch of one pale brow she added with an easy smile, "And to me."

"That is what I wanted to hear." He brushed her lips with his. Just as he pulled her in closer, a beeping noise filled the air. "Damn," Ernst swore as he grabbed his beeper and looked at the number.

"What's wrong?" Kacy asked.

"I have to go. We have to leave." His tone was urgent yet calm.

"Okay," she said immediately. They swiftly moved back up the path to her waiting car. She reached for the keys and slid behind the wheel, turning over the powerful engine.

Ernst admired the way she took his news without flinching. His admiration only grew as she drove her car on the open road. The trees flew by in a flash as she pushed the envelope to get him back to his truck. "Are you going to miss me?" he asked over the roar of her engine.

Flashing him a smile that held a hint of sadness she nodded. "I am."

"Good." He touched her cheek with one hand. "I'm glad. I will miss you as well, *schätzchen*."

Her smile turned shy and she blushed. Her eyes stayed on the road as she took them into town. "That's good to know."

Pulling into her drive, she parked on the side so he could get his truck out. "Here we are," she said and she climbed out of the car.

Not moving into the now-open garage, Ernst gathered her into his arms. "Give me a kiss for luck."

Kacy smiled. "Do you need it?" She arched an eyebrow. "Like last time."

He grinned softly, remembering when he'd first asked the question in Hawaii, but noting these were far more serious stakes. "Oh, yeah," he vowed. "I need it."

Lifting her lips to his, she kissed him, pouring into that one kiss all of her feelings for him. He felt her gratitude for what he had done for her and her sorrow that he was leaving. And even the love she wasn't quite ready to admit out loud.

Reluctantly, he drew away from her mouth. "I have to go, sweetheart." He kissed her one more time. "Don't forget me."

"I won't," she said in a soft voice. "Stay safe." Kacy was blinking back tears.

One strong finger caressed her full bottom lip as his eyes stroked the rest of her. "I will do my best. Goodbye, *liebling*." He dropped his hand and walked to his truck, got in, and drove it out of her garage. As he pulled away from her house, he saluted her briefly with two fingers.

Kacy stayed busy while he was gone. She worked hard and kept herself occupied as much as she could. Every Sunday she spent with Adam. It had been six weeks since Ernst had kissed her and driven off, and she missed him so much more than she cared to admit. She went to her meetings and stayed strong, not wavering in her decision to try a relationship with Ernst.

Monday night she sat eating a quiet dinner when the phone rang. The two words that reached her ears made her heart drop to her feet. "It's Adam."

Kacy kept repeating those two words over in her head. She drove as if Lucifer himself were after her. Pushing her car to its limit, she tore to St. Matthew's Hospital. Squealing into a visitor's spot, she headed for the doors at a run, barely remembering to lock her car.

At the admittance desk she waited impatiently for the woman to acknowledge her. "Can I help you?" the question finally came.

"I'm here to see Adam from St. Lucia's." Kacy paused for a deep breath. "He was just brought in."

The deadpan eyes softened just a tiny bit. "Are you Kacy?"

"Yes," Kacy said as dread filled her heart.

"Exam three. It will be on your right." The nurse responded, pointing in the direction Kacy needed to take.

"Thank you," she replied as her legs took her to where Adam lay.

Knocking briefly before entering, Kacy stepped into the room. Monitors beeped loudly, cutting through the otherwise silent domicile.

"He's been asking for you." The whisper came from Sister Angela who had risen from her seat beside Adam the moment Kacy entered.

With a kiss for the nun, Kacy moved to the bed where Adam rested. His skin was pasty in appearance and covered with sweat. Breathing was shallow and raspy. Tears filled her eyes as she looked at him.

"Adam?" Kacy said as she wiped a cloth over his face.

Those soulful brow eyes were weary as they opened at her voice. "Kacy?" he coughed out.

"Right here, Adam, I'm right here." Kacy sat in the chair beside the hospital bed that seemed too big for the body it cradled.

"I'm scared," Adam said, reaching for her hand.

"Of what? I'm here. Sister Angela is here; the lights are on," Kacy spoke softly.

"I was scared you weren't coming."

"Have I never not come back?" Kacy asked her usual question, trying to pretend she wasn't frightened as well.

"No," he grated out. "You always come back."

"And I always will," she vowed as her hand moved softly over his clammy face. "And I always will."

Ernst wanted to see Kacy so bad. They had been gone for six weeks. One task would end, then and another would line up.

In a black tee shirt and olive green BDUs, he drove to her house. She hadn't answered her house phone or her cell. *Maybe*, he thought, *she had decided to have a relationship with someone who was around more*. Pulling into the drive, he hopped out, anxious to look at the face of the woman he loved and had thought about totally for the last six weeks.

Jogging up the front steps, he rang her doorbell. Nothing. A frown crossed his handsome face as he knocked. "Kacy?"

"She's not there," a voice said.

Those pale eyes swung toward the sound and found her neighbor Mrs. Wilder standing at the edge of her property. "Do you know where she is or when she'll be back?"

Sadness crossed her weathered face. "Don't know when, but I know where. She's at St. Matthew's Hospital." Ernst's heart plummeted. "That orphan boy is in there."

"Adam?" he asked. *Oh, dear God!* "Thank you so much," Ernst said as he bolted for his truck.

Kacy stood listening to the doctor as Sister Angela sat with Adam. Her eyes were full of unshed tears. "Thank you, Doctor," she said, shaking his hand.

Adam was watching her as she sat back down on the stool by his head. "Do you want anything?" He just shook his head and reached for her hand.

A few moments passed and the only noise was the child's harsh breathing and the beeps and pings of the machines hooked up to Adam.

"Kacy?"

"Yes, Adam?" Kacy put her intense eyes on him. She loved this child so much it hurt.

"I'm glad you are my friend."

"Me, too, little man. Me too." She ran a loving hand down his face. "So glad."

His body tensed and Kacy knew he was trying not to cough. "I wish...I wish you could have been my mother."

"So do I." A fresh wave of tears filled her eyes. This time, they flowed down her smooth cheeks. She knew he only talked about a mother when he was in lots of pain.

The lifelessness in his eyes gave way to a spark of emotion. "Ernst," Adam said as another bout of coughing attacked him.

Kacy jerked her eyes to the door. There he stood. Larger than life. Black shirt, green pants, and black shiny boots on his feet. Six feet, two inches of Germany's finest—Ernst Zimmermann.

His ghostlike eyes filled with tenderness as he ran them over her body. Stepping fully into the room he said, "Sister," nodding at the nun. Then he approached the bed. "Hey, Sport," Ernst addressed Adam as his hand caressed the back of Kacy's neck. Looking into Kacy's copper eyes, he put his index finger under her chin and brushed their lips together.

Adam reached for one of Ernst's hands and the Navy SEAL walked around to the other side of the bed so the boy didn't have to strain himself. "Thanks for coming to see me Ernst," Adam forced out between coughs.

"I just got back and wanted to see my favorite kid. Hey, we still have some camping to do. I brought you something." Ernst dug into a pocket on his leg and pulled out a wrapped gift. "Here you go."

Adam smiled his adorable smile and took it. Tired hands tore away the black paper. His large eyes grew wide as he stared upon his gift. It was a small astrology book, Adam loved the stars. "Wow," he breathed. "Will you take me out to see the stars, Ernst?" His eyes were big and full of hope.

"Absolutely, Sport." Ernst met Kacy's eyes. She knew he knew Adam didn't look good.

"Did you see, Kacy?" Adam coughed. "Did you see what he gave me?"

She wiped away her tears. "I sure did, Adam."

His coughing became horrific for a few moments. Kacy sat him up and rubbed his back while he endured it.

"I'm tired, Kacy," the small voice said as he sipped on some water she held for him.

Kacy gathered his hand in one of hers and kissed the back of it. "I know, baby. I know."

"Kacy?" he whispered as one hand held his gift and the other held her hand.

"What, Adam?" The tears falling were ignored.

"Promise," his voice was growing weaker. "Promise me."

"Anything you want," Kacy said.

"I want my picture," he said.

Before Kacy could ask what picture, Sister Angela handed her the one of Adam, herself, and Ernst that was taken the day they'd gone riding together. "He has kept it with him since that day," the nun whispered before leaving them alone.

"That was one of the best days ever," he coughed out. His eyes were full of exhaustion as they moved from Kacy to Ernst.

"Mine too," Kacy and Ernst responded at the same time.

"I felt like I had a family. A mom and a dad." Letting go of the gift, he took a hold of Ernst's hand and placed it on top of Kacy's. Then he held his gift again. "Promise me, Kacy," he begged as his small fingers tightened on hers.

"Anything," she pledged.

"Don't forget me. I'm scared you will forget me."

"I will *never* forget you. You are a part of me forever, Adam. Forever," Kacy swore.

"I wanted to be an electric like you. But I'm so tired," he forced out.

"Then rest, sweetheart. Rest." Kacy bit her lower lip as she watched his eyes land on her face.

"I love you, Kacy. Don't leave me. I'm scared."

"I'm right here, Adam. I'm not going anywhere. I promise."

"Don't let them put me in the dark." His voice was barely over a whisper.

"Never baby, never." Her hand trembled beneath Ernst's.

"Take care of her, Ernst," Adam mumbled, his eyes drifting over to the handsome man standing on the other side of his bed.

"I will, Sport." Ernst had to choke back his own tears. Kacy knew Adam had captured Ernst's heart with his winning smile from the moment he met him.

Those brown eyes landed back on Kacy. "Thank you for loving me. I love you. Love…" His eyes drifted closed as his monitor indicated he had flat-lined.

Kacy sat there holding his hand as the tears streamed down her face. She didn't even notice when the nurse came in and turned off the monitor. It wasn't until Ernst moved around the bed and wrapped her in his embrace that she came to. "I couldn't save him, Ernst. I couldn't!" she sobbed into his chest.

"Oh, *liebling,* I'm so sorry." He kissed the top of her head and held her. He too had tears falling from his eyes.

She remained holding the frail hand of the orphan boy she loved until the nurse came in and said they had to go. It was with great reluctance that Kacy left Adam's side. She leaned down and brushed a kiss over his sallow cheek. "Goodbye, Adam." Her words were whispered as she allowed Ernst to lead her out of the room.

Two days later at the orphanage there was a funeral. The day was bright and sunny, but the mood was extremely somber as they laid Adam to rest in the cemetery. Ernst stood beside Kacy in a black suit. She wore a black dress and stood ramrod straight as the Father gave the eulogy, her hand entwined with Ernst's strong one.

She was stoic until they lowered his small body into the ground. Then her tears came. Unchecked they rolled down her face. As Adam was being set in his final resting place, the loud cry of a hawk filled the air.

Ernst looked down at the woman beside him. He knew he was in love with her; seeing her in pain like this killed him. Unsure of what to do, he had called Scott for some advice; support her and be there for her was what he had been told. So here he stood next to her dressed in a black suit and watching a small boy he had come to love in a short amount of time being lowered into the ground.

Afterwards, he waited beside Kacy's car as she kissed and hugged each of the nuns and children there. When she looked up at him, his eyes were gentle as he watched her. Ernst held out one hand and inside he smiled as she moved easily to him and took it.

He drove her home and walked her into the house. Kacy still hadn't said a single word. In fact for the past two days, she hadn't said much of anything.

"I'll make some coffee," her quiet voice said.

"I'll make it. You sit down."

"I need to stay busy," she protested.

"Okay, you make coffee. I'll get us something to eat." He understood her need. He was experienced it as well.

Soon, they were sitting at the small kitchen table. Kacy's eyes were empty as she stirred sugar and cream into her mug of coffee. Ernst had found a cake and cut them each piece.

"What was wrong with him?" Ernst asked.

CHAPTER EIGHTEEN

Taking a bite of the marble cake in front of her, Kacy remained silent as she washed it down with a splash of coffee. Turning dull copper eyes to Ernst she whispered, "He had AIDS. Over the past few months, his CD4 count had been dropping rapidly."

"Why didn't you tell me?" he asked, holding his cup closer to his chest.

"It wasn't my place to say. I knew he would never be an electrician. That's why I let him do things with me. Why he got his own belt and I sometimes took him on estimation calls. Nothing dangerous since safety was primary importance." She picked at her cake.

Ernst put his haunting eyes on her face. "Is that why you couldn't adopt him?"

She nodded. "They told me I wasn't a good choice for a boy with his needs." Her voice shook. "So I did what I could with him."

He got out of the chair and gathered her into his arms, pressing her face to his suited chest. "*Liebling*, I'm so sorry."

"I don't know what I will do without him in my life." He felt the dampness of warm tears on his chest. "For seven years he has been a part of it and now he is gone."

As if knowing there were no words that could take away her pain, Ernst held her and allowed her to cry it out. Eventually, he picked her up and carried her back to her bedroom where he laid them both on the bed and continued to hold her.

Exhaustion prevailed and soon they were both sleeping.

The chime of her doorbell woke Kacy. Blinking, she untangled herself from the strong man who held her. Wiping away dried tears, she shuffled up to the door and opened it.

Ilanderae stood at the other side. "Sweetie, I am so sorry I wasn't there for you." she said as she wrapped her arms around Kacy. "I know how much Adam meant to you."

Hugging her friend back, Kacy blinked away more tears. "Thank you, Landi. I know you would have been here if you could've." Stepping back, she pulled her friend into the house. "Come on in."

"Hello again, Ilanderae," a rich voice said.

Both women turned to see Ernst in the kitchen entryway. He had taken off his suit coat, leaving him in the white dress shirt and black slacks. His shirt sleeves had been rolled up to expose muscled forearms.

"Hello, Ernst." Ilanderae responded even as her eyes flashed over to Kacy. "Nice to see you again."

"I was just going to make some dinner. Will you be joining us?"

"I would love to," she answered, grabbing onto Kacy and pulling her back to the bedroom. "Excuse me; I have to talk to Kacy."

Ernst nodded silently and went back into the kitchen.

Alone in the bedroom, Ilanderae crossed her arms over her chest and said, "Explain what Mister Gorgeous is doing here."

Heading to her closet for a change of clothes, Kacy told her. "He came to the funeral." She shrugged out of her dress and slipped on a pair of workout pants and a baggy tee shirt. "That's all."

"Oh, please," Landi scoffed. "That man is here for way more than that. Admit it, Kacy."

A faint blush ran up her dark cheeks. "I admit nothing," she protested.

Her brown eyes sparkled. "You don't have to. I already know."

"Shut up, Landi."

Before she could say anything, Kacy's doorbell rang again. "Do you want me to get that, sweetheart?" Ernst's voice rang throughout the house.

"I got it." Kacy yelled back, brushing away Ilanderae's mouthing of the word "sweetheart."

Her friend right on her heels, Kacy opened the door to come face to face with another member of the Megalodon Team. Behind her she heard Ilanderae's sharp intake of breath. "Hello, Dimitri," Kacy said, stepping back. "Come on in."

Ilanderae Nycks was speechless, clearly approving what she saw. The man in front of her was jaw-droppingly gorgeous. He had thick, black hair trimmed to look disheveled. His tanned skin was stretched tight across his muscular body. He was the same height as Kacy and his eyes were golden like a lion's.

Eyes moving between the two who were staring at each other, Kacy cleared her throat. "Dimitri, meet my friend Ilanderae Nycks. Ilanderae, this is Dimitri..."

"Dimitri Melonakos," the man finished as his eyes scanned the pink-garbed beauty standing beside his Chief's woman.

"Nice to meet you," Ilanderae said.

"And you." Those golden eyes moved back to Kacy and he held out a bouquet of flowers. "This is from the rest of us. We are sorry for your loss, Kacy." Dimitri nodded at the man who had materialized behind Kacy. "Chief," he said respectfully.

"Staying for dinner?" Ernst asked as he took the mixed bouquet from Kacy to put in a vase.

"I wouldn't want to impose," Dimitri began even as his eyes moved back to land on Ilanderae.

"No imposition," Kacy insisted. "Please stay. And thank you for the beautiful flowers."

"You're welcome and thank you for the invitation," Dimitri said coming fully into her house.

Dinner was a lighthearted affair, just what Kacy needed to lift her spirits. The attraction between Dimitri and Ilanderae was unmistakable and it left all of them wondering where it would lead in the future.

Landi kissed Kacy on the cheek and the two women walked out to where Ilanderae had parked her car. "You know I will come if you need me," Ilanderae said as she unlocked and opened her door.

"I know." Kacy nodded. "Love you, Landi. Drive carefully." Gently, she shut the door after her friend had climbed inside.

With a smile, Ilanderae blew Kacy a kiss and started up her car. She backed out of the drive and went down the street. Turning around, Kacy saw Ernst and Dimitri behind her.

"Thanks for dinner, Kacy," Dimitri said as he leaned in to kiss her on the cheek, much to Ernst's dismay.

"Don't thank me; he cooked. But it was nice having you here." She smiled as she squeezed his hands.

"I had a really nice time." Dimitri took in the glare that Ernst had and added quickly, "Unfortunately, I need to go as well. If you change your mind about getting married, let me know." He winked at her, knowing that Ernst couldn't see.

"I'll do that," Kacy replied with a smile. "Thanks." They both knew she was talking about the flowers.

"Goodnight, Dimitri," the masculine voice intruded on their conversation. Ernst stood beside Kacy as he sent a meaningful look to his teammate.

"Night, Chief. Night, Kacy." With one more squeeze of her hands, Dimitri had climbed into his Jeep and driven off, leaving Ernst and Kacy alone in the waning light.

Ernst and Kacy sat in the dark on her porch swing. The chirping crickets provided the only noise aside from normal city sounds. His arm was slung casually over the back of the swing and she was curled up against him.

"Welcome back," Kacy eventually, said breaking the silence.

"Thank you." His hand dropped to caress her shoulder.

"And thank you for being there for me during these past few days."

"I loved him too," Ernst said in a smooth voice.

Unable to form a single word as the tears threatened to overtake her, all Kacy could do was nod. Wiping the first few tears away, she closed her eyes and prayed for strength.

"Cry it out, sweetheart," Ernst told her, pulling her even closer to his strong body.

For what seemed to be the umpteenth time in the past few days, Kacy gave in to the tears. She cried for the next thirty minutes. Ernst said not a single word; he just sat there, offering silent support.

Smearing away the remaining streaks from her face, Kacy sat up. There were no more tears left in her. "Thank you," she sniffed as she stood, needing to distance herself from him for a second.

As if understanding her need to be alone, he remained sitting. "Anytime you need me, I'm here for you, Kacy."

Turning back to him, Kacy touched his shoulder, in awe of the strength she felt in his body, as always. "I know." Her words were whispered but sure. "I am going to go clean up." She disappeared inside her home.

Ernst remained sitting on the swing for a few more moments. The need to possess her totally was so strong. He didn't want to share with anyone.

What the hell is wrong with me? He rubbed his hands over his face. Glancing up at the night sky, he sighed. Seeing her interact so freely with Dimitri had been hard. *It wouldn't have been if I was sure about her feelings for me.*

Their relationship wasn't defined. Standing abruptly, he moved towards the door. That was going to change. Tonight. He needed her like a fish needed water.

"Kacy," he began, sliding open the door.

As she turned her head, the smile that crossed her face banished the sadness that had lingered there. Her brown eyes remained on his face as she waited for him to speak.

But he didn't speak, just stood there watching her with those staggering eyes of his. "What?" Kacy asked, shifting under the intensity of his gaze.

"We need to get something straightened out," his deep voice said as he leaned one hip against the countertop he stood beside.

Kacy shook out the rag in her hand and draped it over the sink, resting her hip beside it. "Okay. What about?"

"About us." Ernst crossed his arms over his chest, bringing her attention to the defined muscles in his arms. Even the material of his shirt seemed to caress him tightly.

"So talk," Kacy stated as she lifted herself up to sit on the now-clean countertop.

With a deep breath he started. "I know I have been gone for the past six weeks, and before that, we were just beginning a relationship. So, I don't know what's happened these past few weeks with you and your love life."

Kacy opened her mouth to say something in return, but Ernst just held up a hand and shook his head. "I don't want to know, Kacy. It would tear me up to think of you with another man. But if you aren't dating anyone, I want to fill that spot."

He watched as she cocked her head and hooked her ankles. A sparkle flickered in the back of her coppery eyes. "I want to date you, Kacy. Exclusively."

Kacy's heart tripled in speed as she sat on the smooth counter. Was she ready to try the dating thing again? With Ernst? A man who left at any time for any place and she couldn't know where or for how long?

Ernst unfurled his body from its position and flowed towards her. From the flaxen hair on his head to the soles of his feet, this being moving toward her was downright, mouth-wateringly sinful with his handsome looks.

"Well?" he murmured as his fit body wedged itself between her legs.

A few blinks later, Kacy was able to pull her gaze from the blue one that held her. "'Well' what?"

A sexy grin flashed across his face as he leaned in closer. "I wanted to know what you though about being exclusive with one another." Ernst trailed a finger through the loose tendrils around her face.

Kacy trembled. "Exclusive?" The word was babbled as his eyes made love to her face.

"That is what I said," he acknowledged, sliding one hand up and down her leg.

"What about when you're gone?" Kacy questioned.

Ernst didn't immediately respond. "Well we'd still be exclusive. Why?"

"I've heard the stories about sailors and a different girl in every port." She reached out to fiddle with his collar, not meeting his gaze any longer.

"Look at me," he implored. When her endless metallic gaze met his, he continued. "I don't want anyone but you. I want to be *your* boyfriend, Kacy." His voice was thick with sincerity as he continued. "My feelings for you have only grown since we met. I know before I said we were boyfriend and girlfriend, but now I am putting it to you."

Kacy shook with untold emotion. This man had come to mean so much to her. Licking her lips she spoke, "Is this your way of asking me to be your girlfriend?"

His wraithlike eyes narrowed as he tried to control the grin threatening to cross his face. "Yes, ma'am, I am. But perhaps I need to be a bit clearer with my question."

Her legs tightened around his waist. "Probably should. You were a bit vague there," her teasing remark came.

This time the smile won. He took one of Kacy's hands and bowed over it. "Will you, Ms. Koali Cynemon Travis, electrician extraordinaire, be my girlfriend?"

Using her free hand, Kacy covered her heart. Those thick lashes of hers batted as she drawled in a syrupy voice, "Why this is such a surprise. What shall I say?"

"Yes would be a great choice," Ernst replied, grinning softly at her.

"I think you're right. Yes, Ernst..." she trailed off, waiting for him to supply his middle name.

"Greeley."

"Yes Ernst Greeley Zimmermann, Navy SEAL phenomenon, I will be your girlfriend."

"That's the best thing I've heard in a long time." Both of his strong hands held her face as he brought their lips together in a gentle kiss.

Moving his hands down to cup her ass, Ernst walked her over to the couch in his arms. With extraordinary gentleness, he set Kacy down before following her to the softness of the couch.

Adjusting them so her head rested upon his chest, Ernst enjoyed just holding her and watching her fish swim around in their tank. A while later he spoke, "So what do you want to do tomorrow night?"

No response.

Tipping his head so he could see her face, Ernst saw she was sound asleep. Sooty lashes rested against her cheeks as she slumbered. He didn't say another word, knowing full well she was exhausted from the past few days.

Brushing a kiss over the top of her head, he carefully moved out from under her. Standing, he immediately bent down to scoop her off the couch and place her in her own bed.

Undressing her, Ernst covered her with the thick duvet and kissed her tenderly. "Sleep well, Kacy." It was so hard for him to leave her there. He wanted nothing more than to slip in beside her and enjoy her body against his, but he didn't.

She deserved to get a good night sleep. Losing Adam had been hard on him, but nothing like it was for her. So with one final kiss, Ernst grabbed his suit coat and left, turning off the lights on his way out.

Walking out onto her porch, he double-checked to make sure her door had locked before walking to his truck. For a moment, he sat there and watched her home before he started the engine and headed back to his apartment.

CHAPTER NINETEEN

Ernst was in Kacy's kitchen chopping vegetables for dinner when the phone rang. He cursed under his breath as Kacy wiped her hands on a towel and picked it up. Since he had left her sleeping alone in her bed after the funeral, four days had gone by and this was the first evening they had managed to spend together. He really didn't want to share her.

He eavesdropped but continued dicing the things in front of him. "Hello," her husky alto came. Ernst saw the grin cross her face in response to the voice at the other end. "Hey, Sherri. How are you doing?"

Setting down his knife, he put the veggies in the pan and began to sauté them. "I miss you too. Good, I'm good. We lost Adam." Her voice caught with that but soon the joy returned.

His gaze followed her easy movements as she listened avidly to the other person. "I am so happy for you! He sounds like a great guy. Really?" Her copper gaze met the pale one of Ernst as she smiled. "No, I can understand it. Hon, I am so happy for you! Keep me posted. Love you, too, bye." With a small shake of her head, Kacy hung up the phone.

"Good news?" Ernst asked, moving towards her and ignoring the items on the stovetop.

"Very," Kacy said, reaching around him for the wooden spoon and stirring the stuff in the skillet. "Don't let it burn."

Capturing her around the waist, he kissed her neck. "Coming from the woman who had to unpack these dishes. The only appliance out was your coffee pot, and you are telling me not to let food burn?"

A delectable flush scurried up her face. "Sorry. But I want to make sure dinner is okay."

"Dinner will be fine. It's on a low simmer. Tell me the good news." Ernst wanted to be included in the happy moments of her life as well.

Kacy just grinned and placed herself in front of the salad makings. "That was a call from Sherri who was letting me know she had met someone and they are getting married. She was one of the first women who joined our battered women's group. She's been gone for about two years, so it was great to hear from her."

Ernst watched her cut tomatoes for the salad. "So, are you going to the wedding?" *Will you let me go as your date?*

"Perhaps." At his confused stare she clarified, "They haven't set a date yet."

He nodded before stirring the vegetables. "I have a wedding coming up. Do you want to come with me?"

"When is it?" Kacy asked without turning to look at him.

"Three weekends from now." Her head was shaking "no" before he had finished speaking. "Why are you shaking your head?"

"That's the three-day bike event to raise money for the orphanage. And if that wasn't it, I have a friend getting married that Saturday as well. If I was free, I would go to her wedding." She turned and sent him an apologetic smile. "Sorry."

Ernst knew about the ride and wouldn't make her feel guilty about picking it over him. "Well," he sighed lightheartedly, "I guess I'll go stag."

Her eyes softened as she watched him. "I am sorry. Truly. I wish I could go with you."

"The ride is very important. Don't worry." With a wink, Ernst took the sautéed shrimp and veggies off the stove. "I expect you to make time for me at our wedding."

Momentarily stunned by his comment, Kacy was silent. "Well, maybe if I get more than three weeks' notice," she sassed back.

With a predatory grin, he warned, "Consider yourself notified."

"Not quite what I meant," she responded, smiling back at him.

Heading back to the stove, he took off the pot of linguine, pouring the contents into a bowl. He put it on the table as well. "What can I say?" Those broad shoulders of his shrugged as that smile remained in place.

"Dinner's ready?" Kacy said as she brought the salad to the table.

Pulling out her chair he held it for her. "Okay, dinner's ready," Ernst quipped as he slid her and her chair up close to the table.

Kacy just shook her head.

After dinner was finished and the kitchen was spotless, Ernst and Kacy took a walk around her neighborhood. The evenings had cooled off a bit, so it was very comfortable as they strolled.

They were hand in hand and moving in a companionable silence. As they rounded the corner and were back on Kacy's street, Ernst broke it.

"What are you doing Saturday?" he wondered as his thumb teased the inside of her wrist.

"Just gonna go over some bids...why?" She began going up her steps. Ernst stopped her and turned her back around to face him. They were eye-level.

"Come to dinner with me," he paused, "at my parents' home."

Meeting the parents…big step, Kacy. Sure you're ready? "You want me to meet your parents," she muttered.

"Yes," Ernst said without blinking. One hand wound into her hair.

Kacy swallowed. "What time is dinner?"

"Late afternoon." He flashed a winning smile. "Does that mean you'll come with me?"

"Only if you help me figure out what to take as a gift."

"You don't need a gift." At the instant purse of her lips Ernst added, "But we will find one anyway that they'll love."

She smiled. "In that case, yes, I will go with you."

"Wonderful."

Copper eyes grew serious. "Did you tell them about me?"

"Tell them what? That I would try to bring you? Yes." He held her gaze in the yellow porch light.

Kacy frowned at him. "You know what I mean."

Ernst lifter her and carried her to the top of the porch where he put her back on her feet. "Don't begin those thoughts, Kacy. Yes, I know what you mean; I was choosing to ignore it. It's not relevant."

In what and whose world? "I don't want it to be an issue. That's why I don't want it to be a surprise to them."

Ernst appeared to think it over. "I'll tell them," he murmured and ran a thumb over her cheek, "if it will make you feel better."

Not really, but it's a start. "It will," Kacy stated, stepping away from him and unlocking her door.

Ernst remained silent as they entered her house. "Ice cream?" he asked as he removed his shoes.

"Always," Kacy returned with a smile before heading directly to the kitchen, Ernst following right on her heels.

Lying with her in his arms, Ernst thought about the woman in his embrace. She had changed after the incident with the phone message and understandably with Adam's death. But still he felt she was holding part of herself back, had a piece of her heart he wasn't able to access.

Idly running his fingers up and down her bare skin, he tried to figure out what it was nagging at him. The sex was amazing…sublime really. They had the passion, the emotional connection, and the intellectual one.

It was her eyes, those gorgeous copper eyes. The times she didn't think he was watching her, they would put her in a far away place that he couldn't reach.

Kacy stirred against him. Her naked, silken curves slid against his body. Groaning, Ernst readjusted their bodies and guided his erection into her heat, swallowing her moan of pleasure as he kissed her.

Later that morning, they sat at the table eating breakfast. The clock said six-ten as Ernst got up for more toast. "Wanna go out to eat tonight?"

She grabbed the jam and put some on her toast. "I'm meeting some friends."

He spread some peanut butter on his toast. "Oh, well, maybe tomorrow, then?"

Copper eyes narrowed. "Do you have something planned?'

Ernst grinned. "No. I just want to spend all the time with you I can. But I don't want you to give up spending time with your friends. So have fun. Just so I get you all day Saturday."

Her eyes darkened and she licked her lips. "I'm all yours."

Something primal flared in his pale gaze as he nodded. "Saturday." The look turned promissory as it traveled over her top half.

"All yours." She winked.

"All mine," he vowed.

Kacy toasted him with her glass of juice. They finished breakfast with discussions about their plans for the day. Together they cleaned up the breakfast dishes and then took a long shower together.

It was seven-thirty when Kacy drove off in her van the opposite direction of Ernst and his truck.

The remainder of the week was extremely busy for KT Electric. Kacy worked long hours, not seeing Ernst. Only short chats on the phone allowed her to hear his voice.

Friday night, she pulled into her drive well after ten. Her eyes hurt; her body was exhausted. The van's headlights swung over an older truck in the drive. It brought a smile to her dog-tired body.

Ernst was here.

She pressed the opener for her garage and the grin grew almost foolish as she saw him illuminated by his vehicle's dome light.

By the time Kacy climbed out of her van, his strong body was there to embrace her. Sliding her arms around his shoulders, she murmured against his lips, "Hey, handsome."

His lips were tender upon hers. "Hey, yourself, beautiful."

Drawing back, she met his ethereal gaze. "I didn't expect to see you until tomorrow. What's up?"

"I wanted to see you. I missed you." He kissed her again. "You're getting home late." The remark was casual.

Kacy groaned. "Tell me about it." She moved towards her van and shut the garage door before opening the side and back doors of the vehicle to restock items. "I have a new client, but he lives two hours away."

Into the van went different types of switches until she had about thirty-five boxes of each type. More rolls of wire went in as she made sure everything was accessible and set so it wouldn't move during drive time.

"How'd it go?"

"Not bad." Kacy kept stocking her vehicle. Breakers. Clamps. Screws. "It's a big job so it is going to help immensely with bills."

"How long will it take to finish?"

"Don't know. Hopefully not to long." She closed the doors and smiled tiredly at Ernst. "I would like to be done by the time of the bike ride. Part of it depends on if all his stuff comes in on time." Tilting her head to the side, she asked, "Ice cream?"

Soon they were eating big bowls of ice cream and toppings. Ernst gestured to the potted plant on her counter. "Who's that from?"

Kacy looked between him and the vibrant purple orchid. "From? No one. That is a gift for your mother. You said she liked plants and flowers. A box of cigars is over there for your father." A flicker of panic crossed her eyes. "Do you not think they'll like it?"

Talking quickly to reassure her, Ernst said, "It's more than enough. My dad loves cigars and my mother will love the flower."

Her relief was palpable. "Good. I took a guess since I hadn't seen you all week. I didn't want to not have anything."

"You are amazing." Ernst scraped the last bit of ice cream from his dish.

"Just paranoid," she responded. Her head dropped to the table as she released a lament. "I'm so tired."

"You work too hard," he said.

Rotating her head on the tabletop so she could meet his gaze, Kacy rolled her eyes. "I'm a workaholic, but this week has kicked my ass. I'm not usually this tired."

"Maybe you should go to the doctor," Ernst suggested.

Kacy shrugged. "I'm fine." She yawned and added sheepishly, "Just tired."

"Well, we can sleep in tomorrow. We don't have to be at my parents' until sixteen hundred."

Her eyebrows rose and she sat back up. "Sixteen hundred?"

Ernst smiled. "Sorry. Habit. Four o'clock."

"Gotcha." Kacy removed her dish from the table and put it in the sink. Moments later, Ernst was reaching around her to place his in there as well.

"Let's go to bed." His whispered words sent amperes of electricity through her.

The next morning, Kacy awoke feeling so content, protected, and comfortable that she almost thought she was dreaming. Eyes opened slowly to absorb the bare, pale chest of the man in her bed. Steady even breaths moved the chiseled art work rhythmically up and down.

With a sigh, she closed her eyes again and snuggled closer to the man who had made his way into her heart.

As her lush body burrowed closer, a ghostly pair of eyes opened to gaze down upon Kacy's rich beauty.

Hair tousled, she had one bared leg draped over him. The oversized shirt she wore only tantalizing him more. But, he too shut his eyes, tightened his hold on her, and went back to sleep, also perfectly content.

Later, they awoke again, this time electing to stay that way. They ate a leisurely breakfast before going for a bike ride.

Ernst found himself continually distracted by the smooth brown skin of her legs as it flashed with every pedal she turned. The ride was silent as they worked on building up heart rates.

"How ya doing?" she asked as they crested another hill.

"Good," he responded. "You?"

"Not bad." She down shifted to a lower gear. "I'm gonna hurt after the charity ride, though. I definitely haven't been riding enough."

"Why don't you cut back on the amount you work?" Ernst wondered, keeping pace with her on the paved trail.

"My goal is to pay off some big bills as well a putting some into retirement. I figure—work hard now and save, play later when I retire."

As much as I hate to admit it, she makes sense. Ernst nodded. "Okay, but you're running yourself ragged."

"Naw," she protested. "I'm just not used to having someone around who wants to do things with me. That's why I'm tried. My body'll adjust."

Her response, so matter-of-fact, was such that Ernst couldn't feel bad. "I don't want you to get hurt on the job because you're exhausted."

Kacy laughed and glanced at him. "Coming from a Navy SEAL?" At his silent message she finished with, "I know how dangerous electricity is. Don't worry. I don't take chances. Safety first."

He sent her a "good answer" smile and changed the subject. "How far are we riding?"

"Not far. It's only about thirty miles total."

"Oh." Ernst wiped some sweat off his brow and kept on. "How far is your charity ride?"

"We do almost four hundred miles—Washington D.C. and back."

Wow! That's impressive! "Damn. Where do you stay?"

"In tents. There're vans that come along to keep an eye on us. They carry the food, lodging, spare parts, medical. You know, a bit of everything."

"Sounds well organized." *You're sleeping in a tent?!*

"Oh, very. Riders ride for their orphanage of choice. The group I'm going with rides for St. Lucia's."

"So you get sponsors," Ernst observed.

"Right. Some pledge per mile, some a flat rate. Each one is important." Kacy checked the mileage on her trip odometer. "We will turn around at that circle and head back."

I'm gonna get you some more pledges. "Okay. Tell me more."

She told him all she could as they biked back to her house. Ernst was continually impressed with the woman he had run into in Hawaii outside a bar.

CHAPTER TWENTY

After they got cleaned up, Ernst read quietly on her porch swing as Kacy did some bid reviews. When he was tired of being out there, he went into the house.

Looking around, he noticed the differences between their two places. Hers was clean and homey; his screamed bachelor pad. Well, he didn't have magazines lying around with naked women in them, but there weren't any feminine touches in it.

He moved to stand in front of her fish tank. Slowly the fish swam back and forth, not a care in the world. And why would they? There were no predators to threaten them; no reason food wouldn't be available. They were safe and protected in there.

Protection.

What he wanted to offer Kacy. Marriage was a very prevalent thought to him now. The other day he found himself standing in a jewelry store looking at engagement rings. He didn't purchase one, however. He knew Kacy wasn't ready for that yet.

"What'cha thinking about?" the feminine voice broke into his musings.

Marrying you. "Just watching your fish. They are beautiful." Ernst turned towards her.

"I like my fish. They are calming to me. I think it's time to change the background, though. I want something else."

Moving behind her, he wrapped his arms around her waist. "Want to go today?" *I would love to go shopping with you.*

"You want to go to a pet store with me?" Kacy asked, leaning against him.

"Why not?"

"Well, okay. We could go before dinner."

His lips teased her ear. "It's one now; we should get going soon."

"Just let me change." Kacy unhooked his arms and went to her bedroom. Ernst went to his truck and got his clothes before going to her room as well.

Kacy stood in front of her open closet. "Is dinner with your family formal?"

He almost said yes just to see her in a formal gown. "I'm wearing slacks and a turtleneck," Ernst responded as he opened his garment bag.

"What color?" Her question came as she still stared at her options.

"Midnight blue shirt and khakis."

"Okay." Making up her mind. Kacy pulled two items from the interior of her closet, then went to her bathroom.

Ernst whipped his shirt off his torso. It didn't take him long until he was zipping up his slacks.

Going to the bathroom door, Ernst stopped to take in the vision she presented. She wore a pair of black dress slacks and a pale blue silk shirt. The color was almost identical to the shade of his eyes.

She was gathering her thick hair away from her face, allowing two tendrils to hang down and frame it. She had a clip that was the same hue as her shirt. Standing upright, she ran her hands down her shirt. "Look okay?" Kacy asked as she shrugged away from her reflection.

Ernst lost his words. Her copper eyes shone from behind her sooty lashes that were even more pronounced by the blue of her shirt.

"What?" Kacy wondered. "Not good?"

Swallowing to get moisture back in his mouth, Ernst held up a hand. "No. You look great."

"Then don't look at me like that. Gonna give me a complex."

"You have no idea how beautiful you really are, do you?" His eyes roamed over her natural, makeup-free beauty.

She scoffed, rolling her eyes. "Whatever. Let's get going." Kacy brushed past him trying to ignore how good he looked. It was similar to what he wore on their first date.

"Okay, let's go. However, I meant it. You are beautiful."

"Thank you." She kept walking. Falling into step behind her, he followed her into her bedroom. Kacy grabbed a pair of low-heeled shoes.

Ernst wouldn't let it go. "Why are you so down on yourself?"

That stopped her. Kacy looked at him with genuine surprise on her face. "What are you talking about?"

"The way you blow off my compliments, like I'm making a joke." His gaze was straight forward and held hers.

"I'm sorry. I don't handle compliments well. I wasn't fishing for more. Just that talking about my looks makes me nervous and kinda uncomfortable. I know I'm not ugly, but I'm also no Halle Berry or Angelina Jolie. I'm nothing special." She spoke so emotionlessly Ernst knew it was truly how she felt.

Ernst shook his head. *I can't believe she doesn't see what others see.* "I'll let it go for now, but we need to talk about this."

Arching a brow, Kacy slid on her shoes. "Turning into a psychologist on me, Doc?"

Those blue peepers burned hot. "I'm far from a psychologist, but I'd be more than happy to play doctor with you."

That brought a smile to her face. "Perhaps later. Right now, I thought we were supposed to be leaving."

"I can call and reschedule with my parents." His hands reached for the bottom of her shirt.

Kacy smacked his hands away. "Stop it. Just grab the gifts and let's get going."

Muttering under his breath, "I was grabbing the gift I wanted," Ernst did as he was told. He took the keys she handed him without question.

Kacy parked his old truck in her garage and joined him in her car. "Do you know *Mike's Pets & Supplies* on Virginia Beach Boulevard?"

Putting her car in reverse after the garage door had shut, he shook his head. "No, but I know Virginia Beach Boulevard. Which end?"

Pulling into the lot, Ernst parked and turned off the Camaro. They had passed two pet supply superstores to get here. He kept his mouth shut and followed her in after locking her car.

Kacy stood by the counter talking happily with a woman there. Ernst moved beside her and waited to be introduced.

"Gretchen," Kacy said, "this is Ernst Zimmermann. Ernst, my good friend Gretchen Swann."

"Nice to meet you," he told the blonde woman as they shook hands.

"And you," Gretchen responded.

"Well," Kacy started talking again, "I'm going to look at backdrops." She sent Gretchen another grin and headed off.

Gretchen yelled after her, "Mike wants to talk with you before you go."

"Got it," Kacy said without turning around.

Ernst nodded to Gretchen and followed his woman. *Who the hell is Mike?* "Who's Mike?" he asked, stopping next to her in front of the different background rolls.

"The owner." Kacy pulled out one sheet that was a beautiful Caribbean blue. "This is nice."

Ernst bit his bottom lip. "You don't want one with plants on it or some other design?"

With a slight shake of her head she explained, "I want something that won't be busy. I figured plain background, and I would put in a few of their castles, treasure chests, and things like that."

"Okay, that sounds good." Still, his eyes wandered to ones with more designs on them.

Kacy laughed. "Why don't you pick out one you like as well?"

"'Kay." He turned towards her and said, "You going to see Mike? We need to go soon."

"Going right now. Be back in a few."

I will not be jealous. Ernst focused on picking a backdrop and tried not to imagine her and Mike together. *Jesus, calm down, Ghost! Trust her.*

A short time later, his body told him Kacy was near. Ernst turned and saw her walking with an older woman. Stopping before him Kacy spoke, "This is Ernst. Ernst, meet Mike."

Ernst shook her hand. "Nice to meet you."

"He's good lookin', Kacy. Have babies with him."

Covering her face, Kacy groaned in embarrassment.

"Sounds like a good idea to me." Ernst agreed, waiting with a wink for her eyes to meet his.

Kacy changed the subject. "We need to go."

Gretchen came over and cut the two choices they made and put them in a bag.

Kacy took Ernst by the arm and walked to the door. "Bye, ladies. And thanks."

"Bye, y'all." Gretchen called out.

"My pleasure, girl," the smoker's rasp of Mike's voice came. "Jus' hurry up n' give me my grandbabies!" Her chortle followed them out the door.

Kacy was still blushing as she put her purchase in the trunk. "Sorry about that. Mike is very…"

Ernst slid behind the driver's seat. "Brash?"

Kacy nodded as she climbed inside. "That's one way of putting it. But she is still a great person."

Soon, they were on the interstate heading towards his parents' house. Glancing at the woman beside him, Ernst picked up on her nervousness. With his right hand, he lifted her left one and brought it to his mouth for a kiss. A gentle smile was on his lips as he laced their fingers and rested them on her leg.

"Relax, Kacy. It'll be fine." He hoped he was calming her frayed nerves.

"I am," she protested even as she shifted yet again in her seat.

"Uh, huh." He chuckled. "Trained to interpret reactions, remember?"

"Great. I end up with frickin' James Bond," Kacy muttered.

His hand tightened around hers. "I don't like martinis and I definitely don't want his women." Briefly taking his eyes off the road, he arched a blond brow while looking at her. "My hands are full with the one I have."

Two and a half hours later, Ernst drove up a dirt driveway to stop in front of a German colonial home. As he shut off the engine, the porch's screen door opened.

Slanting a glance at Kacy, he smiled and reassured her. "Breathe and relax. Everything will be fine." He squeezed her hand before getting out and opening the door for her. After she was out of the car, he reached behind the seat and grabbed the gifts to give them to her.

Kacy took Ernst's strong hand and let him help her out. Side by side, they went to the steps to meet his family. Her eyes took in the three figures she recognized from his portrait. *It will be okay, Kacy,* she repeated in her mind.

The woman who was robust and shorter than Kacy herself came down the steps. "Ernst," she cooed as her arms opened to embrace her son.

"Hello, Mother," Ernst returned with affection along with the hug.

Patiently, Kacy stood by and waited for the reunion to be over. Finally, Ernst pulled back and said, "Mother, I'd like you to meet Ms. Koali Travis, better known as Kacy. Kacy, my mother, Nonnie Zimmermann."

With a smile that hid her nervousness Kacy said, "It is wonderful to meet you. You have a lovely home." Extending the orchid, she continued, "This is for you."

Nonnie Zimmermann took the stunning orchid and smiled at the woman beside her son. When Ernst had told them Kacy was black, Nonnie had been upset and extremely unsure of what she would be like.

The woman before her had a quiet dignity that Nonnie liked from the moment she saw her being assisted out of the car by her son. Her eyes observed her son's girlfriend handing a box to Otto, Nonnie's husband, as he too joined them on the ground.

"Well," Nonnie ordered as her husband sniffed on of the cigars he'd just received. "Let's go in and chat in the kitchen while we wait for the food." Her sharp eyes watched the protective way Ernst watched over Kacy as she was introduced to Adolf.

Nonnie entered first followed by Otto and Adolf. Kacy and Ernst brought up the rear. She watched as Kacy stopped by the door briefly until Ernst shook his head at her and whispered softly into her ear.

In the kitchen, Adolf began to flirt with her, helping to put her more at ease. "Can I do anything to help?" Kacy offered.

"You two can just sit there." Nonnie stated, pointing to some chairs. "I haven't seen this boy of mine in a long while. Ernst, fill us in," her order came as she filled some drink glasses.

With an eye roll to Kacy, Ernst leaned back in his chair, draping one arm around the back of her chair and idly running his hand along her shoulder. "Let's see…" he began.

"So, that's where the two of you met?" Otto asked as they sat around the table eating dessert. "In Hawaii?"

"Yes, sir," Kacy said as she took a bite of the cake before her. Ernst had updated them on what he'd been doing until he'd gone to Hawaii.

Eyes that were like his son's watched her. "And why were you there?"

"I was attending a conference," Kacy shifted in her seat, only to calm at the gentle touch of Ernst's hand on her leg.

"What do you do?" Adolf asked leaning back and watching her.

"I own my own business. I'm an electrician." Her body remained relaxed thanks to the soothing caresses Ernst put on her leg and ultimately her soul.

Adolf sucked his lower lip in his mouth. "I see." He shifted on his seat. "And how long have you been doing that?"

"Adolf," Ernst warned in a low growl, only to fall silent at the light touch of Kacy's fingertips.

"It's okay, Ernst." Her burnished eyes held the blue ones of the man who sat across from her. "I've been an electrician for eight years now."

Ernst's father broke in. "Impressive. I bet you stay pretty busy." He sent a frown to his eldest son.

Kacy nodded. "It keeps me going." Her answer was modest.

Shaking his head Ernst added, "Busy enough I don't see enough of her." He winked at Kacy before resting his arm across the back of her chair.

Otto and Nonnie shared a glance. It was obvious their son was smitten with the woman beside him. And for once, Nonnie was okay with it. Normally, there was no woman good enough for her son, but she genuinely liked this Kacy Travis.

CHAPTER TWENTY-ONE

Relaxing in the passenger seat as Ernst drove, Kacy had a content smile on her face. There were containers of leftover food in the trunk Nonnie had insisted they take.

It was dark as Ernst drove them to her house. He kept his attention on the road, not willing to risk the precious cargo he transported.

Sensual jazz played throughout the vehicle. "Thank you for inviting me today," Kacy said.

"I loved having you with me." One hand drifted over to rest on her thigh. "Thank *you* for coming with."

Turning in the seat so her eyes could take in his profile illuminated by the faint lights from the dash, she claimed, "I must admit it wasn't as bad as I allowed myself to believe it was going to be."

"I told you my family would love you, especially when you were willing to play cards with them." His hand tightened on her thigh. Ernst thought about the game. They'd played with both two and four people. The object was to move your peg around the cribbage board to the end first. Depending on the number of people playing, a player was dealt a different number of cards; but when the hand started, the player had four. He knew that if all five had played, it would have been different, but the men had switched out. Points were acquired for card combinations totaling fifteen, flushes, runs, or if a player had a Jack of the same suit as the card flipped over on the pile. Though there were lots of rules, the game was tons of fun.

She grinned in the dark. "I like learning new things. Who knew a game called cribbage could be so fun?"

"Wait 'til we get home. I have something to teach you," he said seductively.

Kacy sighed deeply. "Not sure I want to learn from you," her teasing remark came.

"I promise you'll like this one."

Not electing to dignify that with an answer, Kacy silently shook her head and closed her eyes. At least tomorrow was Sunday and she could relax.

"What do you want to do tomorrow?" His question brought her copper eyes back over to his profile.

"I am going to visit Adam's grave. Other than that, I only planned on doing some riding, assuming the weather cooperates. Why?" She placed her hand on top of his as it stayed on her leg.

"I wanted to spend the day with you. If you didn't mind, that is." Spreading his fingers, he waited until her fingers slid in-between his and then he squeezed them gently. "But if you don't want company when you go visit Adam..."

"Having you with me would be wonderful. Does this mean you are staying the night?"

Letting go over her hand, Ernst shifted gears as he slowed down for the stoplight. "Is that an offer?" His pale gaze turned to look at her face.

Kacy smiled. "Sure, I have a guest room."

"So you do." Putting his eyes back on the road, he drove as the light turned green. "However, I would rather stay with you in the same bed."

"Oh. I get it."

"You will." He promised.

Trembling with the prospect of making love to the man beside her, Kacy looked out the window as they drove through her neighborhood.

❀ ❀ ❀

"I miss you, Adam." Her voice was full of memories of the little boy as she laid the bouquet of flowers down beside his headstone. Kacy's fingers gently traced his name that was carved into the marble as she blinked back tears.

When she began to stand, strong hands were there to help and support her. Ernst had been at her side the whole time. He silently allowed her to do what she needed to do, but gave her some of his strength at the same time.

Slipping her arms around his waist, Kacy rested her head against his shoulder and whispered, "Thank you for coming with me."

"You don't need to thank me for doing this, Kacy. I miss him too," Ernst said as he turned them towards her car.

Kacy waved goodbye to the nuns and orphans who were out as she slid into the driver's seat and started up her gray car. "I have to go grocery shopping. Do you want me to drop you off at your truck first?"

"Do you want me to leave you alone for the rest of the day, Kacy?" His words were somber as he looked at her.

Sitting at the end of the road at the orphanage, Kacy faced the man in her car. "No. I just didn't know if you had things to do yourself."

"I'm doing it." He trailed two fingers down the side of her face.

Shivering at the gentle touch she nodded. "Okay, then." Turning back to the road, Kacy drove to the store.

Walking through the aisles at the grocery story together, Kacy put a few items in her cart. Ernst had stopped in front of the cereals and answered his cell phone that had begun to ring. Kacy kept moving. *What am I doing?* Kacy asked herself as she headed down another aisle, leaving Ernst behind to finish his conversation in private.

Am I setting myself up to get hurt? Standing in front of the soups, Kacy became conflicted. Shaking her head, she admonished herself for trying to sabotage her relationship with Ernst.

"What's the matter, sweets?" a voice asked from nearby.

A bolt of fear coursed through her body. Bile rose in her throat and her knees trembled with trepidation. Kirby.

He chuckled menacingly as he witnessed her reaction. It only increased her dread. "Now I warned you about seeing someone else. You should know better than to test me. And a white guy at that?" His scorn was blatant.

Eyes wide, she looked at the man who had beaten her and enjoyed it. He stood too close for her comfort, but not crowding her. To the people who walked by, their interaction seemed innocent. Unthreatening.

Kacy couldn't say a single word. She was having a hard time breathing. This was the closest she had been to him since they'd split. Never before had he been so forward with approaching her. Her jaw was clenched as she tried valiantly to keep her teeth from chattering. All she could do was stare into his dark-brown eyes and try not to cry.

"Get rid of him, Kacy." The warning came. "Or you will pay." The odious man grabbed some soup and disappeared around the corner of the aisle.

Kacy couldn't move. His threat played over and over in her head as her whole body shook. She wanted nothing more than to vomit right then and there.

"Kacy?" The question made her jump and almost scream. Spinning towards the man who had spoken to her, she gave into the tremors that engulfed her body as she looked at the one with whom she'd felt safe. Until now.

Ernst felt immediately sick at the amount of devastation and fear he saw in her eyes. It was similar to the look her beautiful copper eyes had when she'd showed up at his door the night she had gotten that message.

Reaching for her, his heart shattered as she pulled back from him. Dropping his hand, Ernst tried staunchly to control his emotions her rejection caused. "Let's go," he said softly. Unable to not hold her a second more when he saw her chin quivering as she tried not to cry, he ignored her rebuff and gathered her close to his chest. "You're safe, Kacy. You're safe."

"No," she blurted out even as she tried to get away from his touch.

"Yes. You are." Ernst held her closer, refusing to let her back away.

"No. You don't understand. He told me to get rid of you!" The tears came, soaking the front of his black shirt.

I am going to kill *that man!* Ernst blinked a few times to gather his uncontrolled emotions back in line. He saw a few people back away from the hardness of his gaze and didn't even care. "Let's go home."

"Yes," her muffled answer reached him. "You need to go home."

I don't think so, liebling. I don't think so. "Come on." His voice was gentle despite the rage flowing through his veins.

Ernst kept his arm around her as they went through the checkout line and even out to her car where he sat her in the passenger seat before driving them back to her place. His eyes were alert to anyone following them, watching them, but he didn't see anything.

Pulling into her garage, he closed the door after the car was securely inside the enclosure. He got out and went to the trunk to grab the bags. Letting her follow at her own pace, he went inside the house and began to put things away.

"You have to leave." Her voice was tortured as she spoke from behind him.

With a deep breath, he shut the fridge and turned to face her. "Why?" His gaze took in the stress lines around her face. She still looked terrified.

Her eyes looked everywhere but at him. "I don't want you to get hurt."

Glancing at the ceiling before moving across her open kitchen to stand before her, Ernst reached out one hand and captured her chin, bringing her eyes up to his. "That man can only hurt me by forcing you to push me away. I'm not scared of him. Trust in me, Kacy. I won't let him hurt you."

She stared into his hauntingly pale eyes. "You don't understand; he's evil!" she protested as she closed her eyes against his handsome face.

"I would fight the devil himself to stay with you, Koali Travis. Haven't you figured that out yet? I love you."

Her eyes sprung back open. "What did you say?"

Ernst stepped even closer to her. Both of his hands cupped her face as he held her gaze. "*Ich liebe dich.* I love you."

It was the first time he had ever said that to her. Kacy began to shiver again. "Don't let him win by making you push me away." Ernst's sure voice continued.

"You don't know what he is capable of."

"And he has no idea what I am capable of," The words were lined with steel even though his eyes were still gentle.

"I don't want you to get hurt," Kacy admitted as she took his hands off her face.

"What do you think is happening right now?" his voice cracked. "I am getting hurt, but by you because you are pushing me away." Ernst grabbed her shoulders and shook her gently. "I just told you I loved you. I have never said that to a woman before, and all you are doing is pushing me farther away."

Tears welled up in her big eyes and flowed over to run down her smooth cheeks. Shaking her head, Kacy bit her lower lip. "No. It's the only way I can protect you. You have to go. I can't see you anymore."

It was as if someone pushed him into a dark pit. The sun was suddenly blotted out and darkness had consumed him. "We can get through this, Kacy," he tried again.

"No. Goodbye, Ernst." She wiped her nose with the back of her hand and moved away from his stimulating touch.

"I love you, Kacy. If you ever need me, I'm just a phone call away." Ernst reached for her only to stop as she shrank back. With a small shake of his head he pulled her to him and kissed her one last time.

He tasted her sweetness and the saltiness of her tears as he kissed her. Devoured her. Loved her. "Goodbye, Kacy." Picking up his truck keys, Ernst walked away from her without a backwards glance, shutting the front door quietly behind him. He had every intention of turning around to go back inside, not leaving until she understood he wasn't giving up on them; but as he turned around, it happened. His beeper went off. He had to go to work, so he left.

Kacy crumpled to the linoleum floor of her kitchen the moment she was alone and gave into the hysterical sobs that overtook her body. Deep within her soul, she'd been expecting him to walk right back in the door and tell her all was going to be right with the world. But, it never happened. Three hours later, she was still curled on her kitchen floor in a little ball.

Not having much of an appetite, Kacy didn't eat dinner. She just focused on her workload for tomorrow as she sat at her desk. Every time she closed her eyes, she was staring into Ernst's ethereal gaze.

"I love you, too, Ernst," she told her office. "But I am not going to have your death on my conscience."

Kirby was very unstable; and although it broke her heart to push Ernst away, it was the only way to keep him safe. That was what one did when in love with someone. Protect that person.

"Keep telling yourself that, Kacy, and maybe we will believe it," she mumbled as she left her office and walked to her bedroom to go to bed where earlier that day Ernst had made love to her.

Draped over the side of the bed he'd been on was an old tee shirt of his. Reaching for it, Kacy brought it up to her face and inhaled Ernst Zimmermann's masculine scent. The aroma made her miss him even more. Undressing, she slid his shirt on and climbed into bed to fall into a restless sleep surrounded by his scent and memories.

It had been three weeks and Kacy had heard nothing from Ernst. Not a single peep. Throwing herself into her work, she tried to pretend it didn't bother her. After all, she was the one who'd told him to leave. But it didn't work. She missed him horribly.

Wanting to call him, she refrained since he had said he was going to a wedding this weekend and she was already running late to get to the start of the charity bike ride. A horn's honking shook her out of her mental wanderings and she went outside to see Paul waiting in her driveway with his truck.

She waved with a forced smile on her face. "Hey, Paul."

"Let's get going hon; we don't want to be late," he said as he put her bike in the back.

"I'm ready," Kacy said, locking her house behind her. "Sorry to keep you waiting."

"I was running late myself. Youngest was sick this morning so the wife needed a bit more help."

Smiling, she nodded her understanding even as a sharp pain lanced her heart. A child. She wasn't going to be having one anytime soon, especially without a man in her life. And she knew she wasn't pregnant with Ernst's baby. Easily getting into his truck, the two friends were soon on their way to the start of the ride.

Paul had her in a better mood as they pulled into the crowded parking lot. For once, the ever-present memory of Ernst had been pushed into the back of her mind, allowing her a brief respite.

It didn't take long and soon four hundred people were beginning the ride to Washington D.C. The vans were following behind them with the exception of the lead van that had a sign reading "Charity Bike Ride — Please Yield to Riders" on the top and sides of it.

Kacy settled into the speed her group had set and they were moving along at a very steady pace. The burn from the workout just what she needed. Chewing on her lower lip, she focused on the ride ahead of her, determined not to let Ernst or his memory back into her thoughts.

CHAPTER TWENTY-TWO

Ernst stood in his tuxedo, leaning against the bar and holding a drink in his hand. The wedding had been beautiful. Ross and Dezarae were dancing on the floor. Even as he watched them, his mind kept going back to Kacy.

She would be on her ride right now. He wanted to be with her. The Team had barely made it back in time for the wedding. Ernst was nursing a shoulder wound, but it would be fine. Swirling his drink, he took a sip and kept his eyes on the wedded couple.

"You doing okay, man?" a deep voice asked from beside him.

"No," he admitted honestly as he looked over to see his friend and teammate Maverick standing there in his own tuxedo.

"Have you called her since we got back?"

"Nope." His voice turned hard. "I told her I loved her and she told me to leave. I really don't think there is anything else for us to say to one another," Ernst snapped.

"You were the one who said if we hadn't been called away, you would have gone right back in her house and not given up." Maverick took the drink away from Ernst and set it on the bar. "Why are you giving up now?"

"Maybe I like the single life like you do." Ernst grumbled, reaching for his drink again.

"Not buying it." Moving the drink away again, he added, "I think you've had enough."

Ernst glared at his friend. "Since when did you become my father?"

"I'm not. But I am your friend. You haven't been the same since we left. You need to work this out, with or without her, but it needs to be worked out inside you." Maverick looked at him with jet black eyes. "You are losing control."

Not wanting to hear that, Ernst looked away. "I'm not," he denied.

"Yes, you are." Maverick insisted. "How many have you had tonight?"

He had no idea. "I don't know." Grabbing the shot, he downed it quickly. "But add one more to it."

Maverick latched onto his arm and said, "Say your goodbyes to the bride and groom...and Ghost, don't embarrass Jeb or Dez." There was a not-so-subtle warning in his tone.

Ernst swallowed and did as he had been told only to find Maverick and Dimitri waiting for him at the door. Going out into the night, the men walked in silence down the street.

They continued on until they reached a pier that overlooked the Atlantic Ocean. Three handsome men in tuxedos leaned on the railing in the night air.

Ernst heard a voice that shifted his body into instant battle mode. It was the same malicious voice he'd heard on Kacy's machine that day. The men with him noticed him stiffening and looked at him to figure out what was going on.

The blond man had turned around and was focused on a big black man talking to another person. Pushing lithely away from the railing, Ernst flowed over towards him. Maverick and Dimitri followed in complete understanding of their teammate's manner; it was combat ready.

"Soon," that man was saying. "Soon Kacy Travis will be mine again. And I'll be damned if I let her go. I will kill her first."

"What about the restraining order she has against you, Kirby?" the other man asked. He ran his scarred hand over his shaved head.

"She will just go to the cops and get it lifted. She does what I tell her to. Just like she got rid of that white boy 'cause I told her to," the smug man bragged.

Ernst walked in-between the two men and looked at the one he now knew as Kirby. He saw the second he was recognized for the man's face flashed full of fear before it turned arrogant.

"This is him, Dave," Kirby said as he looked over Ernst. "The one who Kacy kicked to the curb."

Ernst punched him in the face and the two men went down on the ground fighting. For a few moments, the other three men just watched as the two went at it. Ernst quickly got the upper hand; and as he held Kirby in a position that could easily turn deadly, the men acted.

"Get off him, man," the friend said as he took a swing at Ernst. Dimitri stopped him while Maverick went to Ernst and touched his shoulder.

"Let him go, Ernst," the deep voice said.

"No," Ernst refused. "This is the bastard who beat Kacy!" Ernst shook his head and tightened his hold on the man beneath him. Kirby tried to mumble something, but stopped when Ernst shoved his face into the dirt more. "Shut up, you asshole!" he hissed.

Maverick grabbed his wrist and said, "Stand down! That's an order!" The eyes that looked at him flared defiantly for a moment before Ernst did as he had been told. Ever so slowly, he got off the man and pulled him, none to gently, up after him.

Once both men were back on their feet, Ernst grabbed him around the throat and squeezed. "You come near Kacy again, call her, or even breathe in her direction, you will be the one who needs the cops. I will find you wherever you go and make you pay." His voice was as warm as the artic color of his eyes. "Trust me when I say there isn't a single place you can hide from me."

Eyes wide from lack of oxygen, Kirby moved his mouth soundlessly; when Ernst let go, he snapped. "I will file a report on you!"

Maverick spoke up. "All I saw was him helping you up from the ground."

"Me too," Dimitri said as he moved in closer.

Grabbing the man by the shoulder, Ernst put a pinch on him that made the feeling on the left side of Kirby's body leave. "Don't make me come after you. You won't like the results. If I even *think* you are bothering her I hunt you down. I love her, and I will be damned if I let you terrorize her. Are we clear?" His fingers tightened, making Kirby stumble.

Eyes that had once been smug as he'd scared and tormented a woman were fearful as Kirby was terrified of a man who was seriously intent on doing him some harm. "Clear," Kirby muttered. "I won't bother her."

"Good. But if you do," the warning came, "there are so many pressure points that I would love to test on you." Applying even more pressure to his hold, Ernst watched the man's eyes fill with pain. "Glad we understand each other." Abruptly, Ernst let go and Kirby dropped to the ground, unable to hold himself up anymore.

Looking at the two men with him, Ernst brushed the dirt off his tuxedo and said, "Let's go back to the party."

Understanding that he was done with Kirby, the men nodded. In the back of his mind, however, Ernst wondered what would've happened had Maverick not pulled rank. Silently, the three men disappeared, leaving Kirby and his friend alone in the darkened area.

Back at the party, Ernst endured stares from the rest of the Team, but none of them said anything to him. He danced with a few of the bridesmaids, but didn't drink anymore alcohol.

He left when Dimitri did. Getting into his truck, Ernst drove himself home to his empty and quiet apartment. Turning on some music, he changed and began to workout until his body was drenched in sweat.

Showered and once again clean, he sat down on his leather couch. It was well after two in the morning, but his head wouldn't give him a moment's rest. Standing abruptly, Ernst walked over to his stereo and turned off the heavy metal, turning on some light jazz instead. It was a CD he had bought so Kacy would have some music to listen to when she was at his place.

Kacy. "What am I going to do about us?" he asked the walls of his domicile. "I know I love you, and I know Kirby was a big reason you didn't want to get involved with me. But how do I convince you he won't bother you anymore and that I would die before I let anyone hurt you again?"

Ernst stretched out on his couch, draping his leg over the back as he tried to find a solution for his dilemma. Kidnapping her wouldn't work, although the idea of taking her far away so it was just the two of them held gigantic appeal to him.

"I'd go to D.C. but I don't know how she'd take that," he muttered as his leg dropped back to the cushion with a thud. "She will be back tomorrow..." he paused and looked at his wrist, "later this morning." It was already early on Monday morning.

So Ernst stayed on his couch for the rest of the night, listening to smooth jazz and imagining him and Kacy making love as the music played around them. Didn't she understand she was the other half to his soul? How could she not know how important she was to him?

The clock read six when his beeper went off again, jarring him awake. Grabbing his gear, Ernst jogged down the steps to his truck and drove to the base. Just when she was coming home, he was leaving.

❀ ❀ ❀

Kacy shut the door to her van. She was back at that creepy house to help Brett finish up the last little bit. At least he had done that small room in the basement so she didn't have to go there again.

As he was settling the bill with the owner, a sleazy-looking man, Kacy remained by her vehicle. She, Brett, and his new wife Lisa were going to go to dinner this Friday night. She was waiting for Brett to tell her where they were going to eat.

He walked towards her. "Thanks so much for the help, Kacy. I am going to write you a check right now for your part." Brett opened his van and took out his checkbook.

"Don't worry. I trust you. Where are we going to eat? I want to get cleaned up first." *Just being in that house makes me feel dirty,* she shivered.

"Lisa hasn't made up her mind. Why don't you go home and I will have her call you when she makes up her mind? I know she thought we would be here longer than this; so knowing her, she is probably still trying to figure it out herself!" He laughed at his wife's inability to make up her mind.

"That sounds like a plan to me." Kacy got into her van. "I will see you in a bit then." Starting her van she waved to Brett and drove away.

Kacy was feeding her fish when her cell phone rang. "KT Electric."

"Kacy, it's Lisa. Brett said for me to call you when I finally decided on a place to eat."

"Hey, Lisa. I'm ready so tell me where to go." Kacy put the fish food away and picked up her car keys.

"Well, since I love teriyaki food I was thinking of that place by *Fountains* that serves it. It is called *Bento Teriyaki*. What do you think?"

"I know that place. Works for me. How long before you want to meet there?" Kacy knelt down to tie her hiking boots.

"We are on our way now. How long before you can be there?" Lisa's friendly voice questioned.

"Not much more than fifteen minutes. I'm on my way out the door now." She walked into her garage and slid behind the wheel of her Camaro. "See you both in a few."

"Great," Lisa said and hung up.

Moments later, Kacy was parking her car at the restaurant. She climbed out and met Brett who was outside waiting for her. "Hey, Kacy," he said with an easy hug.

"Hey, yourself. Where's Lisa?" she asked, brushing her hair back from her face.

"Left something in the car," Brett said, rolling his eyes playfully.

"I see." Kacy turned to face in the same direction as Brett and wait for his wife to reappear. She sat down on the bench and stretched her legs out.

"Oh, here you go." Brett handed her the check.

Kacy took it without looking at the amount, folded it up, and slid it in her pocket. "Thanks." Looking at the man who took a seat beside her made her smile. "You look so much happier now that you have that band around your finger." She nudged him with her shoulder.

"I am." He turned his brown eyes to her copper ones. "Kacy, I never dreamt I would be this happy." His smile flashed bright against his dark skin.

"Well, I can think of no one more deserving. She is great for you." Kacy looked at the approach of his wife Lisa and added, "Even if she is forgetful!"

"Good thing she doesn't want to work with me," he teased as his wife got closer.

"I wouldn't want to see that mix." Kacy said as Lisa tripped over something small in her way. The two friends stood and Kacy hugged Lisa when she finally made it to where they waited. "Good to see you again, Lisa," she whispered into her friend's ear.

"Sorry, but I forgot something in the car. Well, I thought I did, but it was in my pocket the whole time. I swear," Lisa bemoaned as she leaned up to kiss her husband. "I would lose my head if it wasn't attached!" With an easy shrug she added, "Let's eat!"

Brett and Kacy exchanged glances, but neither of them said a word about her losing her head. It was nothing short of the truth, so both of them bit their lips and kept silent as they walked inside the building.

The three friends sat at an outside table drinking coffee and hot chocolate. It was getting cold out, but all of them were outdoorsy people and so were content to sit in the chill of the evening.

They chatted about work, and future plans of Lisa and Brett. When Lisa was talking about starting a family was when Kacy saw him.

Ernst. Chief Ernst Greeley Zimmermann. He was walking down the boardwalk with another man she didn't know. They were accompanied by two women. The one holding onto Ernst tugged his face down for a kiss, an act that put the final nail into the coffin that surrounded Kacy's heart.

Forcing her attention back on Lisa, Kacy stayed focused on her friend's face, determined not to look at Ernst as he passed their table. She even shifted her body so it was facing away from the man who could set her traitorous body on fire.

CHAPTER TWENTY-THREE

Ernst pulled away from the woman on his arm. The only reason he was there was because a fellow Chief had asked him to do this double date. This woman didn't seem to get the hint that this was only a friendly dinner. Ernst wanted nothing remotely sexual to do with her.

"Stop kissing me," he said for the umpteenth time.

"All the women are jealous of me. I have such a handsome man on my arm," the blonde cooed as her long nails curled possessively around his bicep.

Rolling his eyes, he kept walking. A shiver ran through his body, a shiver only Kacy Travis had been able to create in him. Looking around, he saw one of her electrician friends, Brett, who was sitting with a woman, but no Kacy.

"Kacy," he whispered.

"What did you say?" Jamie, his date, asked.

"Nothing. Just thought I saw someone I knew." Disappointment filled him as he didn't see her, but his body told him she was near.

They walked past the table and all Brett did was meet his gaze before looking back at the woman sitting next to him. Not one word crossed his lips.

Ernst and the three people he was with moved further down the boardwalk and eventually disappeared from sight.

"He's gone, Kacy," Brett said.

Moving back to their table from where she had been hiding, Kacy took her seat again. "Thanks, Brett."

"Is that the one, Kacy?" Lisa asked as her hand covered the still-trembling one of her friend.

"That's him." Her voice only shook a little bit. He still looked so handsome. His hair was longer than she remembered, but he still moved with that natural flowing ability she loved about him. It had been four months since he'd walked out of her house, and he still affected her all the way to her core.

"I thought you were dating," Brett said.

"I told him that it wasn't working out." Kacy admitted.

"Then why hide from him?" Lisa wasn't as dumb as people thought her to be.

"Because I am not ready to face him, especially when he has a date on his arm and I am without one." *Because I am ashamed of my stupid behavior.*

"You love him," Lisa observed as she leaned against her husband.

All Kacy could do was shrug her shoulders. "Maybe."

"Have you told him?"

"Lisa, I told him to get out of my life. Why would he want to hear anything that I have to say now?" Kacy drained the rest of her hot chocolate.

"Because I saw the way he kept staring at me as if I was going to acknowledge him in some way," Brett added his perspective.

"Right," Kacy scoffed, needing to find some anger to hold onto or she would find herself calling him. "He was scared you would tell me he had some hoochie on his arm."

"Sounds to me like someone is kinda jealous," Lisa observed, arching her perfect eyebrows.

"Am not," Kacy huffed, crossing her arms defiantly. "I don't give a rat's ass what that man does."

Standing up, Lisa kissed her husband on the cheek and looked at the pouting Kacy. "Come on, Kacy. We are going out. Brett, I will be home later, but I think Kacy needs to just go out and have some fun."

Nodding his understanding, Brett said, "Okay. Stay safe and have a good time." Kissing his wife on the lips, he gathered their trash and walked away, leaving the women alone.

Lisa pulled on her arm. "Let's go, Kacy. We are going out."

"I don't want to go out. I have work to do at home," Kacy protested. Seeing Ernst made her want to curl up in a small ball and cry over her stupid loss. He had confessed his love to her and now he was kissing another woman. *It's your own damn fault, Koali Cynemon Travis,* her mind taunted.

"It'll keep. Let's go. I want to play a game of pool," Lisa said.

Why not? "Okay," Kacy replied as the two women walked to her car. She had to admit she did like to play a game of pool every now and then.

Despite how clumsy Lisa was normally, the woman was a kick-ass pool player. She and Kacy had teamed up against a couple of guys. The place was well-lit and atmosphere was relaxed and friendly.

Leaning on her pool cue and sipping a soda, Kacy watched as Lisa sank another ball, much to the chagrin of the men there. The guy next to her just groaned causing her to look over at him. "Didn't think she was going to be that good, did you?"

He laughed a rich, kind laugh. "Not really, especially when I saw her stumble in through the door." His dark eyes sparkled as he shook his head.

"That makes two of us," Kacy admitted. Her heart felt light and she was glad Lisa hadn't taken no for an answer.

"Makes me glad we are just playing for fun and not money," the man who'd introduced himself as Jake admitted.

"See, now I am feeling just the opposite. I could have made some cash." Kacy's grin was full of teasing mischief. "What do you do, Jake?" she asked as she lifted her hair up off her neck for a moment.

"I'm a cop."

Releasing her hair, Kacy looked back at him with wide eyes. "For real?"

He nodded. "For real."

"Well, then, I guess it's good we *aren't* betting on this game." She pointed to his friend. "And Rick, is he a cop as well?"

"Yes, ma'am. We're partners. Been partners for ten years now." Jake took a swig of his beer, all the while watching the woman beside him.

Kacy turned to face him totally. "Can I ask you something?"

Jake nodded. "Anything."

Before she could speak, a cackling laugh filled the air, grabbing both of their attentions. It was Ernst again with the same people. This time, however, their eyes met across the establishment.

Frozen to the spot, Kacy could only stare as Ernst brushed the blonde woman's hand off his arm and headed towards her. Swallowing hard, Kacy tried to remain calm and collected.

Wanting nothing more than to end the date and get home to plan how he was going to get Kacy back into his life, Ernst had agreed very reluctantly to go to the bar with his group. It was one he didn't know.

The woman on his arm was driving him crazy. Nothing but endless babble came out of her mouth. He would bet she didn't even know what she was rambling about half the time. But he owed the Chief a favor, and so into the place they went.

As one patron inside said something to the woman on his arm, she cackled like a hyena and grated out about how lucky she was that the man on her arm was her date and a military man. Her laugh was like nails on a chalkboard to his ears. It made his skin crawl.

Looking across the room to try and regain control of his rising temper, Ernst felt his knees go weak. Kacy. She was standing next to a tall, good-looking black man by a pool table. They were talking, but her conversation stopped as their eyes met.

Immediately his body responded with surging lust, desire, and jealousy. *She was with a man.* The warrior in Ernst wanted to rip him limb from limb for daring to look at his woman, but the man who loved her witnessed the pain she unsuccessfully tried to conceal at seeing him with another woman.

As if the woman beside him was no more than an annoying insect, he brushed her off his arm and flowed towards the woman he knew was his soul mate. Walking past the pool table she stood behind, Ernst recognized the woman who had been sitting with Brett at the table along the boardwalk.

His spectral gaze didn't relinquish its hold on Kacy, however. He moved right up to her so her head had to tip back to maintain eye contact. The subtle scent of the lotion she wore filled his nose, his senses. Filled his heart. Filled his soul.

"Hello, Kacy," he spoke in his deep timbre.

"Mr. Zimmermann," she responded.

Something foreign flared in his eyes at her greeting. "How are you doing?" He could feel his fists clenching to keep his hands from entwining themselves in her thick locks.

"Never better," she chirped, sounding false to his ears. "You?" It was like no one else existed in the business.

"Better now." His response fell gently. *Kacy, I love you so much.*

"I see you are out on a date so I won't keep you from her." Swallowing hard, Kacy tried bravely to keep from showing how much it hurt her to say that. "It was good seeing you again."

Ernst saw the final brick fall into place around her heart when she stepped closer to the man beside her. Finally focusing on someone other than Kacy, Ernst looked at the man beside *his woman.* "Sorry, nice to meet you. Name's Ernst Zimmermann."

Reaching out one strong hand, he shook the offered one and responded. "Nice to meet you. My name's Jacob Trask."

Staunchly refusing to let them continue their date Ernst asked, "What do you do?" This time there was unconcealed hostility in his words.

"I'm a cop." Ernst didn't bother to hide his possessive stare on Kacy. "And you?"

A cop? Kacy was dating a cop? "I'm Navy." Those unforgettable eyes focused back on Kacy who reluctantly answered the mental call he gave her to look at him. "Well, I should get going. It was *really* good to see you again, *liebling.*" Ernst turned and walked away before he touched her.

Jake looked down at the cute woman beside him. Her hand was pressed to her mouth as if she were trying to keep from calling out that man's name as he walked away from her. Tears swarmed in her vast eyes and he was amazed they weren't running down her face.

"Ex-boyfriend?" he asked as he handed her a napkin to wipe her eyes.

"You could say that," she mumbled as her trembling hand dabbed away the traitorous tears. How could Ernst still call her that?

Lisa stood in front of her. "You okay?"

Taking a deep breath, Kacy nodded. "I will be. Is it my turn now?"

Lisa nodded and soon Kacy was battling it out with Jake at the pool table. One of the hardest things Kacy had ever done was ignoring the tall, blond German who kept watching her the whole time they were in there.

Ernst was still watching them as the four walked outside. He followed under the pretense of getting some air. He saw her friend climb in the car and then watched Kacy stand too close to that cop and his friend while talking.

They chatted for a long time until Kacy reached up and kissed Jake on the cheek before slipping behind the wheel of her gray Camaro. Both men remained until the car had left the lot, and then the two got in their own vehicles and went their own ways.

At least she didn't go home with him. Ernst felt hollow as he walked back inside. Finding the Chief, he made his excuses and left. The blonde date had tried to get him to take her with him, but Ernst refused.

Back at his apartment Ernst climbed the stairs to get to his floor. He didn't want to feel trapped in the elevator. He wanted to go to Kacy's house and make her listen to him, make her understand there was nothing between him and that blonde woman. Make sure she knew they belonged together.

Glancing at the machine, he felt saddened there was no message for him. It was three in the morning. He wanted to call Kacy. Instead, he went to bed after washing off the smell of the blonde woman's perfume from his skin. Ernst fell asleep dreaming of Kacy beside him.

When he woke up the next morning, her image was just as clear as it had been when he'd seen her in the bar: her full and succulent lips, luscious curves, and those eyes that made him want to protect her for the rest of her life.

"I'm not letting you give up on our love, Kacy," he vowed as he stood beneath the pounding water in the shower.

Dried, dressed, and determined Ernst walked to the elevator and headed to his truck. He really should go to the base; but first, there was something more important he had to do.

Chapter Twenty-Four

Pulling along the sidewalk, Ernst looked across the street to Kacy's house. There was an unknown car in the drive — a white Camaro with tinted windows. It was much newer model than Kacy's.

He watched as her front door opened and she walked out followed closely by who'd been with her at the bar. Jacob Trask. A low, lumbering growl rose up from Ernst's throat as he observed them together. They made a very attractive couple.

She seemed completely at ease with that man. They were gesturing around and nodding as they spoke. Kacy walked him to the waiting car and smiled as he leaned down to whisper something to her.

Stepping back from him she laughed. Jacob leaned down and accepted the kiss she placed on his cheek before opening the door to his car and sliding in behind the wheel.

The window rolled down and as Jake backed out of her driveway and Ernst saw his hand reach out of the car and wave to Kacy before he drove away. With an answering wave and smile, Kacy waited until Jake was at the corner before she turned to go back in her house.

Standing on her steps, she turned around and Ernst knew she recognized his truck, for she briefly froze like a deer in headlights. Then, a somber expression crossed her face and she stared deliberately at him, only to look away and walk into her house without a backward glance.

Once the door was shut between them, Kacy crumbled to the floor. Her heart felt like it was going to pound out of her chest. Her legs couldn't hold her any longer. Why did that man have such a dominant hold over her? It took all of her willpower not to run across the street and beg him to give them another chance.

"What is he doing here? Maybe he wants the clothes back he left." Moving slower than a snail in winter, she rose and gathered the small bag of his clean clothes she had. Time stood still as her fingers drifted lightly across the top shirt in the bag. Each touch filled her with such memories.

Ding-dong. The doorbell chime jolted her out of her reverie. It didn't take a rocket scientist to figure out who it was. Taking the bag with, she forced her feet walk back up the hall to answer the door.

Placing the bag by the door, she didn't even look out the peephole before opening it. Her eyes filled with the delectable and scrumptious vision that stood before her. The door swung open and she stopped it with one hand, holding the solid wood of the door that consequently held her up.

The affect he had on her was astounding. Every one of her nerves cried out for his touch. Her eyes roamed up and down his hardened physique. He wore a black leather jacket under which she could see a brown shirt. Moving lower, she saw he was poured into another pair of black jeans and on his feet were gray hiking boots. Unconsciously, she licked her lips even as a soft moan escaped her mouth.

Ernst was having the same issues himself. When the door opened, it was like his life had meaning again. Being in her presence gave him such hope, joy, and elation. Like at the bar, the scent of her lotion wrapped him in a cocoon and held him close. The smell was gentle like she was, and he knew how soft it made every inch of her skin.

"Hello, Kacy," he managed to mutter.

"Hey." Her greeting seemed forced as well.

Again silence fell as they just stared at one another. He moved his gaze over her gorgeous body. She wore a pair of worn blue jeans that he knew settled so perfectly around that ass of hers. Covering the top half of her body was a sage green sweater. Even as bulky as it was, hanging down to her knees, it did nothing but accentuate her full chest and inflame his lust.

His tongue snuck out to wet his lips. Ernst almost gloated at the raw passion that flared in her eyes at the sight. But he still wasn't any better off. One thing flashed through his mind and that was to take her and make slow, sweet love to her until the only words that left her succulent mouth were his name and "yes!"

"Can I come in?" Ernst asked.

Kacy's hand clutched the door harder. "I was on my way out."

Seeing her feet clad in her fuzzy slippers, he blinked. "It won't take long." Ernst stepped closer, knowing she would step back. Kacy did. Putting one strong hand on the door, he shut it behind him, sealing them away from the outside world, closing out the cold autumn morning and the nosy neighbors.

Her home was warm and he felt like he belonged in it. With her. Turning his head, he glanced into the kitchen where he saw two cups sitting on the table. A fierce spurt of anger filled him. The fact that Jacob Trask had sat with her made him instantly furious.

Taking a deep breath, he slowly glanced back down at her face, which seemed delightfully focused on his midsection. Standing there, he felt himself twitch and grow beneath her heated stare.

"How are you doing?" Ernst questioned as her head flew up to meet his gaze.

Skepticism filled her fathomless copper eyes. "Don't tell me you left your hoochie to come ask me how I am doing."

A warm feeling surrounded him. *You're jealous, my schatzi.* "I didn't leave anyone."

The brief pain that crossed her eyes shattered that warmth. Ernst realized she figured that woman was waiting for him. "I have the things you left right there," Kacy blurted out before he could speak again. "Don't worry; everything is clean."

His pale gaze followed her extended finger to find a brown bag sitting by the door. *If I take that bag, it will be over for us.* Intentionally ignoring the bag, he focused back on her face. "What was he doing here?" The question seemed to throw her for a moment and she didn't answer. Ernst stepped closer, engulfing her with his size alone. "What. Was. He. Doing. Here?"

Again, Kacy clenched her fists. "Jake?"

"Yeah, him, *Jake*." Ernst didn't stop his hands. One finger trailed down the soft curls that framed her face. Her hair always felt like silk to him, especially when it flowed across his skin as they made love. "Kacy?" he murmured as that lone finger turned to two with his thumb caressing her bottom lip.

"He…he…he was telling me about some more things I can do to make the house more secure. About my options in dealing with Kirby."

Ernst knew this was the first time she had ever willingly told him that man's name. Swallowing his rage at the thought of the man who had laid a hand on her body, Ernst ran his other hand up her arm to slip around the back of her neck, sending those electrical impulses through her. "Why were you out with him?"

"I just met him last night. We weren't out." Smacking both his hands away from her body, she took a step back. "Which is more than I can say for you. What gives you the right to ask me about dating when you were out on one?" Kacy's tone had grown cold.

"I was doing a favor for a friend." Ernst didn't like the way her eyebrow rose. "I didn't want to go out with her. Jesus, Kacy, all I have thought about is you since I was dumb enough to walk out of your door four months ago."

Her arms crossed under her breasts, drawing his attention to them for a brief moment before he looked back into her eyes. "And the kiss on the boardwalk? That was what, your way of telling her you weren't interested?" Sarcasm laced her voice.

I knew she was there. Damn it! Why did she have to see that? "I didn't kiss her, she kissed me," he explained.

"So that makes it okay?" Her tone was almost understanding and Ernst fell for the trap.

"Yes."

Her eyes grew twice as hard as diamonds. "That's nice to know. So when Jake kisses me, if I don't kiss him, it is okay."

"Hell no!" Ernst shouted.

"If it is good for you, then why not for me?" Kacy taunted.

"No man kisses you," he growled. His hands grabbed her shoulders and pulled her so there was no light between their bodies before his lips covered hers. It was a dominating kiss and when he pulled away he added, "Except me."

Kacy's hands wound into the supple leather of his jacket as his mouth lifted off hers. Apparently, that brief contact wasn't enough and she jerked him back so their lips mashed together.

Understanding what she wanted, Ernst took control of the kiss as he slid his hands around her ass and lifted her off the floor only to carry her back to her bedroom. Along the way, his jacket was removed and dropped in the hall; and when they got to the room, his shirt was partway up his chest.

Ernst ripped it off the rest of the way and his mouth found its way back to hers. Her fingers were busy lowering his jeans and boxers, shoving them over his lean hips. Ernst mimicked her action and soon footwear and both pairs of jeans were on the floor. It didn't take him long at all to dispose of her sweater and bra.

Once they were both naked, he laid her on the top of her bed and entered her velvet warmth in one smooth stroke. Their mouths stayed connected as he began to move deep within her core.

Her body rippling with pleasure, Kacy drew back and buried her face into his shoulder. Ernst in turn put his face into her neck and left his mark on her. Orgasm after orgasm overtook Kacy as he moved within her. His touch was amazingly tender as he allowed her to find her releases first.

No words were spoken as he increased his speed and depth at the feel of his own approaching climax. One final thrust later, and he came deep within her body, covering her with his sperm and praying this would make her pregnant. Staying within her, he rolled to the side and gathered her as close to him as he could, draping their sweaty bodies with the comforter folded at the foot of her bed.

Exhausted and finally content, both fell into an entrenched and much-needed sleep. They were relaxed for the first time in four months. For unknown reasons, they were allowed undisturbed dreams as they traveled through the world of Morpheus. No restless turning, no unwanted awakenings. They were slumbering in the perfect place — one another's arms. All was right in their world once again.

Kacy awoke first. *It had to be a dream, just like all the other times Ernst has come back and made love to me.* Slowly her eyes opened, expecting the warm feeling that coursed her body to fade only for the usual disappointment to replace it. It didn't, and what met her eyes was the chest of the man who had been in her dreams every single night for the past few months.

The realization of what she'd just done filled her with a maelstrom of conflicting emotions. On the one hand, she felt so perfectly content lying in his arms. But the part of her predisposed for sabotage wouldn't let her forget him with that other woman.

Unconsciously, her body began to tense. The reaction from the slumbering man who still held her was to bring her closer to him and tighten the grip he had on her body. His square jaw covered with morning stubble rested on the top of her head. "Shhhh," he murmured as they both fell back to sleep.

This time when Kacy awoke, she was alone in the bed lying on her belly with her hands under her. She groaned in dismay. "I knew it was a dream." Bracing herself for the pain and loss, Kacy rolled over to get out of bed.

Those feelings never made it. Striding through her bedroom door was the man from her dreams. Ernst Zimmermann.

He only wore a towel that hung dangerously low on lean hips. The midmorning fall light from the windows bounced off the few water droplets remaining on his tanned skin. In one hand he had a glass of orange juice.

Their eyes met and Ernst smiled gently at her as he placed the juice beside her on the bedside table. Hands pulling the blanket up to cover her nakedness, Kacy swallowed as he sat on the bed near her. Her body slid towards him as his weight shifted the mattress.

"Hello, *liebling*," he said softly as he brushed their lips together. Kacy could feel his smooth skin for he was clean shaven now.

Kacy pulled back and stayed silent. Wariness filled her gaze as she glanced around the room before settling back on his face.

"Oh, no, Kacy," Ernst began with a shake of his still-damp head. "I'm not letting you chase me off again." Those amazing eyes of his grabbed hers and wouldn't let go. "I never should have left the last time."

"This was a mistake," she blurted out, tugging nervously on the blanket covering her nudity.

"You're right," Ernst agreed immediately.

Kacy's eyes grew wide with amazement that he would say such a thing. "I am?"

Ernst nodded. "Yes, you are." At the glimmer of sadness and acceptance of loss on her face he continued, "We should have talked it through first before we made love." One hand gathered her chin and stared straight into her eyes. "Making love with you Kacy can never be anything but perfect. In no way could it be a mistake."

Unsure of what to say or how to respond to his words she just stared at him. Her fingers tried to wring out the color of her comforter. *He was with another woman before he came to you. Get rid of him!* her mind yelled. Kacy whimpered in distress as she tried to get the voices to stop. "I need to get dressed," she mumbled for lack of anything else to say.

Ernst reached behind him and handed her the thick robe she wore in the wintertime. "We are going to talk this through, Kacy," he vowed before leaving her alone to get out of bed and dress.

Kacy took her time in the shower. Part of it was spent with the hot, pounding spray washing away her salty tears. She knew she was in love with the man waiting for her in her house. What she didn't know was if she were strong enough to deal with what being in a long-term relationship with him meant.

Wiping the mirror with a towel, she glanced at her reflection as it became visible. Her features were haggard. Eyes were puffy and red, her skin sallow and pasty. Slipping the robe on, Kacy made sure the towel on her head wouldn't move and she walked out of the bathroom.

"Brunch is ready," the masculine voice that had a million ways of affecting her spoke from one end of the hall.

Pasting on a weak smile, Kacy turned and walked towards him. He had put on his clothes with the exception of his shoes. Leaning against a wall, his eyes never left her progress.

Stopping her with a touch he whispered, "Do you want to change first?"

"Why are you here, Ernst?" Kacy asked point blank.

"Because four months ago, I told you something and then left, something that I had wanted to say to you for a long time. Something I never should have left after saying."

Licking her lips, Kacy searched his face for the truth. His gaze was guileless as it stared directly back into her coppery one. It didn't waver, shift; all it did was hold hers. "I just don't know," she grated out.

He fixed the thick collar on her robe. "Don't know about what? Me? Us? What don't you know about?"

"I don't know what to believe," Kacy said, closing her eyes and trying to block out his image.

"What does your heart tell you?" Ernst took one of her hands and placed it over his chest, allowing her to feel the rhythmic beating of his own heart. "What does mine tell you?"

With a deep breath, Kacy held her hand still. She moved her free hand into the fold of the robe to rest upon her own damp skin. After about a minute, her eyes opened to meet his uncanny yet steadfast gaze.

He nodded knowingly. "As one," Ernst spoke in a low velvety tone. "They beat as one."

Opening her mouth, Kacy shut it to nod. Ernst took the hand on his chest, kissed the back of it, and tugged her towards the dinning area. "You need to eat something." His words were followed by another kiss as he helped her into a chair.

CHAPTER TWENTY-FIVE

Glancing over to the digital readout on the microwave, Kacy was amazed to see it was nearly eleven. Blinking, she looked at the spread before her on the table: scrambled eggs, dry wheat toast—the way she liked it, bacon, sausage, fresh fruit, diced potatoes and a batch of sweet rolls. There was orange juice and coffee as well.

Ernst didn't take his usual seat across from her. Instead, he sat beside her and never gave her a moment's rest from his spectral-hued but watchful stare. Ernst dished her up a little bit of food and placed it before her. "Please eat something," he said as his voice broke with huskiness.

Tilting her head so she couldn't see his piercing eyes, Kacy picked up her fork and took a small bite of eggs. One thing was for sure, this man sure could cook! Her appetite back, Kacy began to eat. When she reached for her cup of coffee, she noticed that Ernst was just sitting there. Watching her. One hand around a glass of juice.

"Aren't you going to eat?" she asked as her fingers picked up a piece of crisp bacon.

"I love you, Kacy." Ernst spoke from the heart.

Setting the bacon back on her plate, Kacy sighed. For so long she had waited to have a man like him say that to her. Biting her bottom lip, she looked everywhere but at Ernst until he captured her chin.

"Why are you still trying to push me away?" Ernst questioned as his thumb traced the lip she had just bitten. "He can't hurt me. And I'll be damned if I let him hurt you." His tone never changed, but anyone would have been able to hear the conviction in his voice.

"I'm scared," Kacy admitted.

"Will you tell me of what? Please, Kacy. We can't get farther if we don't talk." Ernst let go of her chin to reach for some fruit. If eating honeydew wasn't supposed to be sexy, then the rules needed to be changed.

She squirmed in her seat as she watched him enjoy the succulent fruit. "I'm not sure I have what it takes to be in a relationship with someone like you." Her hands began to rip up her toast.

"Explain further, please," he ordered gently.

Eating a small piece of toast, she washed it down with some juice. "I don't know if I can live with what you do for a living. All the leaving for however long and never knowing if or when you are coming back." Her eyes glistened with unshed tears as she looked at him. "I don't think I am strong enough for that."

"Do you love me?"

"Yes," she responded without hesitation, "I love you." Kacy glanced away from his face.

"But...?" Ernst drew out.

"There is also Kirby. I don't want him to hurt you, either." Her hands toyed with the fork on her plate.

"Kacy." Ernst waited for her to look back at him. "Kirby can't hurt me. You are the only one with the power to do that. I'm not scared of him. He is only a man who is used to picking on those physically weaker than him. He's a bully and I've never liked bullies."

Kacy sat in the chair and watched Ernst as he spoke. He seemed so sure of himself. So confident. Except when it came to her, that was when she noticed hesitation from him. *Give it a chance,* her heart told her.

Drinking the rest of his juice, he licked his firm lips and said, "As for the other. Kacy, I wish I knew how to make it easier but I don't. All I can tell you is that my love for you will not wane. No matter how long I am gone, it will be you I long to see, yearn to hold, touch, and kiss. Being a military wife is hard; there are many who don't have what it takes. You do. You may not see it in you, but I do."

Kacy sent him a shy smile. "Why are you talking wife? I was just talking about a relationship."

Brilliant white teeth flashed. "*Liebling,* so am I. One that lasts fifty...a hundred...hell, all eternity."

"Let's try to make it through brunch first, okay?" Kacy muttered.

"Deal." Ernst filled up his plate and together they ate a Saturday brunch.

Kacy and Ernst walked around her neighborhood. Since it was a Saturday afternoon, there were children playing in yards and in the street. The air was full of autumn's chill and everyone knew the Indian summer had finally come to a head.

Ernst had his arm around her shoulders as she had one slid around his lean waist. Deep in the back of his mind he knew they hadn't really solved anything. Kacy was still scared of something.

Glancing at the woman beside him, Ernst couldn't stop the smile that crossed his face. She had that affect on him. If he could just pinpoint what the source of her fear was, he knew they could find a way to overcome it together.

"What are you thinking about?" he asked, loving the way her eyes sparkled with life as she looked at him.

"Nothing, really. Just thinking about the here and now." Kacy smiled at his boyish expression.

"Good thoughts?" His fingers tapped lightly on her shoulder.

She nodded. "Good thoughts." Snuggling her head closer to him, she put the question to him. "And you? What are you thinking about?"

"You." Ernst tipped his head and brushed his lips over her forehead. "I'm thinking about you." He stopped and cupped her face in both his hands. Lowering his mouth until it brushed lightly against hers he whispered, "And they are definitely good thoughts."

"That's nice to know," she murmured back. Kacy linked her arm through his and shoved her hands in her pockets. The wind had picked up and it was getting chilly.

They began walking again and people who knew Kacy waved to her as they passed. Before long, they were walking up toward her driveway when Ernst tensed again. That white Camaro was parked in her drive next to his truck. Jacob Trask sat on her porch steps.

"Hey, Jake," Kacy said as they got closer.

The cop stood and smiled affectionately at the woman who approached him. "Hey, Kacy. Hello again, Mr. Zimmermann," he greeted politely.

Ernst looked at the man on Kacy's porch. He was as tall as Ernst but appeared taller being that he was on the steps. Dressed in blue jeans and black boots with his black leather bomber jacket on, Jacob Trask made a very appealing visual—a fact that Ernst noticed and didn't like at all. "Hello," Ernst responded, sounding very surly.

Looking between the two men, Kacy rolled her eyes and heaved a big sigh. "Come on in, Jake." Walking past him on the steps, Kacy unlocked her house and entered followed, by the two men. "Do you have time for some coffee, Jake?" she asked over her shoulder as she kicked off her shoes and headed for the kitchen.

"Sure do. That sounds great." He followed, leaving Ernst to close the door behind them. His pale eyes watched Jacob with mistrust and jealousy.

Jake was sitting at the table eating a piece of chocolate pie when Ernst made it to the kitchen. The coffee was brewing and Kacy was setting out the mugs for the hot beverage. Ernst wanted to be mad, but the smile that Kacy sent him when he walked in the room chased all those feelings away. It was a smile to rival all smiles, lighting up her face and those gorgeous eyes of hers.

Sitting down, Ernst accepted the slice of pie that Kacy slid in front of him. "Thanks, love," he said as he picked up a fork.

Kacy winked at him and went back for the coffee. Setting the pot back on the maker, she fixed her drink the way she liked it and sat down to focus on Jake. "What brings you back, Jake?"

The lightness on his face disappeared as seriousness overtook it. "I got some news over the wire today." His gaze settled on Ernst then focused back on Kacy's dark beauty.

"And?" Kacy prompted.

"It deals with the situation we were discussing last night and this morning."

Ernst had no problems guessing who they meant. Kirby. Hands trembling, Kacy gripped her mug of coffee tighter until his tan hand covered hers, offering his strength.

Letting go of the cup, Kacy latched onto Ernst's hand like it was a lifeline. "You can talk in front of him. He knows about it."

Holding her gaze for an extra moment, Jake assessed whether or not to go on. When her eyes remained steady, he nodded. "Okay. He was picked up today for a domestic disturbance."

Ernst began caressing the back of Kacy's hand the second her body tensed. Kacy bit her bottom lip, no doubt thinking of someone else going through what he had done to her. "And the woman?"

"She died en route to the hospital. He is up on murder charges now. The DA wants you to testify about what he did to you, even though the office has access to the reports you filed on him. The restraining orders and all of that." Jacob sighed and Ernst tightened his hand over hers. "The DA thinks it would be an even stronger case with your testimony."

Shaking her head, Kacy trembled. "No. If he is up on murder charges, then you don't need me."

Ernst moved his chair closer to Kacy but remained silent. His intelligent and shrewd gaze watched the man across from them both. Ernst would allow Kacy to make up her own mind and not say anything to influence her decision; but at the same time, Ernst wasn't about to let that cop pressure her into doing anything she didn't feel comfortable doing.

As if reading his mind, Jake met his gaze and nodded just slightly enough that Ernst knew his silent message had been understood. "I was told to put it to you, Kacy, so I did. But I am not going to bully you into doing it. I can't vouch for anyone else, but I won't," Jake said, draining the rest of his coffee. "So I will let you think about it. You have my card; call me anytime, day or night."

Pushing away from the table, Jacob Trask stood and momentarily looked at the woman sitting there holding the hand of the man beside her. Ernst saw him smile wistfully, and he could guess what the other man thought: *If only I'd met her sooner.* "I'll see you later, Kacy, okay?"

She reached out her hand and squeezed his. "Thank you, Jake, for telling me, for understanding, and for not pushing me." Kacy let go of his hand. "I'll see you out."

"Nice to see you again, Ernst," Jake said as he followed Kacy out of the kitchen to the door.

As Jake walked past her out to the porch Kacy asked, "Are we still on for tomorrow?" She leaned against the door staring into dark-brown eyes that made her feel like there were good cops out there who cared.

Eyes flickering with anticipation, Jake smiled. "Absolutely. I'll be here at five."

"Okay, I will see you then." She flashed him a grin. "Have a great day."

"You too," Jake said as he trailed his knuckles down the side of her face in a tender gesture.

"Bye!" Kacy waved as he got to his car and climbed inside. She closed the door when he closed his.

"That man is half in love with you," Ernst's voice reached her.

Turning around, Kacy rolled her eyes. "I don't think so."

"I know so," Ernst swore. Moving closer to her, he gathered her back where she belonged — in his arms.

"Whatever," Kacy mumbled against the hard planes of his chest.

Ernst rubbed his hands over her back. "How you doing?"

Kacy knew immediately what he was talking about. "I'm losing it. I want him in jail so bad, but I don't know why I have to go be on the stand. I will be in the courtroom, but I don't want him staring at me." Her body began to quiver.

"It's okay. It's okay," he murmured against her hair. "You don't have to do anything you don't want to."

"I just need time to think about it," Kacy confessed.

As Ernst put the pasta on the table for dinner, he observed Kacy some more. She tried hard to play it off as if the news was not bothering her, but he could tell she was extremely conflicted about what to do. Her body was completely tense and she constantly worried her bottom lip, a trait that while adorable, Ernst had come to discover meant she was unsure about a decision.

"Ready to eat?" he asked as another strong wind shook the frame of the small house. They were in for a nasty night of weather.

"Absolutely," she said, walking back into the room. She had spent part of the afternoon going over some bids and doing some work for the upcoming week while Ernst had made dinner.

Grabbing the wine glasses, Kacy set them on the table and let her gaze rove over him. A secretive smile crossed her face.

Ernst hid a knowing grin. "What are you grinning about?" he asked as he poured the wine.

Blushing, Kacy shook her head. "Nothing."

One brow rose with unconcealed disbelief. "Really?" Ernst set the bottle on the tabletop before pulling out her chair for her.

Slipping into the chair, Kacy bobbed her head. "Really."

Leaning down to brush his lips over her ear as he slid her in close, he verbalized in a crystal clear yet extremely seductive tone, "Well, it's a shame I wasn't taught how to read body language, then." His deep chuckle reached her simultaneously as the blush ran over her body.

It took a while for the blush to recede. Ernst was nice enough not to point it out, although he was ninety-eight percent sure of what she had been thinking about. He loved it when she enjoyed his body like that.

"Thank you for making dinner," she said as she wiped up the last bit of sauce with her breadstick and popping it into her mouth. The meal had been very enjoyable and delicious.

Swirling the wine around in his glass, Ernst watched her lips before he took a drink. "You're welcome. I'm glad you liked it."

"Liked it?" Kacy gestured to her empty plate. "I damn near ate all of it!" Leaning back in her chair, she picked up her water and drank it.

"I guess that means we will just have to work all that off later on tonight then, huh?" Ernst stated with a lecherous wink.

He saw her body tremble at the thought. "I guess so. That is going to be one hellacious bike ride," she teased.

His pale gaze burned with passion. "You'll be ridin', all right."

Licking her lips, Kacy swallowed. Her eyes grew hooded as she watched him. With a careless shrug, she crossed her arms and tried to look bored.

Ernst laughed. It was like he could read her every emotion. "Let's take a walk." He stood and offered his hand to her as he walked around to stand beside her.

"Okay." Kacy took to her feet and together they cleaned up her kitchen.

Slipping on their boots, the sound of rain on the roof reached their ears. Ernst glanced at Kacy who knelt near him lacing up her boots. "Still want to go?" he queried.

Her eyes traveled up the lean length of his body. "A little rain isn't going to hurt me." A loud clap of thunder shook her house. "On the other hand, I don't want to get soaked, either."

Pale brows furrowed in thought as he watched her stand. "Well, since we're ready to go out, we could grab some ice cream." Ernst smiled as her eyes lit up at the prospect.

Her response was lightning fast. "Okay!"

Grabbing his keys, he waited for her to slip on her coat. "Ready?"

"Always," Kacy responded, pocketing her house keys. As they stepped out on the porch, the driving force of the rain momentarily stopped them. "Wow," she breathed in awe. "This is getting bad."

"Maybe we should stay in," Ernst said as he looked at the water rushing down the street.

"I think you might be right." Casting a glance at him she grinned. "Guess you are staying the night."

He sent her a heated look. "It appears so." He winked. "And since I'm scared of thunder, will you let me sleep with you? I want you to protect me."

Unlocking her door, Kacy went back inside and chuckled. "I'm sure we will think of something that we both like."

"I know I will," he whispered in her ear as his hands cupped the firm, denim-clad ass in front of him.

CHAPTER TWENTY-SIX

Kacy and Ernst sat on the floor in her living room. Empty ice cream bowls were beside them as they played bezique. Ernst had taught it to her and she was holding her own as they competed. It was a game where players took as many tricks as they could from a sixty-four card deck consisting of Ace through seven of each suit twice, trying to reach a thousand points before the other player.

"Where the hell did you learn this game?" Kacy asked as she took the trick.

"My mother." Ernst shook his head. Kacy was a bleedin' card shark. She was kicking his ass.

"I must say, I don't think I've spent a more enjoyable night in a long time." With a quick raise of her eyebrows she added, "One with my clothes on, anyway."

Ernst smiled at her. Kacy was sitting tailor style and her hair was gathered in a haphazard way out of her face. The joy on her face was real and he loved that it was there because of him. "The same for me. Growing up, we played cards all the time at night instead of watching television. Especially on nights like this. Or board games."

Kacy smiled as she took another trick. "I envy that. There are times when I really wish I had a 'family' childhood. Not that the orphanage was bad, but..." she trailed off for a moment. "I guess I had my fantasies like every other child."

"Will you tell me what it was like growing up there? And why you were there?" Ernst questioned as he finally got a trick.

"I don't know why I was there. The same reason as everyone else, I reckon—my parents ditched me or died. The nuns never offered told me and I didn't want to know. They are all the family I can remember, so I never saw the reason to pry into it." Kacy put the cards down and began pulling on the fuzz on her slipper.

"Of course," she continued, "there are times that I think it would be nice to have a medical history and find out if I have any siblings out there."

Her brown hand picked up the cards again. "Growing up was not bad. Beds weren't soft, but we had food and a roof over our heads. The nuns did the best they could with what they had to work with."

Ernst hated the emotionless tone she used to talk about her past. He loved every bit of spice that she brought into his life, and listening to this bland manner didn't sit right at all. Aligning his cards, he laid them face down and focused all his attention on her. "When did you leave?"

Keeping her metallic gaze on her cards, Kacy said, "I left at seventeen. After high school." She flashed him a brief glance. "I went into college right away and became an electrician."

"Well, how did you find out you were born in Hawaii?"

"Sister Teresa told me one day. We were looking at pictures of there and I said something about how I wanted to go, and she told me I had been born there." Kacy was talking softer and softer.

Reaching across their playing area, Ernst took one of her hands in his and pulled her to him. As her weight sank into his, he leaned back into the couch. "I'm sorry; I didn't mean to pry," he whispered.

Her head shook slightly. "It's fine. I guess I wasn't as okay with it as I told myself I was. I'm glad I told someone. I'm glad I told you."

"Me, too, Kacy, me too." He readjusted her so they were both able to see the calming view of the fish tank.

The faint chimes of a cell phone broke into their cuddling time. With a frown, Ernst took his phone and answered it.

Untangling herself from the man who held her, Kacy took the empty bowls into the kitchen and rinsed them out. With a groan, she looked at the weather out her window. *I hope it clears up by morning.* Lifting a shoulder in a helpless gesture, she opened the dishwasher and put the bowls and spoons in their appropriate places. Closing the door, she glanced at the clock and that ten-thirty.

When she turned around, Ernst was standing in the doorway watching her with those eyes of his. On his face was an expression she couldn't quite make out. "Bad news?" she inquired, drying her hands on a blue-green seahorse hand towel.

He prowled closer to her. "Just a call from a neighbor in the building. They are having issues with all the rain and wanted some help."

Her words were soft as she walked her fingers up his arms. "Guess you should be going, then." *I am not jealous.*

His fingers looped into her belt loops, drawing her closer yet. "I don't know how long it will take to fix."

"Even longer the more time you spend here with me." Tossing her hair back, she met his gaze squarely. "You should go help them out."

"I suppose," he complained. "I was really looking forward to spending the night with you." Ernst backed her up until the small of her back pressed against the edge of the counter.

Inhaling deeply, Kacy allowed his stimulating scent to immerse itself in her pores. She felt inundated by pure, raw, masculine power. "I'd be lying if I disagreed with that, but you were asked to help. So you need to."

His lips teased the side of her neck. "I'll be back in the morning."

Morning. "I won't be home tomorrow," she barely managed to get out as her knees trembled.

Drawing back, he looked into her eyes. "Where are you going?"

Kacy swallowed. "I'll be in North Carolina."

Determined to believe the best, he nodded. "Oh. That sounds like fun. Going with some girlfriends?" Dead silence. Arching a brow, he boxed her in as he asked again, "Kacy?"

Her tongue snuck out to wet her dry lips before she answered him. "I'm going with Jake."

Muscles twitched in that hardened body of his as he stepped back and crossed his arms over his chest. "Jake? As in the cop, Jacob Trask?" Fury lined his words.

"Yes. That's the one." Kacy watched the array of emotions that traversed his face.

"No!" he blurted out.

Dark eyebrows rose. "No? What do you mean 'no'?" Kacy demanded.

"I mean you aren't going with him! I won't let you go!" Ernst spoke without heed to the words coming from his mouth.

"Excuse me?" Total disbelief filled her tone. "I wasn't asking for your permission to go. I was telling you I'm going and with whom."

"You are not going to spend the day with a man in love with you, Kacy," Ernst ordered.

To many years of having Kirby tell her what she could and could not do pushed her right over the edge. Harsh laughter exploded from her. "You know what? I don't care that you don't like it. There is nothing you can say that will make me change my mind."

Blue eyes narrowed. "I thought you said you just met him that night in the bar?"

"I did. What are you implying?" Flames of anger began to build in her eyes.

"What would possess you to go with him anywhere? What about us?" Ernst ground out.

"There was no 'us' when I agreed to go." One hand slashed the air heatedly. "Jesus, Ernst, you were out on a damn date, and I hadn't seen you in four months since you walked out my door."

"Because *you* told me it was over!" he thundered at her.

"Well, I'm *sorry* for wanting to keep you alive and not have Kirby hurt you!" Kacy yelled back right in his face. "Not that it matters; you were on a date yourself. I have every right to agree to go out with a man."

"Not as long as we are together!"

"We. Weren't. Together," she growled at him, "and I'm going."

Ernst glared at her with a very pronounced tick in his jaw. "Would you have accepted his proposition if you hadn't seen me with another woman?"

"Yes," Kacy responded immediately. "Yes, I would have."

Ernst moved farther away from her. "So what is this talk of you loving me?"

"Ernst, I didn't lie. I do love you. But I have a right to go out with friends who are male. Regardless or not of whether we are a couple." Kacy saw a gap forming between them again.

He shook his head. "I don't like it."

Kacy made an effort to soften her words. "I'm sorry. I'm going."

Ernst had moved into the living room and gathered his coat. As his arms slid through the sleeves, he walked back towards her. "So you are giving up on us to go out with this other man?"

"We aren't going on a romantic date, Ernst. Jake and I are just friends. That's all." Kacy tried to get him to understand.

"Who's driving?"

"Jake is picking me up at five in his car."

Devastation filled his gaze. "This man is coming here to pick you up at five in the morning to go to another state and you want me to believe there is nothing romantic in it?"

"I would hope you would. I would hope you would trust me." She shrugged. "I guess you don't." Turning away from his handsome face so he couldn't see the tears she mumbled, "You know the way out."

"If I go out that door this time Kacy, I'm not coming back."

"We all do what we must." Her words were shaky as if trying not to cry.

Kacy stayed in the kitchen long after her front door opened and shut with Ernst's exit. "How did it come to this?" She wailed to the emptiness of her home.

Ingesting a few deep breaths, Kacy wiped away the remnants of her tears and set her shoulders. She had managed to regain and lose her man in a matter of hours. Determined not to give Ernst Zimmermann the benefit of any more of her thoughts, she walked down the hall and got ready for bed.

Unfortunately when she closed her eyes, all she could see was a tall man with flaxen hair and the palest blue eyes God had ever created.

Sobered by the thought of having lost Ernst, Kacy cried again as she stood under the shower's spray at four in the morning to get ready. Her mood had improved greatly as she opened the door to admit Jake.

"I have some coffee on so bring your mug and we will refill it before we go." Kacy said as she smiled at him.

"Great," Jake responded as he followed her into the kitchen. "Love the outfit."

Kacy winked at him over her shoulder. "Well, I love my team. I can't thank you enough for taking me with you!" She looked back at the mug she was filling for herself, taking care not to spill anything on her Carolina Panthers jersey. Her hair was pulled away from her face into a ponytail. The holder matched the team's colors as well as the colored ribbons that fell beside the wavy strands of her dark hair.

"I can't wait to get there," Jake said enthusiastically.

"Me, neither. I love the tailgating parties almost as much as the game itself!" Kacy reached for his cup and refilled it.

"Well, let's get going, then. I know it is going to get crazy down there. And there is a group of friends really looking forward to meeting you." Jake took his mug from her and walked with her to the door. He waited as she slipped into her team jacket.

They walked outside into the pre-dawn. It was cold. Despite it still being fall, there was a winterlike bite in the air. Inhaling deeply, Kacy grinned. "Great football weather." Locking her house, her steps fell easily beside with the tall man's.

Jake opened her door and closed it after she got inside. As he moved back to his side of the vehicle, Kacy smiled. Today was going to be a great day.

❀ ❀ ❀

Today was going to be a shitty day. Ernst knew that the second he rolled out of bed. The events of last night replayed in his head over and over, not giving him a moment's rest. "Kacy," he moaned her name to the emptiness of his apartment as he moved to his workout room to release his frustrations.

Hours later and standing under the water in his shower, Ernst washed off the sweat of his extended workout. He had pushed his body much further and harder than he had ever done before. Nevertheless, he couldn't outrun the image of Kacy's dejected body turning away from him.

"I'm such an idiot. I have no right to tell her what she can and can't do." Smacking his hand against the shower wall, he cursed as pain laced its way through his wrist.

Naked, he walked through his apartment, toweling off the hair on his head. Passing the answering machine, he noticed the light flashing. Eagerly, he pushed the button, hoping that maybe Kacy had left him a message.

"Hey, Ernst. It's Scott. We are having a get-together at the house today. Bring that Kacy of yours so we can get to know her better. Lex won't take no for an answer. Be here whenever; we eat about noon."

That was it. Well, hell. Ernst swore under his breath, something he realized he was doing more and more of lately — at least when he was away from Kacy. Ernst headed to his room and began to get dressed. A dark long sleeve polo shirt went over his head before he tugged a hip hugging pair of jeans on followed by a pair of socks on his feet.

Glancing at his reflection, he shook his head. Ernst reached for his watch and put it on before grabbing the towel to hang up in the bathroom. At the apartment's door, he slipped on a pair of tennis shoes. God, he had even begun to take his shoes off at the door as to not track dirt further into his place.

Picking up wallet, keys, phone, and pager Ernst left his apartment and headed for his truck. He waved at some people he passed but kept his pace quick so he wouldn't have to stop and hold a long conversation with them. It was nine now, so he had some time to kill. He would stop by on the way and pick something up to take to the gathering. He was determined to have fun today.

CHAPTER TWENTY-SEVEN

Pulling up to Scott's home, Ernst took a deep breath. He was one of the first to arrive. Getting out, he picked up the bags of drinks he had stopped to purchase on his way.

Lex opened the door before he got there. "Hey, Ernst," she said with a smile. Her brown eyes flickered around him, yet she didn't say anything but, "Come on in."

"Hey, yourself, Lex," he responded as he followed her inside. Habit made him slip his shoes off by the door an action that Lex silently noticed.

"Let's put that in the kitchen. Scott is in there with the babe." She touched his arm, momentarily halting him. "It's really good to see you, Ernst."

All he did was smile at her.

"Hey, Ernst," Scott's deep voice carried to them both. "Get in here, man."

Setting the bags down on the counter, he helped Lex take the stuff out of them as Scott walked over to shake his hand. "Good to see you." His blue eyes looked between Ernst and the door. "Where is she?"

"Jesú, Scott," Lex scolded. "It's none of your business." Shaking her head over her husband's lack of decorum, she began putting finger foods on trays.

Scott set his son down in the playpen that was in the kitchen and put his eyes on his friend and teammate. Cornflower blue met artic blue. "Well?" Scott demanded.

Folding the paper sack, Ernst shook his head. "She's not coming." He leaned on the marbled countertop and stole a cracker, topping it with a piece of salami and cheese before popping it in his mouth.

"Why not? Is she working?" Scott went to the fridge and grabbed two beers. Handing one to Ernst, he opened the second one for himself.

"No. She is in North Carolina with another man," he ground out from behind his clenched teeth.

"What?" Scott and Lex asked as one.

Helping himself to a healthy swig of beer, Ernst swallowed it before he repeated himself. "She went to North Carolina with another man. Told me last night."

"So you aren't a couple anymore?" Lex was totally confused.

"According to her, not since I walked out of her house about four months ago. Right after I told her I loved her."

Scott and Lex exchanged glances. "But now that you're back, I don't understand what happened."

Ernst looked at the leader of SEAL Team Seventeen. He seemed so damn happy with Alexis at his side, although he did remember how testy he'd been before she was his. "She saw me when I was out with another Chief from the base on a double date. She saw that woman kiss me. Later that night, we were at the same bar and it was like we were strangers. Like I'd never loved every inch of her body." He blushed. "Sorry, Lex."

Lex shrugged. "So she had made this date prior to the two of you being back together?" She asked.

"It doesn't matter," he hissed. "She shouldn't be going out with any man!"

Scott clamped a hand over his wife's mouth. "Lex, don't. Ernst, if she saw you out with another woman, why wouldn't she make a date?"

"Five!" Ernst ranted. "He was at her house at five this morning to drive her to North Carolina. And she has the gall to tell me it isn't romantic!"

Tightening his hold on his wife who had begun to spit fire with her eyes, Scott questioned, "Don't you trust her?"

"Man, she met him that night in the bar! What am I supposed to think?" Ernst put the bottle back to his lips.

"Oww!" Scott's voice yelled. "You bit me, woman!"

Lex yanked Scott's hand from her face. "Then get your hand off my mouth! And you, Ernst, you listen. I can't believe you think that she is supposed to forgive seeing you kiss another woman, but you can't trust her enough to let her go on a date she had planned before you showed up at her door!"

"She told me she loves me," Ernst interrupted.

"So?" Lex snapped. "I loved this one but still went out on dates. 'Cause we *weren't* together." Scott growled low and wrapped his arms around the love of his life. She patted his arms and focused back on Ernst. Her voice calm and soothing when she asked, "Did you keep control of your emotions or demand she not go?"

Looking at Lex like she were crazy, Ernst said, "I demanded!"

Scott opened his mouth to say something but Lex hushed him. "So, after all that talk of wanting to protect her from the man who basically held her prisoner, you go and do the same thing he did to her. Demand obedience. Not trusting her."

Moving out of her husband's arms, Lex moved around the breakfast bar and laid her dark hand on Ernst's arm. "Do you really think that Kacy is the type of woman to sleep around?" She cupped his face in a tender, mothering gesture and smiled gently at him. "If she loves you and you love her then don't give up." Lex went back to working on the food.

Eating another cracker, Ernst followed her graceful movements. "How'd you get to be so smart, Alexis?"

She winked at him over the food. "I'm not. I can just look at it objectively. Look, I don't know her. But if I were in her shoes, that is how I would feel. I would be absolutely crushed that you didn't trust me."

Ernst nodded. "So how do I get her back?" At the looks they sent him he amended, "I told her if I left I wouldn't be back."

"You have got to stop being so rash," Scott reprimanded.

"You were the same way, Scott, cut him some slack." Lex stuck up for Ernst.

The doorbell rang halting the conversation for the time. Scott went to answer it as Ernst stayed and helped Lex.

Soon the place was full of the Megalodon Team and their dates. Ernst was the only one flying solo. He didn't mind; he had made up his mind to do whatever it took to gain Kacy's trust again and marry her.

Lex smiled at him as she moved into the kitchen to grab another platter of snacks for the table in the living room. "The game is on, Ernst; why don't you go watch it?"

The game. He'd forgotten about that. "What can I carry?" Ernst asked as he moved beside her. Lex handed him a tray and together they walked back out to the living room where everyone sat watching the start of the football game.

Ernst found he was drawn into the game like the majority of people there. The game was close, both teams doing an amazing job against the other.

The home crowd was doing an awesome job of being the "twelfth man," but it was during the fourth quarter Ernst really started paying attention to it. He'd just walked back in from the kitchen with more beers for people. Remaining standing, he started to take a drink of his new brew, but instead, he almost dropped the glass bottle.

Kacy was on the screen. The cameras were moving over the crowd and stopped on her and the people surrounding her. The spark that he loved so much shone brightly in her copper eyes.

She wore a numbered jersey that was black and blue with the team logo at the bottom of each sleeve. On each cheek was a painted panther. Blue and white ribbons were in her hair and she had a team logo towel that she was whipping around in one hand. In the other was a beer.

He noticed Jacob beside her similarly decked out in team gear. They were both yelling and cheering their team. When Kacy looked into the camera, she held up her index finger, yelling that her team was number one.

There was a woman on her other side and they were giving high-fives and hugs to fans around. Not for one second did he notice anything other than pure elation for being at the game. No hidden glances between her and Jacob.

The camera moved on.

Ernst was glued to the screen from then on. He saw her a few more times since they were right on the fifty-yard line. Her body was always fully energetic and getting the crowd into the game right along with her, waving the towel around, raising her hands to increase the noise from the fans.

The highlight for him was when the man whose number she was wearing ran out of bounds near her after making a 45-yard punt return. He jumped up towards Kacy and the ones around her only to give her the ball and a hug. The blinding smile she gave him made Ernst wish he was there beside her. All Jacob gave her was a high-five. At that moment, Ernst knew he had been an idiot and she was one of the most honorable people he knew; the only difference was he loved her.

Kacy's favorite football team won that day and as the commentators were running over the highlights, Ernst knew his woman was leaving the stadium with a big grin on her face and a souvenir football given to her by her favorite player.

Ernst knew his teammates had recognized her in that moment when the camera hovered on her face. But at the look on his face, for once they remained polite and left him alone.

Standing with Scott by his truck as he was about to leave, Ernst wasn't the least bit surprised when his superior asked, "So, what are you going to do now?"

Glancing down towards the beach before looking at his friend, Ernst licked his lips and grinned. "Humble myself and get my woman back."

"About damn time," Scott said as he clapped him on the back before heading into his house.

❀ ❀ ❀

Kacy was still smiling as she, Jacob and the group they had met there made their way out the Bank of America Stadium. Her hands were holding tightly onto the ball she had.

"Girl, you were so lucky to get that!" Jake exclaimed as they moved with the crowd.

"I know!" she responded. "And a hug! I don't think I'm ever washing this jersey again!"

Jake put his dark eyes on the group. "Dinner?"

Everyone agreed and soon they were driving to a restaurant to have a nice dinner before she and Jake began the drive back. Once it was just the two of them in his car, Kacy looked over at him. "Thanks again for bringing me along. I had a wonderful time."

He grinned at her. "My pleasure, Kacy. I enjoyed having you. I love a sports fan like you."

It was after midnight when Jake pulled into her driveway. Turning his car off, he set the break and glanced over at Kacy. Her eyes were on the ball in her hand.

One hand opened the door and she got out only to have him do the same and walk her to the door. Unlocking it for her, Jake swung it open and looked down at her. "Thanks for a great day, Kacy."

Eyes full of life sparkled up at him. "Thank you. For everything." Balancing herself on his arm, she stretched up to give him a peck on the cheek.

His eyes tender he said, "If you ever get tired of that man of yours, you know where to find me."

Kacy just shook her head incredulously. "Whatever. Goodnight, Jake."

With a roguish wink he stepped back. "'Night, Kacy." Then he turned around and walked quickly to his car.

Inside her home, she closed and locked the door behind her. *What a day!* She danced her way down the hall to her bedroom. Putting her ball in a safe place, Kacy changed and walked back up the hall to feed her fish.

The blinking light on her machine caught her attention. She pressed play as she got the fish food and sprinkled it in the tank. The first three messages were about work, but it was the fourth that perked her interest.

"Kacy. Hey there, girl. It's me, Dez. Give me a call whenever you get this. I have got some news for you. Call me!"

A smile crossed her face. How she had missed her friend. But, she wouldn't call her tonight, waiting wait until morning instead. A hang-up made her check the caller ID. It was a number she hadn't expected to see again on her phone. Ernst.

Perhaps now he wanted his clothes back. Well, she could deliver them for him so there was no reason to call him back. He'd been perfectly clear when he'd said he wouldn't be coming back if he left.

Fighting with her mind to stay happy, she forced the memories of Ernst out of her thoughts. Still pumped from the game, she fixed herself a bowl of ice cream to help soothe her throat, and then went to work on some more blueprints for some jobs she had.

It was near to two in the morning before Kacy slid between her sheets. Her eyes wandered over to rest on the ball one last time before she shut off the light and closed her eyes. Despite the wonderful day she had, her dreams were haunted.

Ghost. His eyes seemed to follow her everywhere she went. She could smell his masculine scent and feel his touch. When she awoke at five, her body was wet with want for the man who frequented her mind all the time. Her skin felt like it were on fire and only his touch could extinguish the flames.

With a groan made deeper by desire she climbed out of bed to begin her day.

CHAPTER TWENTY-EIGHT

"Hey, sweetie," Kacy said with elation as she got her friend on the phone.

"Kacy?" the voice squealed. "Is it really you?"

"In the flesh, so to speak. How are you, Phoenix? I am so, so, so sorry I missed your wedding."

A husky chuckle crossed the line. "I'm great! I know that if the ride hadn't been that weekend, you would have been there. Thanks for the gift by the way. I loved it."

Kacy smiled as she sat at her desk. She had given the new couple crystal glasses. "Good. Now fill me in on this man you married!"

There was silence on the line for a minute before the voice came back. "Would you like to meet him?"

"Of course! Are you visiting the area?" Kacy cocked her head to the side and waited for a response.

"Well, not really. We've moved here."

Kacy took her turn to shriek. "Oh, my God! That is so awesome!" Seconds later she sobered. "What about your business?" Dez was the owner of a car restoration business called Phoenix Rebuilds and Restorations. In fact, Dez was the woman who'd given her the Camaro.

"It moved with me. Part of my reason for calling you—I need an electrician." She paused. "I have a huge warehouse and a second building for an indoor track, but I don't like the lighting."

Glancing down at the stuff in front of her, Kacy said immediately, "I can come out today and look over the place and talk over what you want to do."

"It doesn't have to be today, although I would love to see you."

"No really, I can do today. Where are you?"

Directions were given before the woman asked, "So, how's my car?"

Leaning back in her chair, Kacy laughed. "Your car? Doing wonderful; could probably use a tune up, but doing great."

"Good." There was another pause. "It is really good to hear your voice."

"You, too, Dez. It's been a while." Kacy stood. "Okay, I have the directions and I am going to get going; so after I check this out, we can catch up with one another."

"Great. I will see you soon."

It didn't take long for Kacy to reach the destination given by her directions. As she pulled into the drive, she looked around and whistled. The place was huge.

Parking next to a sports utility vehicle, Kacy hadn't even gotten the car shut off before a woman came running out of the house. "Kaaacccyyyy!" she yelled.

Eagerly, Kacy got out and the two women embraced. "Oh, it is so good to see you, Phoenix! So good." She pulled back and looked at her friend. "You are looking wonderful."

"So are you," Dezarae Connelly told her. "So are you." Her eyes moved to the car and she grinned. "Still looks good."

"Well, what did you expect? You did it!" Kacy draped her arm over her friend's shoulder and said, "Come on and show me this hubby of yours."

The slam of a screen door caught their attention and both women looked up to see a tall man step out into the autumn morning. His features were obscured by the sun's rays.

"Let's go," Dez said, pulling on her friend but refusing to relinquish her hand. "You will love him."

"I know I will. You had no interest in any man who looked at you; so if you married this one, I know he has got to be something special," Kacy reasoned as they walked closer.

Before Dez could respond, the man reached the bottom of the steps and looked at the two women approaching him. The second his eyes met Kacy's, she froze.

"You?" she barely breathed. "You're her husband?"

Dezarae glanced between them both. "You know him?"

"We met in Hawaii," Ross said as he stepped closer. "How are you doing, Kacy?"

"Fine, Ross, I'm fine." She shook his hand nervously.

Dez frowned. "How did you two meet in Hawaii?"

"We were playing pool in a bar she was at," Ross answered, his gray gaze landed back on Kacy.

She fidgeted. His stare was setting her on edge. Looking at Dezarae, Kacy suggested, "Why don't you show me this place and we can catch up as I make an estimate?"

"Sounds good. See you later, honey." Dez kissed her husband and the two women walked off towards the new shop.

Three hours later, the women were laughing and reminiscing as they sat in the living room of Dezarae's home. Every now and then Ross would poke his head in; but for the most part, he left them alone.

It was late afternoon when Kacy finally got ready to leave. Walking out to the car with Dez, she hugged her friend. "I am so glad you are here, Phoenix."

"Me too."

"Well, I will go home and work up some schematics and bring them to you to, okay? I have a few ideas that I think will work for you, unless your taste in lighting has changed."

"Nope. I know I can count on you to do this prefect. Thanks so much, Kacy." Dezarae kissed her friend again. "Of course, you know you are going to have to tell me which of his team you were out with!" That said, Dezarae stepped back and let Kacy climb in her car.

Speechless, all Kacy could do was start her car and drive away, waving to her friend as she left.

As she pulled into her driveway she wondered how Dezarae was going to deal with Ross leaving like Ernst does. *Well, at least I have someone to ask about it.* Kacy didn't know the other two wives married to Team members, so wouldn't have felt right asking them.

Scoffing, she scolded herself. "You don't have him anymore Kacy. So it is a moot point. He thinks you are nothing more than a whore sleeping around." Climbing out of her car she walked inside her home Kacy's answering machine had seven messages on it. Six of them were from Ernst. She deleted them all, not wanting to hear his scorn, and immediately got to work on plans for Dezarae's building.

The next two weeks she stayed extremely busy with work and putting ideas to paper for Dezarae. She ignored all of Ernst's calls and even went to his apartment to drop off the bag outside his door.

He had come to her door but she'd refused to answer it. Every last bit of energy she had Kacy poured into work. It helped having Dezarae around to talk to.

※ ※ ※

Ernst was getting crankier and ornerier every single day that passed. Kacy was avoiding him. She refused to come to the door or answer his calls; and one day, he had come home to find a bag full of his items sitting in front of his door.

After he left the base one afternoon, he tracked down Officer Jacob Trask. The man was sitting at his desk when Ernst entered.

"Mr. Zimmermann," he said politely. "What can I do for you?"

Barely holding onto his temper, Ernst grumbled, "Stay the hell away from my woman."

Raising a black brow, Jake leaned back in his chair. "What makes you so sure she is your woman?"

Eyes spit blue fire. "She's mine. She loves me. You got that?"

Jake rested his fingertips together as he looked up at the imposing man standing there. "My relationship with Kacy is none of your business."

Ernst stepped towards him and Jake held up a hand, knowing he was close to pushing Ernst over the edge. "Hold on there. You don't want to hit me, not in here." The sizzle in Ernst's eyes spoke a different story. "Sit down, man," Jake said.

Tense and still ready to fight for his woman, Ernst sat at the edge of a chair facing Jake. "What?" he snapped.

"I don't know why I'm telling you this. Lord knows I am in love with her myself." He held up a hand again at the hardness that filled the pale eyes watching him. "But, I know she loves you. I've known it since the night in the bar. I may be a lot of things, but I'm not a thief. Kacy and I are nothing but friends."

"And the game?" Ernst asked.

"She loves football and I had an extra ticket. We went and met a group of my friends, tailgated, and had a wonderful time at the game. Afterward we went to dinner, the whole group, and then I drove her home. Where I left her. Alone." Jake never wavered from holding Ernst's gaze.

"All I am is someone safe," Jake continued. "A bunch of pressure is coming down on her about the whole Kirby thing and I am someone she can talk to. I am the closest thing she has to a big brother; and as much as it kills me to be seen like that in her eyes, that is what I am. Nothing more."

Anger whooshed out Ernst, and then returned ten-fold at the thought of her being pressured to face Kirby. Gathering his emotions, he stood and held out a hand. "Thank you. For taking care of her and keeping her safe when I couldn't."

Jake stood and shook his hand. "You're welcome. You know I expect an invitation to the wedding." He arched an eyebrow. "If you can keep her that long."

"I'll deliver it personally." With a nod, Ernst turned around and walked out of the precinct, determined not to rise to the bait.

❀ ❀ ❀

Kacy stood beside Dezarae on the cement floor of the new shop. A blueprint was between them as Kacy explained her ideas. With her left hand, Kacy gestured to marks on the paper.

Her penny-colored eyes focused on her friend. "So what do you think?"

"My God, Kacy," Dezarae said with awe. "You've outdone yourself. I love all of it." She grinned as if envisioning the finished look. "You're a fuckin' genius!"

Kacy shook off the praise. "Well, I just know how you like things."

"Let's go see the track," Dez encouraged anxiously.

"Okay." Kacy put the plans on a workbench and followed her good friend out the door. She stopped when Dez headed away from the track. "Where are you going?"

With a mischievous grin, Dez answered, "Your car."

Shaking her head, Kacy just tossed her the keys before continuing to open the big door.

The building was huge. Leaving the door fully ajar so Dez could drive in, Kacy looked between the two buildings.

"Hey, Phoenix," Kacy began once she was out of the car. "I know some good contractors if you want a covered area between the two buildings."

Brown eyes sparkled. "That would be great. Hey, by the way, I need to do some adjusting on this thing. He's a bit hesitant."

With a shrug Kacy nodded. "If you say so." She shook her head over Dez's use of "he" when talking about cars. Her friend staunchly refused to call a car a "she" not when, as Dez claimed, a good car could damn near give her an orgasm. In fact, Kacy had even begun to think along the same lines; her Camaro was a "he" to her as well, for Dez's logic made sense to her.

"I do." She grinned at Kacy. "Now, what do you have planned for me in here?"

❀ ❀ ❀

Ernst grumbled as he got out of the chopper. They had been gone for over a week and he just wanted to corner Kacy and love her until she agreed to marry him.

"Hey, Ghost!" Ross yelled to grab his attention.

He shouldered his bag and waited for his teammate. "What?"

Gray eyes were direct. "Can you give me a lift?"

Clamping back the groan that threatened to escape, Ernst nodded. "Sure thing." He didn't want to, though; he wanted to go to Kacy's house.

"Thanks, man," Ross said, falling into step beside him.

The two men tossed their bags into the back of the truck and scurried inside. The day was cold; there was no other way to describe it.

"Where's Dez?" Ernst asked.

"At home with Charmane. She dropped me here since we were at the doctor's when I got paged."

"Everything okay?" Ernst turned the heat up.

"I hope so. I left before the results came back. She has just been really tired lately." Ross said with a shrug that was not as relaxed as Ernst knew he wanted it to be.

"I'm sure it will be." Turning into the driveway that led to Ross Connelly's new home, Ernst was amazed at the changes he saw from the last time. There were construction men building an access strip between the shop and the soon-to-be track. "Wow. I bet she is getting excited about opening her business again, isn't she?"

"Man, she lives to work on cars. We already have people lined up for when the new shop opens." Pride was evident in Ross' voice.

He parked next to Ross's sports utility vehicle and put his truck in neutral.

Ross looked over at him and said, "Shut it off and come in, man. You know Dez and Charmane are going to want to see you."

Almost reluctantly, he turned off his truck. Grabbing his jacket, he got out and closed the door behind him. He stood and watched Ross look at the house before facing the shop and waving him along. The faint drone of music could be heard.

"She's working in the shop," Ross stated as the two men headed across the lawn.

With a sigh, Ernst prepared himself to feel out of place while Ross was welcomed home by his wife. Moving into the shop, Ernst found his feet adhered to the floor like they were covered in cement. He couldn't move.

The sight before him made his heart catch in his chest. Kacy's car was there, hood up. Loud, pulsing music filled the shop and the two women in coveralls were dancing and singing along to the music. Hips sashaying, hair bouncing, they were both gorgeous, but his eyes couldn't move away from his own epitome of perfection. Koali Cynemon Travis.

His mouth grew dry and it seemed she was suddenly moving in slow motion. Each seductive sway of her full hips was crystal clear. He watched her hands move up to lift her thick hair off her neck and a full-blown smile bloomed on her face as her eyes stayed blissfully closed. The way her hands followed the contours of her body made him rock hard in a millisecond.

Her full mouth singing along with the music made him ache. She looked so beautiful, so tantalizing, so alluring. So his. When she growled low in the back of her throat he almost lost it, for he could feel that purr vibrate all the way to his soul.

Flicking a glance to Ross, Ernst was surprised to see him wink. Then he jerked his head towards the women. Ernst smiled in thanks at his friend. Side by side, the two Navy SEALs went to claim their loves.

CHAPTER TWENTY-NINE

Kacy felt flushed. Her body temperature had skyrocketed. Her body was crying out for release. Each hair seemed to be charged with electricity. Sexual electricity.

She didn't understand it. Nothing like this had happened yesterday when she and Dezarae were dancing in the shop. Kacy swallowed hard as she tried to moisten her dry mouth.

Opening her eyes, Kacy halted as her eyes found the reason her body was reacting this way. Ernst.

He stood before her. Out of the corner of her eye, she could see Dezarae in Ross' arms. Too soon, however, her gaze moved back to settle on Ernst.

He had on a black leather jacket and she could see a dark gray shirt underneath. Her hungry eyes took in the black BDUs he wore and the heavy black combat boots. He was here, he was breathing, and he was still so damn handsome.

Her tongue swiped across her lower lip, an action that jolted him into motion. Before she could say anything, his hand was buried deep in her hair holding her head immobile as his mouth plundered hers. His other hand grabbed her firm ass and jerked her closer as his fingers dug into the coveralls and her flesh.

Kacy stiffened for two seconds before losing herself in his demanding kiss. Her tongue swirled around his, toying with it. She sucked on it like it could save her soul from damnation.

Drawing his mouth off hers, Ernst fought to regain his breath. The hand in her hair never loosened. He moved the one from her ass up to her face and gently wiped away the salty tears that had begun to fall.

His gaze was ferocious, yet tender as he watched her. "Let me go, Ernst." Her words were raspy with emotion, one of which was plainly desire.

"Never."

"According to you, I made my decision," she snapped, trying courageously and foolishly to hold onto her anger.

"I was an idiot. A stupid, jealous, irrational—"

"Moronic," Ross offered, only to receive a glare from both his wife and Ernst. With a lazy lift of his shoulder, he carried his wife out of the shop, leaving them alone.

Ernst nodded. "He's right. I was moronic. I was so blinded by my jealousy of Jake that I couldn't see straight."

This had to be a dream. Shaking her head, Kacy backed away, brushing his hand from her hair. "No. I can't do this again. I have to protect myself." Turning from him she walked to her car and slammed the hood.

Ernst reached for her. "Kacy."

"No. You hurt me." With a speed neither of them knew she possessed, she jumped in her car and within was tearing out of the garage, heading for parts unknown.

Unloading a string of curses, Ernst ran for his truck. Jumping in, he headed for her house. *Oh ,hell no, Kacy! Not this time.*

Pulling into her driveway, Ernst turned off his engine. Determination set in the planes of his face he climbed out and strode to the front door.

Ding-dong.

He heard movement but she never came to the door. His glacier eyes narrowed as he raised his voice so she could hear him. "Kacy, come open this door. We need to talk."

Nothing.

Finally, her door opened but not all the way. The chain across it prevented his entrance. "We have nothing more to say to one another," she said.

His voice softened. "Don't do this, Kacy. Let me in."

"No." She slammed the door in his face.

A roar of rage tore from him as he put his shoulder into the door and let himself inside. The safety chain couldn't hold up under the force of his hit.

Kacy spun around as the door flew open to admit a cold, furious, and damn good-looking Ernst. Her copper eyes were wide as he whipped the door back closed behind him.

"Did you really think that would keep me out?" Powerful, measured steps brought him closer and closer to her.

"Get out," she whimpered. Her body trembled from everything this man exuded. All of it made her want him, beg him to take her and not stop until they were both exhausted.

"No," he vowed. "Not this time, Kacy. I was dumb. I admitted that. I was jealous; we covered that as well." Closer and closer he came.

The air filled with the power of the emotions flowing off of his body. A feral look was in his eyes and she knew he was almost out of control. Kacy felt no fear from him, though, only arousal.

"You made your choice." Her words were little more than a weak protest.

"I changed my mind." His voice was a low growl of promise.

Shaking her head in denial, Kacy began to back away from him. *I can't let him touch me. It will be all over if I do.* "You don't get to."

That slowed him a fraction. "Why not? I'm only human. I make mistakes."

Her brain twisted that so she could be angry at him. "So, what, now I'm a mistake?" Kacy's scorn raked him.

He moved before she could blink. It was as if he'd leaped the remaining distance between them. One second he wasn't, the next he was…right there. In her face. Surrounding her with nothing but hot, hard, and extremely angry maleness.

"If I was a man taken to hitting women, I would beat you for saying that, Koali Cynemon Travis." His words were barely comprehensible as he shoved them through clenched teeth.

Lean fingers latched like vices on her upper arms. His face lowered to get right into hers. Kacy could feel the sparks that flew from his eyes. "Go ahead," she taunted recklessly even though she knew in her heart he wouldn't *ever* lay a hand on her in anger. "Do you think you can hurt me anymore than you already have?"

"You, Kacy. *You* are the one hurting yourself, hurting me. Not me. I have owned up to my stupidity. I came back." His lips descended until they were scant millimeters away from hers.

Her eyes widened before she shoved him in his chest as hard as she could. "No!" she screeched.

Tightening his hold on her, Ernst jerked her in closer. "Yes!" His voice was just as low as hers had been high. "You are going to have to do a hell of a lot better than that to get rid of me." His head cocked to the side. "Got anything else?" His nostrils flared.

"You are just going to hurt me again!" she wailed.

"Never again," he vowed. "Kacy, I would sooner kill myself than hurt you." The anger left his voice, leaving in its place raw honesty.

"I hate you!" she forced out between her teeth.

"Not good enough. Can't you do better than that? Come on," he goaded her. Ernst knew she had to face the immense anger she had kept welled up in her body for so long if they were going to even have a chance. He would force her to confront it.

Her eyes darkened with uncontrolled rage as she jerked her knee upwards. "Bastard," she seethed.

Turning his hips at the last second, Ernst felt her knee connect hard with his thigh. He hadn't thought she had it in her and was extremely glad he had blocked it. "Nope," he mocked her, laughed at her. "Can't even do that. Try again."

A deep keening cry rose from her throat, one of despair, fear, lust, and a myriad of other emotions. Ernst bit the inside of his cheek to stop himself from allowing her to back away from the feelings she needed to release so badly. He hated to see her like this, but it *had* to be done.

Kacy flew at him in a rage. Arms flailing, legs kicking, she turned him into her own personal punching bag. Tears streamed down her cheeks as she managed to land blow after blow to the man before her.

Ernst blocked most of the blows and allowed her to do what she needed to do. Her rants involved yelling at a nonexistent Kirby to howling over the fact she didn't know her parents.

It took a while before her fury abated. When it did, she was exhausted. Her body sagged and at the feel of strong arms holding her, she looked up. Ernst met her gaze; there were still unchecked and barely controlled emotions in his eyes, but they were amorous as they met hers.

"Better now?" he asked in a gentle tone. He could see mortification fill her copper eyes and she tried to pull back. "Uh-uh, Kacy."

"I'm so embarrassed." Her voice was scratchy from the yelling and crying.

"It had to be done. I'm so sorry I had to push you into it, Kacy, but we didn't stand a chance until you did. *Ich liebe dich, liebling. Ich liebe dich.* I love you." He wiped away the tears from her silken skin.

Looking to the floor, Kacy didn't resist when he tipped her head back up so he could met her gaze. "I hit you," she said remorsefully.

"Yes, you did." A wry grin crossed his face. "A few times." He sobered at the humiliation on her face. "Kacy, I'll be fine. You needed to do this." Ernst kissed her lips lightly. "I love you, Kacy. You know I have loved you for a long time."

Shaking her head, Kacy put her hand over his mouth. "No." At the flare of unbridled emotion in his eyes, she continued. "Let me talk."

And talk she did. Three hours later, they were curled up on her bed. Ernst held Kacy in his arms as she finished what she had to say. He'd stayed quiet, allowing her to find the words she needed at her own speed, only interrupting with a few questions here and there.

"Regardless, Ernst, my feelings for you haven't changed. I love you as much as I did before. Perhaps more." Her hand rested upon his chest, her fingers trailing patterns on the gray shirt he wore.

"I love you, too, Kacy. And I don't want to live without you. Not anymore."

Tilting her head so she could see his face she asked him, "Would we be able to live here?"

Closing his eyes against the powerful wave of emotion that surged over him, Ernst nodded. "Anywhere you want, my love. Anywhere you want." He opened his eyes when he felt her move away. "I want to ask you —"

"Shut up," Kacy said. "I have a question for you."

Ernst sat up and met her gaze. She was still in coveralls and sitting on her bed. "Ask away, *liebling*."

Her eyes were full of hope and love as she watched him. "Will you marry me?"

One half of his mouth quirked up into a grin. He should have known. "That's supposed to be my question to you."

"I know I messed up things between us." She maneuvered her body to straddle his hips. "I don't want to be without you, either, not anymore. Not ever." Her hands cupped his face. "So I'll ask you again; will you marry me?"

Ernst blinked back tears as he captured her mouth with his own, pouring everything he had into the kiss. "Yes. Yes, I will marry you."

I love you, his heart screamed.

And I you, was the message he saw in her eyes.

It was after ten at night when the couple finally left the bedroom to seek sustenance for their weary bodies. They had a late dinner before Ernst swept her off her feet and carried her back to her room.

When she was finally sleeping soundly in his arms, Ernst brushed a tendril of hair away from her face. "I love you, Kacy. *Ich liebe dich,*" he whispered to the woman of his dreams as she snuggled closer to his naked physique. Resting his lips against her head, he realized he had no anger left in him. It had disappeared.

Tomorrow, he would get her a ring and move his stuff over here. He would be with her when she testified against Kirby, which was what she had ultimately decided to do. He would protect her for the rest of his life. A wry smile moved slowly across Ernst's face. Who knew he would've found his life outside a bar in Hawaii?

The woman in his arms was everything he desired and more. His love. Koali Cynemon Travis was, after all…

GREELEY'S SPYCE.

THE END

About the Author

Aliyah Burke loves to read and write. Her debut novel, *A Knight's Vow*, was released in 2004. She loves to hear from her readers and can be reached at aliyah@aliyah-burke.com, aliyah_burke@hotmail.com, and feel free to join her yahoo group at http://groups.yahoo.com/group/aliyah_burke or friend her at http://www.myspace.com/aliyahburke. Please stop by her website, www.aliyah-burke.com for more available titles—just don't forget to sign the guestbook.

Aliyah is also married to a career military man. They have a German Shepherd, a Borzoi, and a DSH cat. Her days are spent splitting her time between work, writing, and dog training.

4139178

Made in the USA
Lexington, KY
27 December 2009